I0744186

Published by: Cinnabar Moth Publishing LLC
Santa Fe, New Mexico

Cover Design by: Ira Geneve

ISBN-13: 978-1-953971-88-3
Library of Congress Control Number: 2023938857

Gibbous Moon

KATIE GROOM

Mid-June
Near Bran Castle, Romania

Zoie flew up out of the water and looked down at her attacker. She had escaped! She had won!

And—pretty exciting—she could fly or levitate or something. This was going to be a neat talent to add to her magic arsenal, which truly only was going to grow from here. She knew that at some point, she had been able to mess with time, but that power hadn't been exercised in a while.

It didn't matter. With her new ability to fly, she was excited to get started on learning what her powers could do. She felt infinite in that moment. But only for a moment.

As she floated above the pool, she watched her nemesis Miles smirk and then saw her mermaid friend Stevie walk calmly out onto the pool deck. It always amazed Zoie how calm and confident Stevie was, even in the scariest of moments. Zoie watched in excited anticipation for her friend to draw the water out of the pool and tear Miles apart in a maelstrom.

Instead, Stevie locked eyes with Miles. "Go!" She ordered. When Miles hesitated, she ordered more firmly. "Get out of here

1

before he gets back here and kills the both of us!"

Zoie had her gaze fixed on Stevie, confused, and barely noticed when Miles exited. Why didn't Stevie take him out? If she didn't want to kill him, why didn't she capture him? Make handcuffs out of the pool water? Use the water as rope to tie him to the chair? Why did she just let him go?

Zoie's concentration had faltered, but it returned when Stevie used the water in the pool to lift something from below the surface.

With a gasp, Zoie startled and jumped back in the air when she realized that the item being pulled from the water appeared to be her. Willing herself closer, Zoie knew that she had to get a better look to figure out what this out of body experience was.

Stevie leaned over the body and spoke sincerely. "I'm sorry, Zoie." Stevie looked around quickly, her black curls bouncing with every move. Then she leaned closer to Zoie's body and whispered something too quiet to hear.

"What? What are you apologizing for?" Zoie asked. Stevie didn't acknowledge her whatsoever.

Soon after, Zoie's mate Hugh came bursting through a door, and to Zoie's side—well, the side of that immobile body that looked like her.

He took that lump of a body into his arms and sobbed. He angrily begged Stevie to help. Stevie told him that she tried—that Zoie's lungs were clear.

"That's a lie!" Zoie yelled. That's when it hit her.

Flying wasn't a new power. This was the afterlife.

—Zoie—

Zoie quickly flew down closer, taking in everything that was going on around her. Hugh had a death grip on her body, and a terrified crowd of hotel employees had gathered in the lobby. One of them was on the phone—undoubtedly calling for emergency help. Not only was it obvious to Zoie that she was dead, but Hugh had literally crashed through a wall of glass to get to her. One police car was not going to cover this.

Stevie and Hugh's best friend Cade were trying to convince Hugh to leave. They tried to plea from every angle—any excuse to get him to comply. "No!" Zoie cried. "Don't leave me." She couldn't imagine that Hugh would even consider leaving her there.

"You need to leave her, and you need to go," Cayden stated as they knelt down in front of Hugh. Their face was so full of genuine concern. It became obvious to Zoie that this was the best choice.

Zoie placed her feet on the pool deck and walked over to Hugh—despite everything going on, she noticed that her shoes didn't make that strange squelching sound that they should have. So her guess was right, then; she was dead.

Hugh ignored Cade's pleas, but Zoie inched closer and put her hand on his shoulder. She lied, "It's okay, Hugh. Go." It was in his best interest and in the best interest of their world for Hugh to leave.

She frowned as Hugh was dragged away by Cayden, but when Stevie put her hands on Hugh, Zoie groaned in disgust. Lying, evil bitch. Zoie made a mental note to haunt the hell out of Stevie and make her life miserable. Maybe take her sanity from her. Zoie didn't care about getting revenge for herself; it wouldn't bring her back. It was more to balance out the pain that Hugh felt. The pain that Zoie, even in death, could feel in her heart on his behalf.

As soon as the others were out of sight, Zoie realized she needed a plan.

"Ok. I need to find a way to warn Hugh that Stevie can't be trusted." She considered figuring out how she could get back to Hugh's house and leave him a note. Could she pick up a pen and paper? She looked down at herself. She had clothes on, so she surmised that she could touch things. Maybe she could write a message on a foggy mirror.

"This is ridiculous." She didn't want to be dead. Maybe she could bring herself back to life. Maybe she hadn't crossed over because she wasn't fully dead. Maybe there was a grace period.

Biting her lip, she decided to lie right on top of her body. "Maybe it will be like Peter Pan and his shadow, and we'll just stick back together." She prayed quietly to herself, "Maybe I just won't be dead anymore…"

She sat back up, still seeing her body lying there. "Maybe I need to be perfectly in that form." She carefully lay back down again, trying to make sure her posture exactly matched her body's. "Come on… work." This was it—if it was going to work, it was this time. Not even a piece of hair was out of place.

Closing her eyes for a second, she made a wish. "Please, please,

please, make this work." Zoie sat up and opened her right eye very slowly. When she noticed that she was still separate from her body, she groaned and jumped up.

"If only I actually had some damn training with my powers, I could maybe reverse this." She stomped her foot—again it was silent. No water shot out from below the sole.

She rubbed her hands together, not confident that this was going to work. Not only did her hands not make a sound, but she couldn't feel them touching each other. Still, she used the trick that her Auntie Lettie had shown her when she was a young girl to "channel" her energy. She held her hand out in front of her, ready to concentrate—but on what?

"Okay, Zoie. You want to reverse death." She gnawed on the inside of her lip. "That seems a little bit like dark magic. Maybe we should try something else." She considered her options. "Well, Stevie pretended that our lungs were clear…" She paused. "Note to self: stop talking in the second person." Zoie went back to the important task and snapped her fingers—silence, but the symbolism was there for her. "Reverse the direction of the water. Clear it from your lungs." Then she quickly added, "and heal the damage to your lungs." She thought about how big of an undertaking this would be for someone who had years of training, and she wasn't sure that she could do it without any training. But she had to try.

She held her hand out and closed her eyes, concentrating on moving the water. She cautiously peaked out of one of her eyes. She had forgotten to take stock of how much water was around her before starting, so she didn't know if it had worked at all. "Well, you're still lying there, grey and blue." Zoie decided to try maybe moving one molecule at a time.

Starting the process over again, all the way back to rubbing her hands together, she tried again. When it didn't work, she stomped her feet as if she was going to start having a tantrum. "Ugh! This is bullshit!"

Pacing, Zoie ran through every single idea that she could. Maybe she would just haunt Hugh until she was able to communicate that Stevie wasn't as good a friend as she had pretended to be.

It was just then that someone walked up and stood next to her body—someone she hadn't seen before.

He was dressed entirely in black—black jeans with a black t-shirt, exposing black tattoos that started at his fingers and crawled up under his sleeves. He bent over and cradled Zoie's body in his arms.

"Hey!" Zoie yelled. She wasn't about to let someone take her body away before she could figure out how to reverse everything.

It was pointless. As soon he stood up, he and Zoie's body were gone. Suddenly, against her own will, Zoie was zipping through the air. At first, she tried to fight it, but when she realized that it was useless, she decided to let it happen. There had to be a reason that she couldn't be far from her body. She strangely felt herself twist and contort—even her face felt like it was being stirred around in the darkness, like soup.

After a few seconds, Zoie felt herself reassemble. She saw that they were in Italy—a few hours outside of Rome, maybe. She recognized it from one of the vacations her mom had taken her on and then left her alone to get lost in a strange place and pray it didn't end up like a Liam Neeson film.

She soon realized that they were in a ghost town, one of those places where they were advertising homes at a price of $1. It was remote, with no one around.

The man—obviously some sort of supernatural—kicked the door with his foot three times, and then someone inside opened it for him. He carried Zoie's body in, and Zoie crept up to the window to be nosy. She didn't feel like this was technically eavesdropping because it was her body in there. Mr. Elder-Emo-Wearing-Only-Black-Because-That's-How-I-Feel-Inside took Zoie's body directly to a wooden—obviously homemade—table and placed her there.

She saw a flurry of red, curly hair run over to the table. "I paid you to protect her!"

"Well, there were others after her," he spat back. "There was a bounty for her. I had some competition." He added, "and, to be honest, I think it was a lot more difficult to keep her alive than it was for that clown to kill her." He folded his arms across his chest, obviously defensive that the woman would even question him.

The woman spun around to yell at the man again, and, as soon as Zoie saw the woman's face, she gasped in shock. "Auntie Lettie?" Lettie looked the same as she always had: wild, curly red hair with wildflowers, a long maxi dress, big jewelry (including way too many rings and mismatched earrings), and flip flops.

"We need to get her to my friend Claudette right now. She may be able to help." She muttered, "She had better be able to."

The man cradled Zoie's body in his arms again, and Lettie put her hand on his shoulder. "I'm ready," he stated. They were sucked back into the darkness again.

Suddenly, they were in a different place—a different country, perhaps a different continent. Zoie had traveled with them, and, while she was the same distance away from them, she was no longer outside. She was in a large room with them.

"Claudette, do you think you can help?" Lettie pleaded. Then she looked over at the man. "Well, Silas, put her on the table," she ordered, obviously beyond frustrated with him at this point.

The woman Claudette, who was tall and slim with long, grey

hair, walked around Zoie's body, inspecting random parts of it. "She looks a little grey." She looked up at Lettie. "How long has it been?"

Silas answered. "About a half an hour. Maybe 45 minutes. That dog wouldn't leave her side without being dragged away by his friends." He looked at Zoie's body, appearing annoyed. "Please say you can help her." His voice sounded as if it had a hint of a plea in it.

Lettie shot him a sideways glance, but immediately turned back to her friend. "If you need me to gather any herbs…"

Claudette shook her head. "No."

"No you don't need herbs or no you can't help her?" Silas growled. He let out an annoyed breath through his nose.

"Be quiet." Claudette glared. Then she turned her attention back to Zoie's body. She turned around to a shelf and grabbed a few crystals, a feather, and what appeared to be a smudge stick. After setting a few things up, she looked at Lettie. "I will try my best. But you know how hard it is to move time back more than a few minutes."

"I am grateful that you are even willing to try, friend." Lettie took Claudette's hands in hers. "Even if this doesn't work, I am indebted to you."

Silas grumbled. "Let's get on with it." He tapped his finger to this wrist. "Each moment that passes is another one you have to go back in time to reverse this."

Zoie shot him a disgusted glance at the same time that both Lettie and Claudette did.

Claudette got to work. After cleansing the area, she rubbed her hands together and then held them gently above Zoie's body. She closed her eyes, and then Zoie felt some wind blow through the room.

Zoie resisted being pushed towards the table. "No! I didn't get to warn Hugh or tell him that I love him!" She grabbed onto a chair, as if that was going to hold her in place. She didn't want to be forced to go back into her body; she had a feeling that she would really be dead then. She had unfinished business.

The chair moved ever so slightly, scraping on the floor. Lettie and Silas jerked their heads towards the chair. Lettie smiled and then mouthed "Let go" towards the chair—and Zoie.

Confused, Zoie looked to see if someone else was standing behind her. When she realized what she already knew—that no one else was there, she let go of the chair and felt herself get sucked into her body's core.

Zoie experienced a strange pins-and-needles feeling all over her body. She tried to move, but her body seemed welded to the table. A wash of cold flowed from her head to her toes, and the pins and needles started to slowly fade—very slowly. Zoie wanted to shake her hands and arms or move her head from side to side, but it was as if she was strapped in place. Things were dark. She couldn't even open her eyes.

"Did it work?" That was the voice from that Silas guy—but it didn't sound as cold and distant as before. There was a hint of worry, and Zoie wondered if she mistook his demand to rush everything earlier. She internally shook her head. No, that didn't make sense. Who is this jerk anyways?

Then she heard that familiar voice—the voice Zoie had missed so desperately for several years—Auntie Lettie. "See her mark? It's returning to its normal color." Zoie felt the gentle touch of her aunt's hand on her wrist. "She's getting a little warmer; and…" she paused for a few moments. "Her heartbeat is there. Faint, but there." A sigh of relief. "Claudette, thank you."

That Silas guy went back to his irritated state of mind. "How long will she be out? How long will she be like this?"

"Her body needs to heal." Claudette sounded as annoyed as Zoie felt. If only Zoie could advocate for herself.

"How. Long. Will. That. Take?"

"Ignore him," Auntie Lettie suggested. "I always do."

Pfft.

"Listen," Claudette replied, "Her lungs were full of water—heavily chlorinated water—for somewhere between 30 minutes and an hour. They need to heal from the burns and aspiration." She added, "There's still a chance she won't make it."

Zoie called out "No!" but no one heard her. She was screaming into her own head. Desperate to communicate, Zoie started doing anything that she could to get out of her own head. Throwing things—who knew that her imagination was vivid enough to create grey chairs, dishes, cutlery, and even curtains to pull from the imaginary windows in her mind? She stomped her feet on black nothingness. She screamed into the void.

She was still alone in her head—and she supposed that was a good thing—but no one even acknowledged her outside of her head.

"You'll take care of her?"

That Silas guy replied, "Of course. That's what you pay me to do, isn't it?" He almost seemed smug about it.

Zoie wished she could have been able to see his reaction to Claudette's jab back at him. "Looks like you did a great job about an hour ago, eh?"

She could hear a deep, annoyed inhalation followed by a low growl and an exhalation. "I couldn't interfere with that. It was fixed."

"Which is why it is doubly—no, triply—important that you keep a watchful eye on Zoie for a bit." Zoie felt her aunt's soft hand over her forearm. "You must make sure that she makes it through." Zoie felt the tension in the silence.

It felt like hours before another word was said.

"Should we stay close in case we need your assistance again?" The floor creaked as Silas paced. Silence again. Was the answer a signal of sorts? Telepathic? Did they just ignore him? "Why not?"

"First of all, and I mean this with all respect to you, Lettie. You know we've been friends for more than a century…"

"I understand, Claudette."

"It's just that if it's found that I've helped her, I'm an accessory to this crime."

A deep sigh. "That's ridiculous."

"Silas, that's not even the biggest reason." Claudette's heels clicked on the wooden floor. "You said it yourself. This is a fixed point in time. I've done everything that I can, and nothing I would do from this moment would make a difference." She added, "It's already likely that the Shrews have felt the disturbance."

Suddenly, Zoie felt herself being lifted from the table. It wasn't until she felt the vibration in his chest that Zoie realized that she was being cradled in Silas' arms. "Well, then there's no reason to linger here." A few steps. "Lettie?"

"Claudette, thank you." There was the sound of two air kisses, and then a whooshing sound, and the air suddenly felt cooler on Zoie's arms.

Zoie heard another door creak and then smelled the familiar, welcoming scent of a wood-burning fireplace. Wherever she was at this point, she hoped that it was the last time she—her body, whatever—was on the move. She just wanted to stay in the same place so she could figure things out.

But the last thing that she heard was Lettie suggesting getting her into some dry clothes and Silas making a snarky comment about how Zoie smelled like wet dog.

—Hugh—

Hugh attempted to concentrate on securing a part to his bike, but Cade singing along with the radio kept distracting him. It wasn't that they sang poorly. No, Cade had the voice of an angel. It was the choice of song, "Ghost" by Justin Bieber.

They hummed the rest of it. Despite all of the tools and equipment absorbing the sound, it still bounced off the walls and echoed.

Hugh slammed his wrench down. "Please, turn this song off." He raked his hands down his face and looked up to the ceiling and groaned.

Cade made their way over to the radio. "You don't like this song?"

Hugh glared. "The lyrics are about being okay with a ghost instead of the person. What do you think my problem is with the song?" He picked up the wrench and started working again.

"Some day you are going to need to move on." They changed the radio station and "One Sweet Day" by Mariah Carey and Boyz II Men was in the middle of the chorus. Hugh didn't even have time to glare again before Cade quickly switched it to a rock station. "Aces High" by Iron Maiden was on, and that seemed to

13

be sufficient. "Seriously, she would want you to be happy."

Hugh replied, "I am happy." He plastered a fake grin on his face. Even that couldn't battle his bitterness—after a few seconds, it was gone.

It was Cade's turn to glare. "Hugh, you're just going through the motions." They pulled a seat up next to Hugh. "Zoie wouldn't want this for you."

"Look, I thought removing Miles from this planet would help, and it did. It did for a little while. But I failed Zoie. I promised her that I would take care of Alvin, and I didn't." He added, "and I don't know when I will have the opportunity again." He put the wrench down and looked up again, hoping that the tears welling up in his eyes would retreat into the depths of his tear ducts.

"How much do you think that it would really help? You could kill everyone on this god-forsaken planet, and that's not going to bring her back." Hugh didn't respond. Cade looked him up and down. "You think she's still out there, don't you?"

"No…" He frowned. "I don't know." Still a lie. Looking down at the garage floor, he sighed. "I still feel her." If Hugh was honest with himself, against all evidence to the contrary, he believed that she was still alive. He believed it was a mistake to just leave her in Romania, and, upon finding out that Stevie had lied, he believed that he had made a grave error by not contacting a witch for assistance.

Beyond that, Hugh regretted letting Zoie's mother take possession of everything that was Zoie's that he hadn't acquired the night she died. Legally, he didn't have a leg to stand on, but he could have taken some things by force—but did that really matter? He had already taken Judy, Zoie's manuscripts, her collection of editions of *Little Women*, and the tie that he had used to make a vow to Zoie. Any of these items would have ended up in the trash if Carol had gotten her hands on them.

Cade put a hand on Hugh's shoulder. "You'll always feel her, Hugh. She's a part of you." Taking a deep, cautious breath, they continued, "but she's gone, and you have to move forward in life."

Hugh took his hair out of the man-bun and put it back, readjusting it. "What, Cayden, do you think that I should do?"

Cade moved back just a little bit, preparing for retaliation for their suggestion. "One date. Go on one date." They got into a defensive stance, ready for assault—physical or verbal.

Hugh scoffed. "You have someone picked out?" He didn't care if there was already someone waiting. He didn't want to go out with her. He didn't want to hold hands, hug, kiss. Hugh had no desire to buy flowers or teddy bears. He certainly didn't want to hold open doors or pay for meals or make small talk. Above all else, he refused to even begin to think about sharing a bed with another woman. As far as he was concerned, Hugh was eternally committed to Zoie, and no one would ever be able to step in and try to replace her. His soul was married to hers, and even if she was gone, the commitment remained.

"Actually, no," Cade suggested, "but I think you should just… find someone—someone that you find attractive or funny or have something in common with—and go on one date. You don't have to take it anywhere further. It doesn't even have to be like a serious date night like Friday. It could be a Wednesday. Brunch."

Hugh shook his head and laughed weakly. "That's ridiculous. What's that going to do?" His patience was wearing thin. This was a conversation that they had had about once or twice a week for the last couple months. After he'd pulled himself out of his depression and torched Miles's remains and shredded Stevie's face, it truly seemed like every Friday, as if on cue, Cayden would try to convince Hugh to move on.

"It. Will. Help. You. Move. On."

Hugh snapped, "I'm not ready!" He tossed his wrench across the garage, where it clanked against some other tools before falling to the cement floor.

Cade stood up and put their hands up in defeat. "You know what? Fuck it."

Hugh stood up. "Why do you care so much?"

Cade's jaw dropped to the floor. "You fucking serious?" They folded their arms across their chest. "Dude, I love you, Hugh. You're my brother. It physically hurts to see you like this. Jesus fucking Christ!" They shook their head. "It's actually painful to see; it's like there's something missing inside of you."

Hugh groaned and then yelled, "There is something missing, Cade!" He tried to fight back tears. He slammed his fist against his chest. "There is a hole in my heart, and any time I think—even entertain the thought—of moving on, that hole erodes even more of what little is left." He wiped a waterfall of tears with his sleeve and looked up at the ceiling. He raked his hands through his hair. "I cannot even begin to formulate the thought of being with someone other than her." Trying to hold back a sob, he took a deep breath. "I've tried to hold back how I feel about this because I know you're trying to do what's best…"

"Hugh…"

He walked in a circle, looking up towards the ceiling. "She still calls to me." His hands dropped and he slumped over. "I feel like she…" He shook his head. "If Zoie isn't physically out there, then her spirit calls to me, so she may not be alive, but I'm not convinced that she doesn't still need me."

Cade narrowed their eyes at him. "Listen to what you just said." Pausing for a moment to collect their thoughts, Cade finally continued. "I hope you realize that what you just said sounds like a big fucking excuse and that, if the roles were reversed, you would be trying to knock some sense into me."

"If I never felt the mating bond, yeah, I would. But I've felt this, and knowing what this feels like, no, I wouldn't be trying to force you to go against it." He sat back down, defeated. He put his face in his hands and, finally, let himself be vulnerable.

Hugh feared that the tears flowing from his eyes would find their way into the cracks in his heart and further erode any pieces left and aid in its complete destruction.

Cautiously, Cade made their way over to where Hugh was seated. They pulled up a chair and hugged him. "I'm sorry." Hugh just sobbed as his friend held him. "I'm so sorry." They continued to hold him and repeated that they were sorry. "I didn't know that it still hurt the way it did when it first happened. I thought you were healing." They quietly added, "I won't bring it up again."

—Zoie—

Zoie sat up, suddenly, gasping for air.

"You're okay. You're okay," Lettie said in a calming tone, as she approached Zoie.

Looking around, Zoie noticed that she was on a bed in an unfamiliar room. "What… where… when… how?" Her eyes stopped on a figure sitting in a chair in a dark corner of the room. "Who…"

"All that's left is 'why'." The dark figure stood and approached Zoie. It was that Silas guy who had taken her from the poolside in Romania to Auntie Lettie.

Lettie sat down next to Zoie on the bed. "Zoie, this is Silas. He's been…"

Zoie interrupted. "Stalking me. He's been stalking me." Her throat was dry, and it felt as if there were cotton in her mouth.

Silas let out an annoyed sigh.

"No. No way," Zoie pointed at him, coughing and swallowing to try to coat her throat with liquid. "You're not allowed to be annoyed right now. I have no idea where or, actually, when I am." She continued. "I have no idea who you are, except that Auntie Lettie paid you to stalk…"

"Protect." His arms were folded across his chest.

"Stalk." Zoie wasn't backing down. "She paid you to stalk me." She turned to Lettie. "And, you! You!" She coughed again. "You led me to believe that you were dead! For years. You were the best part of my childhood, and I needed you these last few years. And you've been lying to me."

Silas huffed and rolled his eyes. "You're so overdramatic."

"Don't speak. I don't care what you say in the slightest bit. I have no fucking idea who you are." She squinted her eyes at him and then turned back to Lettie. "Explain all of this. How long have I been asleep?"

"Four months."

Zoie pushed herself back in the bed, hitting her shoulders and head on the headboard. While rubbing her head, she asked, "I've been sleeping for four months?"

"Healing," Lettie corrected. "Your body went through a lot and, sometimes, when time is reversed there are consequences and uncertainties."

"Consequences?" She looked around the room, in search of a source of water. How in hell could neither of her alleged caregivers think to get her a damn glass of water?

She nodded. "You just needed to sleep it off, but…"

"You've had four months to practice telling me, so spit it out."

Lettie looked at Silas and then back at Zoie. "Well, there's a chunk of your hair at the front that's changed to white and a piece underneath, too."

Zoie wasn't very concerned about this. She could dye it if it bothered her that badly. She looked back and forth between them. "Is that the big issue?"

Lettie took Zoie's hand. "This one, we're not sure, but… you technically did die, so… your bond with Hugh, it may be broken."

Zoie yanked her hand back. "It's not."

"How do you know?" Silas asked, harshly. "You never felt it yourself anyways." How did he know that? While stalking her, had he infiltrated her thoughts?

Zoie glared at him. "Not that I owe you any explanation, but I just know." While Hugh had always explained their bond as electricity shooting through his entire body, she felt it as a fire burning within her.

"If your bond is so strong, why hasn't he come to find you? Hmmm?" Silas rolled his eyes.

Zoie rolled her eyes in return. She definitely hated this guy, who had no chance of turning that around. "He saw my dead body. He held it. I'm pretty sure that would have been enough evidence to deter him." Turning back to Lettie, she asked, "When can I see him?"

"Zoie," Lettie replied cautiously. "Zoie, I think you need to rest a few days…"

"I just rested for four months." Rest a few days? What a bunch of shit.

"…and then we need to work on some of your magic skills so that you can protect yourself. And, I'm not sure that it's safe for you to return yet. Hugh's about to get scheduled to meet with the Council to be held accountable…"

"Then I need to go to him now." She wasn't really planning to negotiate this.

Silas stepped closer to her, leaning over to intimidate her. "What part of 'it's not safe' do you not understand?"

Zoie looked around, pretending to search for something. "I'm sorry, I'm unable to find the fuck I give about your opinion." She turned back to Lettie. "I'm sure that Hugh can protect me."

"Like he protected you in Romania?" The huevos on this guy.

Zoie turned to Silas again. "Seriously? Who the fuck are you?" She turned to Lettie. "Who is this prick?"

"I am the prick that, I don't know, just nursed you back to health for the last four months; saved your ass when you drowned; and kept you from fucking dying for a year before that." He held his hand out for her to shake it. "Silas."

She swatted his hand away. "Hero complex much? Do I owe you something for that? I'm pretty sure that my auntie paid you for your work." Being present for her own resurrection had come with the perk of having background information that she wouldn't otherwise have known.

"Zoie, his work isn't finished. He's going to train you."

Zoie put her hand up in the air, signaling a stop. "I'm done with this part of the conversation right now. I have so many other questions."

"Of course you do," Silas scoffed. "You always have 800 questions."

"Seriously, dude. Shut. Up." Hatred. Definitely fiery, passionate hatred. She looked back at Lettie. "Where have you been for the last several years? I thought you were dead." This excuse had best be gooooooood.

Lettie frowned. "It was at the request of your mother that I left you alone." She then asked, "How is that old… well, I don't have many nice words for that woman." Lettie looked at her nails, trying to be dismissive of any thoughts of Carol.

Zoie shrugged. "The last time I saw her, she was drunk and expected me to apologize for one of her outbursts."

"Typical." Lettie continued, "She wanted all of this 'magic business' to end with your father." Actual finger quotes. "I wanted to send you away for training; she didn't agree, and well, she threatened to tell your world about our world, so I had to leave."

"Why didn't you just put a spell on her? Miles made it so that I couldn't talk about… wait how can I talk about it now?"

"Miles is dead," Silas said flatly. "Your beloved, in a fit of rage, avenged you." He rolled his eyes and grumbled, "total brute" under his breath.

While she was pleased to hear that Miles could no longer be a threat, she didn't want to give Silas the satisfaction of wasting any more of her attention on him, and she didn't want to acknowledge his cowardly insult. She continued "…so the magic just goes away?"

Lettie nodded. "That's why we think that it's likely your bond is severed."

"It's not." She glared at Lettie, annoyed that she had to repeat herself. The fire that had been ignited in her blood for him was still burning, but she didn't feel that she had to explain to anyone the way that her bond with Hugh manifested within her.

Silas interjected again. "Why do you care, though? If you two love each other as much as you think you do, the bond shouldn't matter. You should be able to get back together and everything will be fine." He mumbled, "Only the wolves believe that shit anyways."

The facts that wolves believed it and Hugh was a wolf would have been plenty for her to believe that the mating bond was real, but she knew she also felt it.

Zoie started to stand up. "Shut. The. Fuck. Up. I hate you." Her vision began to shake, and she started hearing muffled dubstep.

When she wobbled, Silas grabbed Zoie by the arm to support her. "Be careful. You're like Grandpa Joe in Willy Wonka—you've not stood up in ages."

Zoie started to chuckle at the reference, then caught herself. She looked up into his eyes—so dark brown that they were nearly black—and got lost for just a moment. Shaking her head, she yanked her arm a little. "I don't need your help. Thankyouverymuch." She quickly sat back down on the bed. She did need help, but she didn't want his.

"Silas," Lettie requested, "Can you go make something for Zoie to eat?"

Zoie quickly added, "I need water."

Reluctantly, he replied, "Sure. I don't want to listen to your girl talk anyways."

As soon as he was out of the room, Zoie turned to Lettie and groaned. "He's awful."

"Zoie, he's actually quite wonderful once you get to know him."

Zoie looked back and forth between Lettie and the door a few times. "Are you two together?"

Lettie laughed. "Lord, no!" She explained, "I've known him since you were a little girl. Your father and I requested his assistance with protecting you."

"I thought he was only watching me for a year." Zoie was beyond over it with people in the supernatural part of the world lying or withholding information. She wasn't surprised that things didn't add up.

Lettie nodded. "He was. But your father knew that some dangerous people were after him, and he wanted to set things up for you to be safe. I was to watch you until you came into your powers a bit more and began training, and Silas would watch you after that, until you were able to take care of yourself."

"Who watched me in the years that you were dead?" Zoie wasn't about to forget or forgive that little lie.

"Actually, I did. But just before you broke up with that horrible fiancé of yours, there was a close call, so I called upon Silas."

Zoie sat up straighter. "Close call—how? Did I nearly die or something?"

Lettie shook her head. "No, I understand how that could have been confusing. There was a close call where you might have seen me."

"I was an adult. You could have come back to me."

Lettie tilted her head a little. "Really? Do you really think that you would have accepted my grand return before you knew about this kind of world?"

Zoie frowned. "It would have been nice to have my friend back." She looked down. "I know it's strange, but even though I was a child and you were my auntie, I thought of you more like a friend." She finally answered Lettie's rhetorical question. "Yes, I would have believed you because, well, it was you, and you would have worked to prove to me that it was true."

"Well, then, Zoie, I'm deeply sorry." Lettie reached over and gently took Zoie's hand.

After a brief silence, Zoie changed the subject again. "How long until I can go back to Hugh?"

"As long as it takes."

This veil of lies and omissions was thick and layered. Annoyed and hungry, Zoie sharply asked, "As long as what takes? I'm not some little child anymore, Auntie Lettie. Explain this shit to me." Then she added, "and when you're done with that, I want to know if you're really my aunt."

Lettie sighed and then smiled. "As long as it takes for you to be comfortable with your powers. You can wield fire, and we can't have you burning a house down because you've seen a spider." Her attempt at humor was lost on Zoie, so with the reply to Zoie's genealogical question, she was blunt. "I am your father's aunt, so I'm your great-aunt."

"How old are you? How old was Daddy?" It almost felt strange to talk about him with someone who'd known him. Zoie's mother rarely spoke of him, and no one else really knew him.

"Well, I'm about 150. Your father would have been about 135 right now, if he was still with us." She added, "You're an adult now. You don't have to call me Auntie. Just call me Lettie. I would much rather us be friends, like you said, before anything else."

"Friends don't lie to each other. Friends don't pretend to be dead for years. Friends don't keep each other from the people they love." She sat in silence for a moment. "Do you think I could shower and see this hair and… just, you know, allow myself to feel a little more human?"

Lettie nodded. "I will be right outside that door, but I would like it if you kept both doors open so that I can hear if you fall or something, since you've not stood in a while." She pointed at a duffle bag. "There's clothes for you in there."

Zoie headed towards the bathroom but paused. "Lettie?"

"Hmm?"

"How did I get clean and stuff while I was sleeping?"

Lettie grinned. "Well, Silas gave you sponge baths, of course."

"WHAT?!" Zoie shrieked.

Lettie laughed. "Zoie, we're witches and he's a warlock. We used magic to keep you healthy and clean."

Zoie narrowed her eyes at her aunt. "That wasn't funny."

She tried her best to ignore it when Lettie replied with "Yes, it was". In the bathroom mirror, she immediately saw the large chunk of white hair, just above her left ear. Since her hair parted on the left, she wouldn't be able to cover it, so she decided to embrace it. The other piece was actually on the right, at the point where the hairline behind her ear met with the hairline on the back of her head.

"It actually looks cool," she said to herself with a smile. Zoie had never feared aging, and, in fact, she embraced it. When her father had passed, she had believed him to only be 35, so Zoie had always thought of aging as a luxury. She wasn't going to let a few white hairs bother her.

Using a new shower for the first time was always like unlocking a portal to a parallel universe. Zoie knew if she asked Lettie or Silas for instruction, she would never hear the end of it.

She eventually got the water going from the faucet. Thinking for a moment, she reached to where the water was coming out and pulled down. "Success!" Water streamed from the shower head.

The first thing she did was drink some of the water from the shower. Her request for a glass of water had been neglected.

While in the shower, she dropped both the shampoo and the bottle of soap, prompting Lettie to come running in and checking on her. Having her privacy invaded really annoyed her, but it was nice that someone cared. It was doubly nice that that someone was not Silas.

After getting out of the shower, she opted to scrunch her hair to help it dry but also avoid frizz. She paused her work when she overheard Lettie and Silas in a quiet argument.

"…Silas, it was part of the contract." Lettie's voice had two parts annoyance—not hard to imagine since she was dealing with Silas—and one part concern.

He put something down on the counter, hard. "Lettie, just take her back to Hugh. He can train her."

"Hugh doesn't know magic, and he's not friendly with any witches or warlocks—at least none with the ability to help."

"Then you do it." Water ran for about three seconds, someone swallowed, and then someone slammed a glass onto a counter.

Lettie stomped her foot. "Damn it, Silas. Victor and I contracted you to protect her, and part of that was…"

He cut her off. "She's too old to be taught, Lettie. Sure, if she came into her powers now, yes, she could be. But they've been lying dormant for nearly 20 years. Wipe her memory and send her back to her mother."

"And make her forget everything she's been through? Make her forget Hugh?"

Silas groaned. "It's an idea, and it would keep her safe. Out of our world." He continued, "You trusted me with her safety, and it's my expert opinion that this would be the best thing for her."

Lettie started to speak but Silas cut her off. "How long has the shower been off?"

"Not sure…"

Zoie shoved past Lettie into the kitchen. "Is there no end to the lies?" She headed towards the door. She could feel the blood in her veins ignite, and her palms started to radiate heat.

"You're going to want to put a coat on…" Silas backed up as Zoie rushed past him.

She flung the door open and slammed it behind her. She pulled her cardigan around her more tightly—she didn't want to admit it, but Silas had been right about the coat.

The door creaked open slowly as if it were haunted. Zoie didn't even turn around. She didn't want to talk to Lettie.

"Hey. Here's one of my hoodies." It was actually Silas.

Reluctantly, Zoie took it and threw it on over her clothes. "I don't want to hear whatever it is that you have to say."

He stood next to her, looking out, just as she was. "I wouldn't either, if I were you."

They stood in silence for a few moments. "Where the fuck are we?"

"Northern Canada. Where, like, no one lives, because I like to be left the fuck alone." From the corner of her eye, Zoie noticed him turn a little towards her.

She turned towards him, arms folded across her chest. "I will never let you take my memories—especially not the ones of Hugh."

"I couldn't do it if I wanted to." She glared at him. He explained, "I'm not the right kind of warlock to do that."

"Whatever." She turned and looked back out at the scenery. "You underestimate me, anyways."

He rolled his eyes. "You can't keep a witch or warlock skilled in memory manipulation from winning that kind of situation."

She scoffed. "I heard you say that my powers have been dormant for too long. You're wrong." Zoie added, "I'm an excellent student."

"Do you see that metal fire ring off to the left of the porch?" When Zoie nodded, Silas said, "It's empty right now—just ashes. If you can light a fire using only your magic, then I'll teach you. Otherwise, I'm leaving you out in the wilderness for the wolves."

Zoie knew she could do this; she didn't know how she knew, but she did. She had to do it—getting comfortable with her powers would open the door to getting back to Hugh. Zoie needed to get back to him. She closed her eyes for a moment, concentrating. She didn't know what she was trying to picture, but Zoie had a feeling that her mind would just figure it out.

She pictured the sun—only it was different than when she normally saw things in her mind's eye.

For starters, it was actually colorful. Not colorful in the sense that it was every color of the rainbow. No—it was predominantly yellow, with sparks of orange and red. The difference was that when Zoie normally pictured things, they were the outlines of them, filled in with grey, so when she saw the bright colorful sun, it was like an entirely new world opened up in her mind.

The second thing that was strange to her was that she wasn't picturing this fiery sun in the sky or even actually in her mind. She was visualizing it just in front of her belly button. Floating there. Solar flares shooting out in all directions.

Zoie also realized that she could feel her Sun. She realized that not only was it a sphere—a moving, shifting ball that rotated—but she could feel the heat that radiated from it.

She thought of igniting the fire, and those solar flares became weaker. She was angry at herself. She would prove to everyone— Silas, Lettie, and, especially, herself—that she could do this. The red, yellow, and orange solar flares shot wildly from the surface. Zoie realized she could really do this. If Hugh were there with her, he would be so proud of her. The solar flares shot up smoothly and returned to the surface, energizing her Sun more.

Zoie's eyes shot open. She smirked. Fire shot from her palms and fingertips, igniting the fire pit instantly. The flames shot up, higher than the roof of the cabin, then quickly settled to a nice, calm, appropriately sized fire, crackling periodically.

Silas jumped back, knocking a flower pot off of a small table onto the porch. Zoie turned to him, and Silas put his hands in the air. "Okay, okay! I'll train you!"

"Thank you." She reacted calmly, but inside, she was scared. Frightened of what she'd just done and what was to come.

He turned back towards the cabin door, mumbling something about her eyes.

"What was that?" Zoie asked, folding her arms across her chest.

"Your eyes. They glow orange when you do magic. I've just never seen anything like that before."

"Why'd you agree to do it?" She asked.

His confusion was written all over his face. "Because you lit the fire...?"

"No. Why did you agree to protect me?"

"Because I didn't think I would have to actually do it." He continued, "I figured, when you were an adorable little five-year-old with bouncy red curls, no one would actually hurt you. When I didn't get called to watch you for a while, I figured that the fear about you father's enemies had died down."

"And when you found out that it hadn't?"

"When Lettie contacted me and I saw the fucking douche bag you were going to marry... Holy shit, Zoie, let me reiterate that he was a fucking loser. A total tool bag. The worst possible person you could have tried to tie yourself to..." He started to chuckle.

She narrowed her eyes at him. "Move on from that, please."

He looked down at his feet. "I legit almost staged it so that you and I would meet—what do you call it? A 'meet-cute'. I almost created one so I could save you from all of that pain because I felt sorry for you."

"Gross." Zoie really didn't like that he was arrogant enough to think that some stupid meet-cute would have made her fall for him. "I don't need your pity."

"No, you don't, do you? You don't need anyone's, really." He turned and stared towards the path leading away from the cabin. "Then you moved to Birmingham, and you were super independent, and, I'll admit it, that kind of courage was kind of..." he hesitated. "Well, it was sexy. I thought it was incredible the way that you put yourself back together and started a new life."

"What are you getting at?"

He admitted, cautiously, "I would have done it. Protected you out in the open, rather than in the shadows. I was going to insert myself into your life and make it happen, even though I find you unbearable most days." She glared at him. "Then you met Hugh, and it seemed like you hit it off." He shrugged. "I've never liked him, but you did. Plus, he could protect you." He paused. "Until he couldn't."

She narrowed her eyes at him. "It's not his fault what happened. And, if I recall correctly, it was your literal job to protect me."

He groaned. "You're kind of difficult, you know?"

Checkmate. "No. I just call you out on your hypocritical bullshit." She turned to go back inside.

"Zoie, yeah, I get paid to protect you. BUT!" He grabbed her arm and turned her towards him. "But, as your alleged bonded mate, he is supposed to protect you with his life. He didn't do that." He looked her directly in the eyes. "It's not real, Zoie. He made up the bonded mate bullshit to draw you in. To make you believe that you have no choice but to love him."

Instinctively, she reached up and slapped Silas across the face and then stepped down off the porch. Zoie took off down a path flanked by thick rows of trees.

"Where are you going?!"

She didn't turn around. She didn't answer. Zoie just kept walking—until she felt a lasso wrap around her and tighten. Did this dude think he was a cowboy?

When she tried to wiggle free of the thick woven vines, Silas called out, "It's no use." He gathered the vine as he walked closer to her. "Victor—your father—made this rope specifically for me so that I could capture my marks and they couldn't get free."

"Your marks?"

"I'm a bounty hunter, Zoie. A damn good one. This," he pointed back and forth between the two of them, "is not my typical line of work."

"Then why did you take the job?"

He admitted, "Your father… he took me in when I first found NightBrooke. He didn't agree with my becoming a bounty hunter, so we went our separate ways, but there was always a mutual respect between us." He stepped closer to her, still drawing the rope in. "I took the job because I wanted to protect a little girl from evil people." He pulled her close. "I had no idea she would grow up to be such a pain in the ass."

Silas wasn't much taller than she was—maybe five or six inches—so it wasn't difficult for her to glare right into his eyes. "Then take me back to Hugh and let him deal with me."

He let out a sigh. "Do you ever stop whining about him? He's not that fucking great, you know?"

"How do you know? You don't even know him." She yanked on the rope again, but it didn't budge.

"Everyone knows your boyfriend. Anyone that's been a part of our world for more than a few years knows him." He placed his hand over the knot in the vine. "Most people are afraid of him— especially now again since he killed Miles." He released her from the rope. "He's not known for being overly nice to anyone other than his friend Cayden, and now you. He's kind of grumpy."

"Oh." Even though she loved Hugh dearly, she understood how others could label him in that manner.

"Yeah, when everyone found out that he'd fallen in love, people were shocked that he could even like someone that much, let alone actually feel love." He placed his hand on her back and guided her back towards the cabin.

She didn't fight him on going back to the cabin, and she didn't swat away his hand, either. "What do people think about you?"

"They don't."

"No, seriously."

He reiterated, "No, seriously, they don't. I'm a bounty hunter, and I keep myself pretty low-profile." He explained, "You know how your power is from the sun?" When she nodded, he continued, "Mine is pulled from the shadows. The dark." He pointed towards a shadow under a tree, and tiny black bubbles of shadow came to his palms.

Zoie jumped back. "Isn't dark magic evil?"

"No." He opened the door to the cabin. "That's a misconception. What makes magic evil is actually the intent behind it, not the source of the magic itself. You have a lot to learn."

Lettie greeted them. "Are you two getting along better? I hope so because I can't stay much longer."

Immediately, Zoie went back into her apprehensive mode. "Are you going to leave me here with him? I'm not convinced that he doesn't know someone who could wipe my memories, and he hates me."

Lettie shook her head. "Oh, no, no, no, dear. Silas loves you dearly." She said it as if this was normal conversation about the weather forecast. "In fact, he's been fighting it for ages." With that, she stood up and grabbed her purse. "I'll be back in a week or so. I have some business to attend to." She immediately disappeared.

"That's not true," Silas said immediately. "I was honest when I told you that I found your courage hot, but that's all it is."

"It doesn't matter. I don't return the sentiment. What I mean is, I don't love you. Not that you're hideous."

He chuckled. "Good to know." He walked past her and sat on the couch. He pull the remote from between two cushions. He scrolled to Netflix and put on *Blown Away*, a glass-blowing competition show.

"Ooh, I really like this show!" Zoie exclaimed excitedly and then took a seat on the chair, to maintain maximum distance between them. Zoie admitted, "I think it's unfair that you have a dossier about me but I don't have the same advantage."

Silas laughed once. "I don't have a dossier on you. I've just been watching you for a while, and you get to know someone pretty well playing their shadow."

"Well…" She dragged out the word as if she expected Silas to say something. When he didn't, she requested, "Can I get some insight into you?"

He sighed. As if he was repeating a story he had told a billion times, he emotionlessly stated, "I was born in Hawaii in 1962. My father left in 1970, and in 1975, my mother died in the same house fire that gave me my powers." He continued, as if this was something he explained to others on the daily and was annoyed. "I was raised by my grandmother, an evil, devoutly and allegedly Christian woman, who was solely focused on image, and forbade me from using my magic because she was afraid that someone would see and ostracize us. She wanted me to lose my abilities so that our family wouldn't reside for eternity in Hell."

"Oh, I'm sorry."

He shook his head. "Don't be. I would have spent my life running or using my magic, slowing my aging process, and would have been essentially 13 forever." He chuckled. "I went to college but quit after one semester. Dear old granny was mortified—what would the neighbors in our tiny town think about my failure, about her failure as a guardian?" Silas acted as if he were his overdramatic grandmother asking the question. "She kicked me out. While wandering around I found this really weird pool of water. It looked like… you know when oil is on water? Being the total jackass that

I am, I jumped in, and I ended up in Nightbrooke."

Seemingly out of nowhere, she asked, "You want hot chocolate?" She couldn't handle just sitting there, and she'd never gotten the food that was allegedly being prepared for her while she was in the shower.

Silas raised an eyebrow at her. "I hope you aren't planning to make it out of that weird powder shit."

Excitedly, she shook her head. "No, I can make it from scratch." She ran over to the kitchen—all six steps away—this was going to be tight quarters and got started. She paused for a moment when she saw a sandwich. "Is this for me?"

"Oh, yeah," he glanced over the back of the couch at her and grinned. "I made that for you before you stormed out of here like a teenager planning to run away from home because your mom told you to clean your room."

She scoffed. "You're a total jerk."

He replied, "and you can't take a joke."

Annoyed and wanting to take the focus off of her flaws, Zoie asked, "Do you have any popcorn? Maybe I'm weird, but I like to eat popcorn when I have hot chocolate."

Silas laughed. "I don't think I have any popcorn, sorry." He got up and checked a couple cupboards. "Lettie may have brought some, so I'll check."

"Um… how long have you and Lettie been living together?" She looked down at the pan as she stirred.

This question confused him. "We don't live together. She hired me for a job, and we've become friends. She checked in on this place while I was watching you. When you lived in Pittsburgh, I didn't have to watch you day in and day out, but once you moved to Birmingham and met Hugh…"

Zoie zoned out. She thought of Hugh, who must have been

mourning her for months without any idea that she was still alive. She hoped that her mother hadn't been too evil towards him and had let him have some of her things—especially the book he had loaned to her. She hadn't gotten to finish it. If they'd had a funeral, what did they put in the casket? Or was she officially listed as a missing person? Did her death satisfy the Council enough to drop the charges against Hugh and end that ridiculous reward for his capture? There were so many things she wanted answers to, but even more than that, she just longed to be in Hugh's arms and feel

the heat that radiated from his body

—Hugh—

Running his fingers along the broken spines of the dusty, old books in the boxes at the outdoor block-party-style flea market, Hugh scanned for any titles that sparked his interest. Most of the books were the usuals—*Moby Dick*, *To Kill a Mockingbird*, *The Great Gatsby*—but there were a few lesser-known titles.

Hugh saw an edition of *Little Women* that he knew wasn't part of Zoie's collection. He picked it up and flipped through the pages, taking in the smell of the paper and ink. A smile crossed his face. Any time he picked up a book, especially *Little Women*, he felt closer to Zoie. It was as if she lived within the pages and opening a book was an escape into a world where maybe she still existed.

"Which of the *Little Women* characters do you consider yourself most like?"

"Huh?" Hugh looked up to see the woman at the table smiling at him. "I'm sorry, I missed what you said?"

"Maybe you're more like Laurie—no, no. You're Mr. Brooke." She placed another box up on the table. "Quiet. Sensible. Don't need many frills." She deftly pulled her long, straight black hair into a braid and secured it with a rubber band. She put her hand out. "I'm Rosalie."

Reluctantly, shook took her hand. "I'm Hugh. I would love to say that I was exciting like Laurie, but I think you're correct. I probably am most like Mr. Brooke." He looked at the hand-written price sticker on the front of the book. He was shocked that the book was marked at a quarter. "Nice to meet you, Rosalie." He handed her five dollars and declined change.

He turned, but before he walked away she touched his arm. "Wait…"

Hugh paused and took a deep breath in before turning to her. He hadn't been touched by anyone—besides Cade when they tried to comfort him—in a long time. It had become foreign to him. "Yes?"

"Why *Little Women?*" When he didn't answer right away, she said, "I was watching you browse, and it looked like you were searching for that specific book because your face both lit up and filled with sadness when you found it."

Reluctantly, Hugh replied, "Well…" Surely she didn't want to hear the long, painful story of his relationship with Zoie.

"Is it for a lady-friend?" Her eyes lit up.

He chuckled. "Sort of." His smile turned into a small frown. "She's gone."

Her face fell. "Oh. I'm so sorry. I didn't mean to upset you."

He shook his head. "You couldn't have known." He wanted out of this conversation, desperately.

"I certainly can put my foot in my mouth. I was planning on asking you to meet me afterwards for some frozen yogurt, but I'm pretty sure that ship has sailed."

"I'm sorry," he replied. "It has nothing to do with what you said, but I'm just not ready…"

Teasing him, Rosalie interjected, "You're not ready for fro-yo?"

He chuckled. "No, I mean, any time is a good time for frozen yogurt, but…" He trailed off for a moment. "She just… It's only been a few months."

She shook her head. "I'm not asking you to marry me."

Hugh put his hand up. "I'm sorry. I would feel as if I were being unfaithful to her or her memory. It's too soon." He didn't give her a chance to say anything more. Hugh left and mounted his bike.

There were many reasons that he'd declined the invitation. The first five reasons were Zoie. Then, there was Rosalie not knowing he was a werewolf. The rest of the reasons were related to her. She was so young, possibly even younger than Zoie. She was selling dusty, unused, not-very-well-loved books. For less than a dollar. Obviously, she didn't read. He couldn't be with someone who didn't enjoy reading.

At home, he placed the newest-to-him edition of *Little Women* on the shelf next to the others he had collected for Zoie.

The front door creaked slowly. His ears perked up, and the glow of his eyes reflected in the glass of a picture frame.

He crept out to the main room, then let out a deep breath and relaxed. "Cade."

They turned around. "Want to go out tonight? Sister Hazel is playing at a bar downtown." No "hello," just straight to the question.

Hugh shrugged. "Sure."

"You really shouldn't sit at home—wait did you agree to go?"

Hugh nodded, walked into the kitchen, and put the kettle on. "Yeah, I did."

"Are you feeling okay?" Cade tried to put the back of their hand on Hugh's forehead, but he dodged.

"Cut it out. I'm fine." He chuckled, swatting their hand away.

———————

The bar was more crowded than Hugh had anticipated, especially since it had been a bit since the height of the band's popularity, and this was a college town. The last time Sister Hazel had a charting hit, most of the patrons hadn't been born.

Cayden and Hugh sat at the bar. It wasn't long before Cade's natural magnetism attracted a group of college students. Their confidence drew people in. The blunt honesty kept the worthwhile ones around. As usual.

A sweet, sing-song voice cut through the noise. Hugh caught the tail end of her sentence to Cade. "…so tell me about your friend." He could almost hear her eyelashes flutter.

He turned away and rolled his eyes. He didn't want to do this. Not on the first night that he had gone out in months without being forced. Definitely not when he actually wanted to enjoy the music.

"Oh, he pretends to be all grumpy and icy, but he's really nice," Cade said. "His girlfriend… she…"

"What happened to her?" The girl leaned in.

Hugh turned around, interrupting the conversation. "She died. Recently. Very recently."

He didn't want to chat with anyone, so he figured telling them the truth would get them to back off. What girl wants to talk to someone that's depressed and in mourning, right?

He was so wrong.

The college-aged girl came right to his side. "Oh, you poor thing. Do you want to talk about it?" Her blue eyes showed genuine concern and she pouted, placing her hand on his forearm.

Unsure of how to react, he pulled his arm back a little. "Ummm… Not sure that I do." What was it with people today thinking they could touch someone whenever they wanted?

She took a sip of her drink through a straw and looked at him through her eyelashes. "We don't have to talk…"

He smiled. "No, let's talk. What's your name?" All those required courses on the university's learning management system about drinking, sex, harassment, and so on were coming back to him.

"Paige." She smiled. "Yours?" She leaned even closer to him.

He replied. "I'm Hugh. What do you do? Do you work at the hospital here? Almost everyone in this city does."

She shook her head. "Not yet! I'm a nursing student at the university."

"Oh, that's interesting." He dropped the bomb that he hoped would stop her flirting. "I'm a professor at the university."

Wrong again. Impossibly, she leaned closer. "What do you teach?"

Over her shoulder, Cade was chuckling about Hugh digging himself in further and further. Apparently, Hugh hadn't flirted in so long that he'd also forgotten how to turn a girl off. He sighed. "English Literature. Specializing in anything pre-19th century." He prayed that she found the subject matter to be dull as dust.

She pretended to think it was interesting. "So, like… Shakespeare and stuff?"

He shook his head. "Shakespeare is wonderful, of course, but not to my taste. Right now, I'm working on a seminar on *Beowulf*."

"Bay of Wolves?" She asked over the music.

How could someone not have heard of *Beowulf*? Hugh couldn't help but laugh. Instead of correcting her, he just nodded. "Exactly."

She ran her finger down his forearm, and asked, "What are you doing after this?"

He took his free hand and grabbed hers. "How old are you?"

She giggled and motioned for him to come closer. "Don't tell, but I used a fake ID to get in here. I'm 19."

He looked at her and sighed. "Paige, sweetheart, I'm far, far too old for you." Older than she could even imagine.

"No, you aren't." She pouted and hopped down off her barstool, standing between his knees and placing a hand on his chest.

He grabbed her hand and looked her in the eyes. "Paige, I am pushing 40. And, more importantly than that, you have had far too much to drink to make this decision."

She frowned. "I've had two drinks, and I like older guys. They don't play games."

"You're underage. One sip is too many." He let out a deep sigh and tried another tactic to let her down gently. "It wouldn't be right of me to lead you on. I'm not looking for anything remotely romantic. My partner…"

Paige wasn't taking no for an answer. She put her hand on his leg. "I can help you forget about her." She slid her hand up his thigh slowly.

"No." He put his drink on the bar and then placed his hands on her waist and moved her back enough so that he could get up. She stood, frozen, with her mouth hanging open as he made his way through the crowd to the door.

Cade excused themself from the group they were chatting with and stopped Hugh just before he reached the door. "You leaving?"

"I need to get some air, but yeah, I'm probably heading home." He shook his head. "I can't do this."

Cade scoffed. "That girl? She's fucking wasted—she'll find someone else and never even remember you." When Hugh refused to stay, Cayden gave in. "Let me get my jacket."

"No, no. You stay. I want to be alone."

"You sure?"

He nodded. "100 percent." Hugh added, "Have a good time. See you tomorrow?"

"Definitely. First thing. Waaaaafflesssss!" They both sang

the word and held the s longer than Gollum would have talking about his precious.

Hugh walked through town, not heading anywhere particular. It was early in fall semester but still warm at night, so there were lots of people out.

It was nearing 11 o'clock. Even being on sabbatical for this semester, he didn't usually stay up past 10:30 on a Friday night. He should get home and start his nighttime routine. He had found in his nearly 200 years of life that having a regular sleep schedule kept him from snapping and going full wolf on someone.

Making his way past a row of bars, he stopped, hearing behind the thumping music that someone was struggling in an alleyway.

"I told you no!" It was a female voice. It sounded as if she was trying to be brave, but Hugh could hear the shakiness in her voice.

"I don't care what you say. I took you on this date, to the most expensive restaurant in the city, and then we went out for drinks. You owe me this." A slimy, evil-sounding man.

"Sex isn't currency." Hugh heard a punch and then a slap and then the woman's voice and screams were muffled.

Hugh made his way into the alley and grabbed the man by his shirt and jacket collar. "She declined, you fucking asshole." He threw the man into the side of a green dumpster, denting it deeply.

The man fell to the ground, still. Hugh could see that he was still breathing. For a moment, Hugh considered killing the man. Then he heard a sob from behind him. The woman was still there.

He gathered his composure. If his eyes glowing when he turned to her, that wouldn't help.

When Hugh turned, he saw her makeup was smeared and her red dress was ripped. Her lip was bleeding. He recognized her. "Rosalie? Are you okay?"

She ran to him. "You saved me." She sobbed into his chest.

"It's going to be okay." He cautiously put his arms around her gently. "We should get you to the hospital."

She shook her head. "I don't want to. I'm so embarrassed." She buried her face in his chest. "Besides, you got here before he could really do anything." She looked around Hugh and then asked, "Is he…"

"No. But I think we should leave before he wakes up." Hugh was certain that the man hadn't seen his face, but he didn't want to chance it any longer than necessary. "You really should consider seeking medical attention, Rosalie." She declined again.

He took his jacket off and gently placed it over Rosalie's shoulders. "Would you like me to take you home?"

She shook her head. "I worry that he may know where I live. I would feel safer somewhere with you."

Hugh paused. "I think you need rest. Would it be okay if I took you to my place? I promise that I have no nefarious intentions."

Rosalie nodded slowly. "I would like that."

They walked in silence for a while until they got to a more well-lit place, and then Hugh ordered an Uber.

"The driver's going to see my face and think…" She tried to hide the tears in her eyes.

Hugh interrupted. "I don't care what they think. We know the truth."

When they got in the vehicle, Rosalie cuddled close to Hugh, and he put his arm around her. He whispered, "It's going to be okay." She cried softly into his shirt.

Once they got to Hugh's house, he led her in. "You wanna shower or something?" She nodded, so he found her some towels.

"Ummm… I don't have any clothes."

He looked her up and down. She was tall—probably about 5'10", but she was thin. He sighed. "I can give you one of my t-shirts, but my sweatpants will fall off of you." He paused. "My girlfriend's pajama pants would be really short on you, but you could maybe tie them at the waist so they fit there…"

"Are you sure you're okay with…"

Hugh cut her off. "Just take them before I change my mind. We can wash your clothes so that you don't have to take her pajamas with you and it won't look like a walk of shame." She chuckled at his joke, but Hugh worried she was trying to avoid processing what had happened to her.

While Rosalie showered, Hugh got a pillow and some blankets and placed them on the edge of the couch and fixed some tea. He sat down on the other end of the couch and started reading.

After a while, he realized that the water in the shower was still running. It had been much longer than was normal for a shower. Hugh knocked gently on the bathroom door. "Rosalie? You okay?" She didn't reply, but he heard her crying. He opened the door a crack. "I'm going to come in, okay?" She still cried.

Hugh's shower curtain was cloth and decorative, and opaque. Hugh sat on the floor. "I'm right here if you want to talk about it."

She cried a little bit more. "I just… I feel like it's my fault. I shouldn't have… I don't know."

"Rosalie, you did nothing wrong tonight. There is nothing that you could have done that would have made you deserve what you went through." He slid closer. "It wasn't too long ago that I sat on the floor of the shower and cried. I've often blamed myself for what happened to Zoie."

She sniffled. "Was she attacked?"

"Yes. She was…" He paused. "Someone…"

Rosalie poked her head out from behind the curtain. "She was murdered?" Her eyeliner had run down her cheeks even further than when she was in the alley, and her hair was stuck to her face.

Hugh looked down at his lap. "Yes. I've never actually said that to someone. Everyone who I've ever really talked about it with already knew." He shook his head. "That's not the point." He continued, "The point was, I've always kind of blamed myself. Why wasn't I with her? Why didn't I get back to her sooner? Those sorts of things." He looked at Rosalie's face. "You can't do that. You can't dwell on what could have been. All it will do is make you live in that moment over and over again, when you could be living a million other moments."

She reached her hand around the curtain towards him. Cautiously, he touched her fingertips and then slid his hand around hers. She looked in his eyes. "Hugh, you need to take your own advice."

He let a small, involuntary smile escape and then stood up. "Stop wasting water," he teased. He paused for a moment and considered what he was about to say. "There's some face soap in there—I think it's rosewater scented."

"Yeah?"

"That was Zoie's. She said it removed even waterproof mascara easily." He decided to poke a little fun at her. "You should use it so that you don't look like a member of Kiss for the rest of the night."

She poked her head back out of the shower. "What's this about kisses?"

"Kiss." He stared at her. "The band." She shrugged. "Detroit Rock City. Rock and Roll All Nite." She shook her head. "How young are you? Christ. The song 'Beth'." When she still didn't know, he started singing it.

"Oh, yeah." She smiled. "My dad really likes that song."

"Your DAD?!" He laughed and grabbed the hand towel from the sink and playfully threw it at her. She giggle-shrieked as she caught it and threw the towel—weakly—back at him. He picked it up off the floor and then left the room to go read on the couch.

Rosalie finished her shower and then joined Hugh on the couch. "I don't know if I could go to sleep just yet."

"Grab a book."

She picked up a random book, obviously not even looking at the title or caring whatsoever, and then grabbed a throw blanket and cuddled close to Hugh. "I was going to suggest we watch a movie."

He placed his bookmark and set the book on the table. "What do you want to watch?"

"Nothing too… thought provoking. Just something mindless, please."

He started scrolling through movies, and then Hugh suddenly asked, "Were you on a date with him?" He tried his best not to sound jealous, but Hugh wondered how many dates she could manage in one day, since she had asked him to meet for frozen yogurt earlier as well.

"It was work."

Hugh sat straight up. "You work with him?" This made him furious. "You absolutely must tell your boss…"

She cut him off. "No, it's not like that. He was a client, and I'll do my best to make sure that he's blacklisted in the industry."

"But your boss still needs to know, if this was a work thing…"

She laughed. "I'm my own boss. I am the owner of the business." She took his hand. "You're so sweet to care." Rosalie moved closer to him. "Thank you for saving me tonight."

"I just happened to be at the right place at the right time." He let her cuddle close to him as he began to scroll again. Hugh felt her hand slowly start to slide down his chest, and his heart started to pound. Determined to distract her, he asked, "What kind of business is it?"

She put her hand back on his chest. "Oh." Sitting up, Rosalie proudly replied, "Well, my business is experiences." It must have been obvious that he didn't know what she was talking about because she explained further. "Sex work. When I was younger, I started out on the streets and stripping, but then I started providing dominatrix experiences, and now I do exclusively girlfriend experiences. I also manage a network of girls that do this across the country. Mostly in the big cities. I plan to add some men to the network and also hope to add some gender-fluid individuals."

"So, is that why he felt you owed him…"

She nodded, sadly. "I think so. That doesn't automatically come with the experience. It has to be consensual—it says so on the website and in the contract, and tonight definitely wasn't consensual. He was a total dud. There isn't any way in the world that I was going to sleep with him."

"Your job—it seems dangerous."

Rosalie was taken aback by this. "Yes, if can be. But if you're insinuating that I should try my hand at something else…"

He took her hands in his. "No. I just wondered, do you do it in Birmingham often? Don't you get recognized?"

She inched closer to him. "No. I usually don't work in Birmingham. Mostly Nashville or Atlanta. Sometimes Destin or New Orleans. I limit myself to one event in Birmingham a year, at most. Some years I don't take any. It has to be worth it." She shrugged. "He was paying a lot, so I took it."

"How many years have you been doing this?"

"Well, I started everything when I was 17, and I'm 24 right now, so about seven years. I started adding others to my network about five years ago. They pay me a fee to be on my site and for help with things like that."

He went to ask her another question but was cut off by her mouth on his. He put one of his hands on her hip and the other on her shoulder. "I don't think we should do this."

"Why not?"

"First of all, I very much love Zoie, and I'm not ready to move on."

She interjected, "If you always live in that moment, you'll miss a million more you could be living."

He softly chuckled at her use of his own advice against him. "And most importantly, you just went through something extremely traumatic, and I don't think that this is what you want." He added, "and even if it is, it's just not a wise idea."

She straddled his waist, and despite knowing that he should move her, he didn't. With her hands on his shoulders, she looked him in the eyes. "No offense, but I don't think it matters that you still love your girlfriend. I'm not asking you to love me." She slid her hand down his chest and then ran her finger under the waistband of his pants. When he moaned, she smiled slyly. "Don't you want to let go a little bit? Get lost in each other for a while?" She kissed him again, biting his lower lip and pulling away.

He moaned a little more, but he couldn't help but kiss her back. "I just think…"

She cut him off. "Don't. Don't think." Rosalie stood up, turned around, and dropped Zoie's pajama pants to the floor. She started to walk towards the bedroom.

"Rosie, I have to tell you—Zoie's the only woman I've been with in a very, very long time." Part of Hugh was screaming at him to stop what he was doing, but there was another part shouting even louder. A piece of him convincing him that this might help him cope with some of the pain. That part of him willed him to stand up and follow her, to take off his shirt as he walked.

She turned when she reached the door. "Doesn't matter to me." Turning the doorknob, she waited in the doorway, biting her lip, while he walked towards her.

It wasn't until she heard birds chirping that Zoie realized she must have fallen asleep at some point. She stretched and squeaked— Zoie insisted that a good stretch is not complete without a good squeak—and then sat up. The front door of the cabin was half open, but the screen door attempted to block whatever woodland creatures—or spiders or bugs—that would attempt to venture inside. The cool breeze that cycled through the small cabin smelled of pine trees, moss, and dirt.

Zoie made her way to the bathroom, and realized, just like when Stevie took her to the island safe house, that she didn't have a toothbrush. "How do I get myself into these situations?" She squeezed some toothpaste onto her finger and did her best.

Where is Silas? She noticed that his bed was made, so she immediately went out to the couch and folded her blankets, putting them in a tidy pile, topped with her pillow. She didn't want to be a sloppy houseguest.

Making her way outside, she took in the scenery. When she had stood outside the day before, she wasn't really in the mood to notice anything, but with fresh eyes, she understood why Silas had chosen this location to live. Not only was it remote, but it was beautiful. Evergreen trees that seemingly reached up into the clouds, impaling them. Moss on every rock. Land that was barely touched.

Zoie stepped off of the porch and made her way towards the back of the cabin. Just off to the side there was a small shed, with a ramp leading up to the double doors—probably where Silas kept tools and maybe a small tractor or lawnmower—or perhaps a deep freezer that he kept dead bodies in. A few yards away was a small chicken coop; Zoie instantly recognized that because her grandparents had one when she was a child. She approached the coop and greeted its inhabitants. "Hi, Ladies." The smell of the pine shavings for the bedding brought back memories of selecting the eggs with her grandmother and then cracking them into the skillet. One time, she recalled, that they had three double yolks in a row.

As she rounded the corner to the backyard, a small garden came into view, and then she saw a wash-line. Several pairs of black pants and black shirts were hanging, pinned along side some towels.

"There's an entire rainbow of colors you could wear, you know?"

Turning around, Silas flatly replied, "In my line of work, staying hidden in the shadows is key." He glared at her. "You need to work on that. I could hear you coming before you came around to the side of the house."

"I wasn't trying to be sneaky…" Everything was a flaw for this guy. A mistake. Something that could be better. She knew that Lettie trusted Silas to protect her from enemies, but what about Silas himself? His constant critical eye could really bring Zoie back down into the dark place she'd been in after her engagement, before she'd met Hugh.

"In our world, you always need to be able to blend in." He continued hanging clothes on the line.

A cold gust of air blew, and Zoie pulled her (Silas's?) sweatshirt more tightly around her. "I've never really stood out, so I think I'll be fine." How could it be any different in the magical world. She was nothing spectacular in the world she'd always known, and she wouldn't be anything more than adequate in the supernatural world.

He shook his head. "You aren't in the same world anymore."

"So I've heard." Tell her something she didn't know—something that hadn't been reiterated one billion times. He was mansplaining to Zoie. Of course she knew things were different. She had known that since the day she'd chosen to follow Hugh into the Storyteller fountain.

Zoie suspected this place was hidden by magic—or perhaps it was just another path in Nightbrooke, one that didn't lead to a door. It could be at the end of a very long path that no one ever went to see what was hiding at the end. Sure, Silas said that it was Canada, but could she trust him at all? Zoie wasn't sure.

After hanging the last item on the line, Silas started back into the cabin. When she didn't immediately follow, he turned around. "Coming?"

She had been staring up at the sky. Zoie was lost in the fact that the trees had grown around each other, giving each their own space, practically creating an umbrella for the land that Silas had made a life on. Still, the trees knew to leave each other enough space to move in the wind—they didn't touch up in the canopy. She was mesmerized by the vivid blue that snuck into the spaces between the branches. "Sorry. I was just taking in this place. It's so…" Zoie twirled with her arms out. "It's so beautiful and free and open."

She caught him smiling a little. "That, Zoie, is why I live here." He closed the space between them. "C'mon." He waved her towards him, almost as if he was offering his hand to her.

She took a few quick steps and caught up to him, but still left enough space between them to keep herself comfortable. Unable to determine what kind of relationship they were building—friends or student and teacher—she didn't want to cross any lines. Still, the best approach was to always start with the truth. "Y'know, I have to be honest that I don't feel like training today…"

He shrugged and said, flatly, "Doesn't matter."

Who did this guy think he was? Zoie looked back and forth as if for people who could stick up for her. "You can't force…"

Silas chuckled. "No, that's not what I mean." Zoie's confusion prompted him to continue, "Lettie left some books about spells and stuff behind, and…"

"…And?"

"Well, even though it's probably a good idea to train you in defensive tactics right now, I figured that maybe you wouldn't really be in the mood." Looking down at the dirt, he added, "Plus, you like to read, so I thought maybe you would enjoy it more."

Zoie rolled her eyes. "Since when do you care what I enjoy?"

His entire mood changed. "Look, we are going to be living together for a while, so I am just trying to make this… tolerable. If you want me to kick right in with the physical part of things, I will." He let out an ugh, and started back to the house.

Reluctantly, Zoie followed. She shut the door behind her and asked, "Do you need it a lot?" Silas wasn't even in the same room.

He emerged from his bedroom with several books. "Need what?" He let out an annoyed sigh.

That little prophecy that Lettie let slip before leaving must have just been just something to stir the pot. This guy definitely wasn't fighting any romantic feelings for Zoie. It was obvious that he found her to be a thorn in his side. From the sound of his sighing, the depth of his eye rolls, and the groans he emitted after any question she asked, it appeared that he actually hated her. Still, she continued with her questions. "The actually physical fighting stuff?" She asked, "Can't you just disappear and reappear somewhere else?"

"Read these." He handed her the books. "Do you think I'm the only creature that can do that in this entire world?"

"Well, no. I mean, I guess Lettie can." She sat down on the couch, looking at the titles of all the books. "So, do you use the fighting a lot?"

He paused for a moment, considering what he was going to say next. "I really think that if you work at it hard enough, you'll be a witch who can transport herself. And about the fighting, actually, in my job, yes, I do have to physically fight at times. Even after you fully have harnessed your powers, you will still need to keep those skills sharp because people in this world… ugh…" He rolled his eyes. "People in this world aren't the nicest, if you know what I mean."

She flipped haphazardly through one of the books. "They aren't the nicest in my world either." Zoie felt her frown in the muscles at the corners of her mouth—she was working those muscles hard. Determined to not freeze her face permanently, she relaxed. Looking at the titles again, she let out a small "hmm" and then admitted, "I bought some of these, actually, when I was building my altar at home and stuff. Back when I only wished that magic was real." She actually missed her altar. It wasn't anything spectacular, of course, but she had candles, herbs, a feather, cards, books, and a small little altar cloth. She'd felt comfortable there, a safe space for her and her thoughts. Zoie wasn't sure she would be able to get any privacy in this little one-room cabin.

He nodded. "You'd be surprised how accurate some of them are." He then added, "There is one that I suggest you get to know pretty well—it's the one that is maybe ten pages long. It's the laws of our world. Everything that we don't have the privilege of doing or having. Kind of like the opposite of the Bill of Rights." He chuckled to himself and said under his breath, "More like the Bill of Wrongs." Zoie shook her head slightly—did this guy think he was actually funny?

Silas pulled things from the refrigerator. Breakfast time. Zoie watched as he did everything by hand—no magic. Silas chopped vegetables with the speed and precision of a chef. Cracked the blue and brown eggs with one hand. Measured nothing. Maybe it was magic, and she just didn't realize it.

"…I would offer to help, but it seems like you've got everything under control." Truth was, she wasn't the best cook and would probably just get in the way.

He looked up at her briefly. "Kitchen is too small for two people." Silas went back to what he was doing.

Zoie struggled to figure out Silas. He was all over the map in how he interacted with her. It was almost as if he would forget for a moment that she was—more or less—his ward, but the moment he caught himself being friendly, he dialed it back. She was determined to break him. She refused to stay somewhere with someone for more than two days if they weren't going to become friends, and she knew she had no choice but to stay here. That meant he had no choice but to become her friend.

She took his advice and read the short book of laws. "Immortal children?" Zoie didn't realize she'd said thought that aloud until she heard a "hmm?" She looked up. "Oh, I just didn't know that immortal children were a thing because… well, you and I…"

"We were born this way, not created by force. Vampires... they don't pass it on from parent to child. They just...the victim doesn't really have a choice."

Zoie thought back to what she knew about vampires—but what was from books and movies and what was from real life? "I thought that they could only change their mate or something?"

"Fake news." The bread popped out of the toaster like a cartoon, and Silas actually caught it. "Unlike your werewolf friends, I can get close to a vampire without gagging, and I actually know a few. They can make anyone a vampire that they want, but..." he pointed to the book in Zoie's hands, "...they have to register them. The max is twelve a year and no immortal children."

"How old is it when someone is no longer young enough to be an immortal child?" When Silas put down the knife, obviously annoyed, she noticed something. "Do you have a mustache tattooed inside your index finger?!"

He laughed. "Yes. Yes, I do."

She jumped up from the couch. "Me too!" She put her finger under her nose to show him.

"Oh, yours is a pencil-thin mustache. Nice." He showed her his. "It's rare you meet someone with a mustache-on-the-finger tattoo nowadays."

How did he not know? Hadn't he watched her sleep for the last four months? Zoie chose to not press the matter because she really didn't want to know how closely he watched her. "It looks like you have a lot of tattoos."

Silas didn't look like he had a lot of tattoos—he did. His hands and arms were covered at least up to his sleeves. He had at least one on the back of his neck, too. Zoie wasn't able to see all of them, but he had more than anyone else she knew.

He smiled at her. "Is there a question in there? I feel like there is."

"Tell me about them. How many do you have? Is there a meaning behind each? What's your favorite? Do you regret any?" She picked up a piece of toast and nibbled at it.

Silas smacked her hand playfully with a spoon. "Breakfast isn't ready yet."

This didn't stop Zoie from eating the toast—she loved bread.

Silas shook his head. "You just asked a lot of questions at once." He looked up towards the ceiling as if the answers were floating up there. "I started getting tattoos when I was still in Hawaii." Unbuttoning the top few buttons on his shirt, he exposed the left side of his chest—a compass. "This was my first one, and it is still my favorite. It's in the honor of someone from my childhood who was really there for me." Continuing, he said, "And, no, they all don't have deep meanings—case in point: the mustache tattoo." As he was plating their breakfast, he asked, "What about you? Or is it just the mustache for you?"

"Well, you've been watching me for so long, don't you know?"

"Zoie, I've never once watched you get undressed." He sat down across from her at the table. "How many do you have?"

"Just the mustache…" She was slightly embarrassed about it. Zoie has always wanted more tattoos, but her mother wouldn't let her when she was still 'living under her roof' while in college, and her fiancé forbade it while they were together. She had gotten the mustache on a whim after acing midterms at UAB. Hugh had never mentioned it, and since he basically noticed and knew everything about her, she had always assumed that he didn't like it. "Do you have any that you really don't like?"

He pulled his shirt up, exposing some work on his ribs. "My artist really screwed me over on this one." He took her hand and ran it along one of the waves in the scene. "Do you feel that?"

She nodded slowly. "Did he go over it too many times or something?"

"The artist also changed the tattoo gun mid-session."

She looked closer. "Is that a tiny sea turtle?"

He laughed. "Yeah, most of my tattoos are really silly." Silas sat back down. "I have a slice of pizza chasing a pineapple while holding a bloody knife on my right ass cheek." He shook his head. "Don't ask because I honestly don't know."

"Were you drunk?"

He shook his head. "I wish I had that excuse. I just got the idea in my head and went and did it."

"Wow," she replied, exaggerating each part of the word.

"Do you ever want more?" His eyes lit up as he looked at her, waiting for her to answer.

She looked down at her plate and shrugged. "I don't know."

Zoie felt his eyes on her. "Zoie, you don't have to hide your desire or lack of one about this with me. I'm not going to judge you."

Cautiously, she admitted, "There's several that I want, but I'm probably too old to start now and maybe I'm just not thinking rationally. And they are so expensive. What if they look horrible?"

He smiled and laughed, very gently. "Zoie, you're not too old, and if you've wanted them a long time, then you're not being irrational. They won't look horrible." Then he added, "But they are expensive." Silas took a bite of food and then said, "But the good thing is that you age very, very slowly as long as you use your powers regularly, and you can save lots of money." He excitedly added, "And you can move time into the future and see what winning lottery numbers are and…"

She cut him off. "We don't know if I can actually do that, and, more importantly, that seems like a bad way to use magic, and I don't want to use my magic for things like that. I want to help people."

The smile that grew on his face was meant to be hidden—the right corner of his mouth had crept upwards, but he caught it and course corrected. It was too late. She had seen it, and she saw a little bit of joy in his dark eyes. Silas tried to cover everything by self-righteously stating, "You would say that you want to help people with your powers."

She sat up straight and squared her shoulders. "What's that supposed to mean, Silas?"

He shrugged. "I told you that you don't have to worry about me judging you. Everyone says they want to help people, but it's just not true." She was still glaring at him. "There are things you desire, Zoie. Be honest. If you could get them with your magic, wouldn't you take the opportunity?"

Angry air pushed out of her nose. "You don't know anything about what I want."

"You wouldn't use your powers to get back to Hugh right now if you could?"

She lied. "No. You and Lettie said that it wasn't safe."

The lie must have been obvious. He laughed and leaned back in his chair. "You are so full of it, Zoie. You would be gone instantly if you knew how to get to him." He continued laughing. "Don't lie to me, Zo."

"Don't call me that."

"Call you what?"

"Zo." She felt her mouth narrow and her eyes squint. The tension between her eyebrows grew. "That's what Hugh calls me, and it's for him only."

Silas rolled his eyes and got up from the table. "You've got to be kidding me. It's two fucking letters."

"He's the only person that's ever called me 'Zo', and I would really like to keep it that way." She wasn't budging on this boundary.

"Well, I just did, so I guess he's not the only one."

Zoie stood up, slamming her hand on the table. "Why are you so fucking bitter about him? Do you have a thing against love? Did someone hurt you?" She wished she could see in his head and figure out why he was so angry all the time—why he really hated Hugh. She concentrated hard on figuring it out.

Suddenly, Zoie felt as if she was zipping through a tunnel, and she was in a foggy place. Everything sounded muffled.

She looked around, and finally her eyes locked onto a man standing under a streetlight near the edge of a driveway; he was carrying a bouquet of flowers. Stepping closer, she realized that it was Silas—but it was strange because he wasn't wearing his typical uniform of black on black. He had on normal, everyday clothes—jeans and a button-down shirt.

He took a deep breath and walked towards the front door of the house. Zoie followed in the shadows. When Silas got to the porch, he took another deep breath and knocked on the door. A man answered. Everything sounded like it was under water, but Zoie thought she heard them ask each other, "Who are you?"

After a few moments, a woman appeared at the door, and all that Zoie could make out was apology after apology. Silas' shoulders slumped. He dropped the flowers as he walked away. He was heartbroken—she could feel it.

He then walked down the sidewalk to where there were some trees and head into the dark, dense forest. Zoie followed, until he stopped and turned to her. "What are you doing?!"

Zoie gasped, and she felt herself come back out of the tunnel. Disoriented for a moment, she looked around to see where she was. Silas' cabin. The sound was no longer muffled, and she could see as clear as day that Silas was furious with her. "That memory— that memory was one that I never wanted to think about again. How dare you!"

She stammered. "Silas, I don't even know what I did or how I did it." She quickly added, "I'm sorry."

He slammed down the towel he was using to dry dishes and walked to his bedroom. With a slam of the door, he growled, "Sure you are."

Zoie stood in awe for a moment. She had entered one of his memories—but how? Because she'd concentrated extremely hard on trying to get into his head? But why that particular memory? How was it selected? Were things always muffled in memory?

She shook her head. That wasn't important right now. She needed to figure out how to get Silas to stop being angry with her. Zoie decided she would finish the dishes. This would give him some space, and it was also a nice thing to do.

When she was placing the last dish away, the door to Silas' bedroom creaked open. He stood quietly for a few moments. "I have been in love one time. That memory was the moment that I found out that she was married. I have spent the last 35 years pushing that memory out of my mind, and…" He gnawed on the inside of his lip. "…Her name was Rhonda, and I was going to propose that night."

"Did she know?"

"That I was going to propose? No."

Zoie interrupted. "No, did she know what you are? A warlock?"

He shook his head. "I was planning on telling her. Her husband— his name was Dennis." Zoie watched the shadows pull towards Silas—his anger was drawing his power to him. "The papers said that Rhonda killed herself that night, but I never believed that." His breathing became deep and he exhaled anger. "I found Dennis a few years later, made him confess what he did. I knew that Rhonda would never do something like that—hurt herself. I found out that Dennis was a police officer, so he likely had someone cover up everything. But he confessed to me, surrounded by the darkness that I drew from the dark corners of the cheap motel that he had been hiding out in on a stakeout, and then I killed him and made it look like a drug overdose."

Zoie wasn't sure if she should hug Silas or run away. Frozen in place, Zoie quietly said, "I'm sorry."

He looked up at her. The anger in his eyes made darker than ever before. Zoie was certain that he was going to have some stern remark, but he softened. "I know you didn't mean to do it."

"I will do my best to not do it again."

Silas shook his head. "No. You have to do it again. Navigating someone's memories like that—infiltrating a memory that someone has repressed—that's a rare power. You must exercise it."

"Silas, I don't know. I really don't know if it's a good idea for me to try and dig through your memories. Plus, I don't even know how I did it." She took a step towards him. "I'm sure there's things that you don't want me to know about you, and what if I stumble on those things?"

He paused for a moment, then looked her directly in the eyes. "Well, I just told you about Rhonda and Dennis, which is something I've been keeping secret a long time. It's probably the darkest secret about something that I've done." He stepped closer to her. "You have to try and unlock the rest. It's the only way to improve your skills."

—Hugh—

The sun somehow snuck into the room through a gap in the blackout curtains. Hugh smiled and stretched, rolling to put his hand on the empty space in his bed. It was still warm. His heart lifted and he softly said, "Zo." He ran his hand over where her body was before realizing that she was not who had occupied his bed the night before.

He rolled onto his back and looked up at the ceiling before raking his hands down his face and neck. "Fuuuuuuuuuuuuuck." He groaned and then got out of bed, pulling his hair up into his man-bun—because he was really in a battle with himself. Finding his jeans, he kept walking as he zipped and buttoned them, found a random shirt on the back of a chair and threw that on.

He wasn't sure if Rosalie had left yet until he heard some talking coming from the kitchen.

"…and that's why I will never go to Australia."

Hugh recognized the laugh that followed whatever story Rosalie was telling. "That's the most ridiculous thing I've heard. It's like you dreamed Australia cheated on you and you got angry at it for real!"

"That's an absurd comparison!" Her face lit up when she

saw Hugh walk into the kitchen. "Good morning, sleepyhead." Immediately, she basically danced over to him and kissed his cheek.

"Good morning." He looked over at Cade, trying to read what his friend was thinking, but he couldn't read them.

Cade smiled. "Rosalie is making waffles."

She looked at Hugh, nervousness in her eyes. "I hope you don't mind. I just made myself at home."

Hugh wasn't sure if he cared or not, so he just said the first thing that came to mind. "I wasn't sure if you would be here or not when I woke up." He went to pour some hot water from the kettle over his tea leaves, seeing as he noticed both of them had tea, but when he touched the kettle, it was cold.

Cade must have sensed the confusion. "Oh, she made the tea in the microwave." Their voice had a sense of laughter behind it.

Hugh closed his eyes and did his very best to hide his horror. He grabbed the kettle and filled it with water. "Oh." He started warming the kettle and then turned around. "So… do you always make your tea in the microwave?"

She shook her head, and for a moment, Hugh thought maybe she just hadn't seen the kettle. "I don't really like tea," she said, "so I didn't know how to make it and he," she motioned to Cade, "told me to heat the water, so that's what I thought to do."

"They." Cade gently corrected her.

"I'm sorry. They told me to."

Cade put their hands in the air. "I want to be clear that I didn't tell her to put it in the microwave."

She narrowed her eyes at them and folded her arms across her chest. "So, you intentionally didn't tell me about the kettle?" Her lip pouted a little.

"No and yes. I didn't want to discourage you from the nice

gesture you were trying for."

Hugh could tell from the look on both of their faces that Cade really did let her microwave the tea intentionally and Rosalie didn't trust them whatsoever.

Cade snapped their fingers. "I almost forgot. Paige asked if you were alright after you left so abruptly last night."

Rosalie's head nearly snapped off of her shoulders. "Who's Paige?"

Cade smirked. "Oh, just a woman that wanted to take Hugh home last night."

"Oh." Rosalie pouted a little and continued to work on making waffles.

Hugh glared at Cade and let out a deep sigh. "I wasn't interested." He nudged Rosalie. "I promise."

Cade rested their chin in their hand and looked back and forth between the two of them. "So... how did you two meet?"

"I bought a book from Rosalie yesterday."

Cade shook their head. "No. After you left the bar. Did you plan to meet, or was this just magical serendipity?" Their voice was dripping with distaste.

Hugh hesitated to answer because he didn't want to share Rosalie's personal business without her permission. She replied, "It was by chance. I was on a bad date, and Hugh actually got me out of it."

"Awww, that's cute." Cade rolled their eyes behind Rosalie's back as she plated another waffle. "You must have really hit it off for Hugh to let you stay here, and to let you wear his wife's pajamas." They took another sip of microwave tea, with their pinky up.

"Wife?" She looked back and forth between the two of them, obviously confused and hurt.

Hugh scoffed. "Zoie wasn't my wife—"

"You were handfast, weren't you?" Cade was obviously pretty proud of themself for that.

Rosalie removed another waffle and placed it on a plate and then said, "Excuse me for a moment." She basically sprinted back down the hall.

Hugh waited to hear the door shut, and then he leaned towards his friend. "Cayden. What was that about?"

"I don't trust her." Cade frowned.

Hugh took a step back. "You just met her."

"You just met her, too."

Hugh couldn't argue that point, so he decided to table it for a moment. He heard soft footsteps and then Rosalie quietly reentered the room, wearing her clean, but torn, dress. She had the clothes that Hugh had let her borrow folded in her arms. "I think I'm going to go."

"Bye!" Cade smiled excitedly and waved.

Hugh glared at them and then turned to Rosalie. "I'll walk you out." He shot a displeased look at Cade over his shoulder as he guided Rosalie out the door. They stood silently for a few moments after she ordered a Lyft. Breaking the awkwardness, he blurted out, "I want to see you again." He didn't even know where that came from.

She grinned. "I would really like that." She took his hand in hers. "Maybe we could have an actual date and get to know each other and make sure that we're in the same place with what we're looking for."

He nodded. "I will wait the customary three days and then text you to set something up."

She laughed. "You can text me as soon as I get in the Lyft and I wouldn't think that you were clingy." Rosalie actually pulled him into a hug. "Thank you for saving me last night. I don't know what would have happened…"

Instead of letting her finish, Hugh pulled Rosalie in for a kiss. For those few moments, Hugh's mind was quiet and his heart didn't ache as much as it normally did. He knew that he had to be honest with Rosalie about what their relationship would be for him—something to push away the pain of losing Zoie.

After getting Rosalie in the car, he took a deep breath and walked back into the kitchen, where Cade was chowing down on a stack of waffles drowned in syrup. "Mmmmmm, that bitch can't make tea but she makes some fucking fluffy waffles." They moaned as they took another bite.

Hugh reached over and grabbed the plate and slid it out of Cayden's grasp and placed it on the counter. "What the fuck was that?"

"Those were waffles. What the fuck, Hugh?"

Hugh crossed his arms. "No, Cayden. Why were you so mean to Rosalie? What was with that?"

Cade put their fork down. "Let me answer your question with another. What do you like about her?" They waved their hand. "No… let me rephrase. What do you know about her?"

"What's the point in this line of questioning? Isn't the point of dating to get to know someone?" Before Cade could protest, Hugh reminded them, "You're the one who told me to date."

They rolled their eyes. "And she is what you're going with?"

"What's that supposed to mean?" Hugh's jaw tightened. His blood was starting to boil. It was like he couldn't win.

"Hugh." Cade looked him straight in the eyes. "Are you fucking kidding me?" Hugh didn't respond so Cade threw their hands up in defeat. "She's like, what, 17? You have, like, nothing in common. She doesn't even like tea. In fact, she hasn't had it in so long, she thought it was made in the microwave—with the bag in the water."

Hugh couldn't help but cringe. Cade asked again. "What. The. Fuck. Are. You. Doing?"

"Okay, which question do I start with? Um… she's 24."

Cade cut him off. "She's too young for you."

"Zoie's 24."

Cade shook their head. "Yeah, and Zoie was leaps and bounds more mature." They stated, "Do you know why she won't go to Australia?" They waited for Hugh to even react—he didn't—so they stated, "A girl with an Australian accent once stole her boyfriend so she hates the accent. She's immature."

"That's one thing. She's mature in other ways. Rosalie owns her own business."

"Yeah, she told me. I'm sure that business made last night a lot of fun for you."

Hugh readjusted his man-bun.

Cade groaned in disgust, rolling their eyes. "You're going to fight me over this chick?"

Hugh frowned. "She takes the pain away." He gave Cade the waffles back. "Last night was the first time since I left Zoie laying on the pool deck that she didn't haunt my every move."

"Just tell me that you realize that this relationship is going nowhere." Cayden shook their head. "Does she know you're a wolf?"

"Are you crazy? Of course not."

Cade put their hands in the air. "Well, you were adamant that Zoie knew right away."

"That's different. I knew I was going to spend the rest of my life… our lives… I knew I was going to spend until death separated us with Zoie." He stirred his tea. "Look, I know that no relationship for me is ever going to work." When he swallowed, it felt like a cue ball was in his throat. "In the moment, with Rosalie, I… I don't feel like Zoie is in the room with me. I feel like she's gone completely. But the moment that there's silence between Rosalie and me—that's the moment that Zoie returns, and I feel like I'm cheating on her." He looked away. "But, for those moments, when Rosalie and I kiss or touch, sometimes even when we hold hands, Zoie steps out of my brain for just a moment."

"I just think you're picking the wrong person to do this with." They shrugged. "There's millions of other supernatural beings on this planet. There are women—age appropriate, mature women— that hit on you constantly, and you're out here getting your dick wet with someone you could easily break in half. Without even phasing into wolf form."

"You're the one who was pushing me to move on. You told me that Zoie would want me to."

Cade rolled their eyes and delivered the biggest blow of them all. "This is not what she would have wanted." They shook their head slightly. "She would have wanted you with someone you could love and have the future you were robbed of with her. Someone who could be your equal—who could challenge you." After a pause, they added, "You are not honoring her memory by fucking around with a glorified hooker."

Hugh slammed his fist on the counter. "First of all, don't insult what she does for a living. But secondly, and most importantly, how in the hell would you know what Zoie wanted? Did she tell you? What if she wanted me to be with someone that I could never love like I love her?"

"I know what Zoie would want because she isn't narcissistic, you fuck head." They turned and looked out the window for a second and then turned back to face Hugh. They pointed at the dining room table. "You sat right there the night that we killed

Miles, and you told me that you never wanted to forget Zoie. And now you're telling me that you're being with someone so that you can? Who the fuck are you? Did some pod person take over your body, Hugh?"

"You don't understand the pain because you've never loved anyone!"

"I loved Stevie! I still love Stevie! It isn't the same as what you had with Zoie, but it is real. And I fucking chose you over her. In the end, I fucking chose you! I chose you and your love for Zoie because it's something I wanted for myself someday, and you're sitting here dishonoring it." They growled. "I fucking hated that chick at first. I loathed Zoie because she was taking your time from me, and I was jealous. But anyone could see that she made you a better man. Happy. Alive. You were truly alive for the first time since I met you. I fucking teased you about it, yeah, but I was so happy for you. And here you are, just months later, doing this. I never thought I would be defending her to anyone, especially you. Was the bond real? Did you even love her or did you just want her?"

Hugh felt his blood boil, and he knew that his eyes had begun to glow. "How dare you." A low growl built in his chest.

"Then don't do this to her."

"Zoie is gone, Cade." It killed Hugh to say that, but it was a fact. "I have to move forward with my life. Stevie said it, you say it, everyone is saying it. I'm doing it." He sighed. "I'm doing it, and you're fighting with me for it."

Cade reached across the counter and tapped their fingers on Hugh's forehead. "Because you aren't moving forward with Rosalie. Get that through your thick skull. You are side stepping at the very best."

Hugh grabbed their hand. "You're going to fucking touch me

right now?! We are *so* going to fight."

"Over a girl, Hugh? A glorified one-night stand." They laughed. "She must have been in-fucking-credible in bed."

Hugh didn't respond, but instead just turned around and looked out the window over the sink. He calmed himself.

"Oh. My. God. I know what this is." After a few moments, Hugh turned around, so Cayden continued with their theory. "You had this amazing night with her. You saved her from this horrible date, and she loved it. You came back here and fucked and now you think you could develop feelings for her. You think you could fall in love with her." When Hugh's gaze dropped back to his tea, Cade continued, gently, "Hugh, you can wish it all you want, but, and I'm telling you this as your very best friend, she's not it for you."

He put his face in his hands. "She…"

"She takes away the pain." Cade waited for Hugh to nod. "You are mistaking that relief from the pain as something else, something more."

"I know. Just let me have this."

Cade paused. "I will let you have it, if you listen to me for a minute." Hugh looked at them, fuming. "This girl, Rosalie. She's going to band-aid the pieces of your heart together. But you need, like, stitches, and this girl, she's not even using name brand Band Aids. She's using Great Value. You know, the ones that don't even really stick. And are the wrong size. Too small. Well, you'll have fun at first, but she's going to tire of you or you won't be compatible or something will separate you, and all of the Great Value band-aids are going to pop off and your heart is going to break again. Only this time, you will be mourning the end of your relationship with Miss Great-Value Rosalie and also with Miss Surgical-Grade-Sutures Zoie. It's going to hurt even more."

"I appreciate your concern." The tone of his voice said otherwise.

Cade grabbed their jacket. "Enjoy your fucking waffles. I'm going for a run. I need some air."

—Zoie—

Living in a little cabin in northern Canada was getting old, and it had only been a few weeks. Wake up. Go check on the chickens. Check the garden. Have breakfast. Read some of a book. Train on something allegedly simple. Try to invade Silas's mind and memories. Fail at getting anything substantial. Lunch time. Try again to invade his mind and memories. Fail again. Train on something simple. Dinner. Read. Watch two episodes of *Star Trek: The Next Generation*. Read. Go to bed. Repeat.

The chirping birds woke Zoie, and she groaned. She didn't want to do this same thing yet again. She was feeling defeated, if she was really honest with herself. Ever since the night that she'd accidentally found a memory Silas had buried deep in his mind, she had not been able to replicate that level of invasion. She could pull little memories—usually happy—of Silas as a child chatting with an older man on a rocking chair facing the beach, or even memories of his mother from when he was very young. She had once gotten him a glow-in-the-dark ring from a gumball machine, and Silas cherished this. It would absorb any light—especially sunlight—and when the lights went out, it would light up a little bit of space around him. He had kept it hidden for years after his mother passed, but eventually his grandmother discovered it and destroyed it, because it was a girl's toy.

But Zoie wasn't gaining anything that was difficult to find. These were all stories that Silas was happy to share with her, which was evident after Zoie found each one. He would give her more little details. Things that weren't actually a part of the memory. Things like how his mother always smelled like waffle cones on Thursdays because she worked one evening shift each week at an ice cream shop to help make ends meet after Silas's father left. Or how she wore mismatching shoes to church on Sundays. This would infuriate his grandmother, but Silas hadn't paid attention to that. He thought his mom was the coolest person on the planet.

Zoie was beginning to build a little dossier about Silas, as he had of her when he had watched over her—she had gotten past the stalking terminology.

After completing her morning self-care routine, Zoie headed out to feed the chickens and check for any new eggs. "Hey, Ladies. What's going on?" One of them responded with a short cluck, and Zoie replied, "I know, Evie. I told Jodi to stay off of your side of the henhouse, but she just refuses." The other chicken kicked up some straw. "Now, Jodi, you need to compromise. Evie is a tidy chicken, and it's difficult to live with someone who doesn't match your level of cleanliness." She let out a tsk tsk and then collected the eggs. Each hen would produce one or two eggs a day, so the amount wasn't overwhelming. Between breakfast and some recipes for supper that called for eggs, there was usually just enough left for Zoie to make some cookies or brownies for after dinner.

When she'd finished collecting the eggs, Silas was working in the little garden out back.

Zoie put down her basket of eggs and hid behind a tree. She

closed her eyes and centered herself for a moment, then found herself flying through that strange tunnel into Silas's mind.

At first, she couldn't really tell where or when she was. Then she recognized the brick street in her hometown; it had been paved a few years ago. Silas turned onto a driveway—a long one—and either transported magically or a piece of this memory was missing because he was suddenly sitting in a tree closer to the house, patiently waiting for something.

Zoie struggled to recognize the exact location of the tree. She had never climed a tree, and so never seen one from the trunk and branches out.

She and Silas were suddenly pulled to alert. In the memory, someone was arguing. A light turned on in the house, hurting her eyes—or maybe she was feeling some of Silas' pain from within the memory.

Zoie recognized the argument. She recognized it clearly because one of the voices was her own.

"...I hope she was worth it!" She then heard the gut-wrenching, painful scream of "Just get out!" A shriek and a slamming door followed.

The man stood on the porch, and Silas's eyes focused on him. Zoie could feel the conflicting emotions build in Silas's body— concern and rage. He moved on the branch, causing the leaves to rustle. The man on the porch—Zoie's ex-fiancé—glanced at the tree but dismissed the noise, likely thinking it was an owl or raccoon creating the ruckus.

The front door opened again, and this time, Zoie's mother, Carol, came out. "What happened?"

The response she heard in Silas's memory broke her own heart. "She doesn't know it was you; she just knows there was someone."

Zoie gasped and then felt herself get sucked in reverse through the memory tunnel. She slumped against the tree, pulled her knees to her chest, and cried.

She didn't hear the door to the garden 's fence swing shut, nor or Silas's footsteps.

He knelt and told her, "I never wanted you to find that one." When she didn't acknowledge him, Silas didn't push. He just sat beside her.

She cried and then leaned into him. His arm wrapped around her, and she felt safe enough to say, "I always suspected, but was never sure." Wiping her tears with her sleeve, she admitted, "I knew she'd slept with a couple of my boyfriends, but I didn't know for sure that…" she waved her hand. "I don't know why I am so upset. I hate him. I always hated him. I just stayed because it was what had been expected."

He ran his hand up and down her arm. "It's okay to feel many things about this. It doesn't matter that you never loved him." She rested her head on his shoulder, and he leaned his head a bit on top of hers. "I'm very sorry you had to see that memory."

"You seemed very angry." When he didn't say anything, she clarified, "in the memory. You actually felt furious."

Lifting his head, he smiled and turned towards her. When she looked up and met his eyes, he admitted, "I remember that night very, very clearly. There was no moon, and it was also cloudy. It was so dark that I knew that I could pull some crazy shit out of it. I was imagining all the ways I could terrify him or… Let's just say worse."

"Oh." She looked at him, not sure how to react. She knew how she wanted to react, but she wasn't sure how he would judge her.

He leaned in a little. "I can tell that you want to know." He pulled from the shadow under a tree, creating a small grim reaper character. "I could have made that huge and had it follow him. Jump out in front of his car, if he tried to drive off." The image dispersed to dark smoke and then disappeared. Dark vines of shadow came crawling towards the two of them. Normally, Zoie would have been terrified to see such a sight, but she felt safe next to Silas. "And if that didn't do the trick, I was going to have these enter his nose, eyes, ears, mouth, whatever, and just destroy him. Fill the bronchial tubes of his lungs with these vines. Have them flow through his veins instead of blood. Just. Kill. Him." He waved those away. "I hated him in that moment."

"Oh. The dishonesty from Rhonda… that really did a number on you." She looked up, picking at smaller twigs and snapping them or flicking away their bark.

He shook his head. "No. Well, I mean, yes. I really hate dishonesty, and the Rhonda–Dennis thing was part of that."

His hand was in the dirt, and Zoie slid her hand on top of it. "But what's the no part?"

"You." He let her fingers slide between his and hold on. "I had never heard you yell at someone like that. You weren't even angry. You were just… destroyed. He betrayed you so badly that you couldn't even communicate with him rationally anymore. My heart broke for you, even though I knew in the end, you were much better off." Silas turned towards her a little more. Zoie released his hand from her grip, and he touched her face.

She leaned into his hand, realizing for the first time since all of this began exactly how starved for intimacy she was.

Silas looked in her eyes and said, "I've not been entirely honest with you."

"Have you been watching Star Trek without me?" She giggled.

He shook his head. "No." He closed his eyes, obviously preparing himself for a multitude of reactions that Zoie would possibly provide. "Lettie wasn't exactly wrong." Not wanting to be wrong, even though she thought she knew what he was talking about, Zoie kept quiet. He leaned in closer. "I do have strong feelings for you." She didn't say anything. "I've cared about you for a long time. And that moment—that memory—was when it kind of started."

She felt him lean closer to her, and despite trying to fight it, her body moved towards his. They closed their eyes, and she felt his nose touch hers gently. He told her, "I'm going to kiss you now."

She nodded slowly. "Okay."

Before their lips could touch, a loud clap of thunder erupted around them, causing the ground to shake, and lightning flashed, sending them both jumping away from each other. Zoie shrieked. Heavy rain started pouring from the sky.

Laughing, Silas stood up and helped Zoie up. He ran over to the garden and grabbed his tools and the basket of vegetables. "Grab the eggs. Let's get inside."

As they headed quickly past the chicken coop, Zoie called out to Jodi and Evie. "Try to stay dry, Ladies!"

When they got to the porch, Silas went straight in, but Zoie stood outside and watched the rain.

He poked his head back out the door. "You coming?"

She took a deep breath. "It smells so nice. It's different from city rain." She stood there for a few more moments. She felt horrible for what had nearly happened. She needed time to come up with how to approach this situation. Another lightning strike and some thunder paired with a large tree branch falling caused Zoie to jump. She laughed nervously and yelled to the storm, "Okay! I'm going inside!"

Silas threw a towel at her so that she could dry her hair. It was obvious that he was trying to avoid looking at her, but he couldn't stop himself. Zoie turned away from him so that she could dry her hair in peace. It worked for a few moments. But eventually, Silas broke the awkward silence. "So… are we going to talk about what almost happened out there, or…?"

Zoie replied, "I'm sorry. I think that it was very irresponsible of me to behave the way I did. Letting you kiss me or, even worse, go any further would have been me just taking advantage of you for attention." She frowned. "I'm embarrassed."

"Oh." He just stood there for a moment. "I see."

"Silas, I'm sorry. Please understand…"

He put his hand up like a stop sign. "No. I understand." He went into his bedroom and slammed the door.

"Silas." She knocked softly on the door. "Silas, please."

He opened the door, doing his best to look angry at her, but he really just looked upset. "What do you want me to say, Zoie?"

"I don't know." She frowned. "I just had a momentary lapse of…"

He rolled his eyes. "Whatever. I'm used to being second to someone else. I always am." He turned away.

She wasn't going to let him manipulate the situation. She replied sternly, "You know what? You are, at best, second to Hugh. At. Best."

"Oh, I know." He turned around and glared at her. "The sun rises, sets, sails across the fucking sky for Hugh. I. Fucking. Know."

"What do you want me to say, Silas?" She let a breath so angry it was almost a growl.

"Just admit that you wanted that kiss, not that it was a 'momentary lapse of good judgment'." He made air quotes and used a whiny voice. "It makes me feel like I'm nothing, Zoie. Nothing."

Zoie considered her words very carefully—and she also considered her loyalty. She didn't know whether Hugh had any inkling that she was alive or if he had moved on with his life. But her loyalty—her commitment—was to him. She pushed away thoughts and desires for touch and the confusion she felt in her mind and heart. "I'm sorry, Silas, but, for me, it's Hugh, until he tells me he doesn't want me anymore."

It was apparent that Silas didn't believe a word that was coming out of her mouth. Still, he put a smile on his face. "Then, if that's the case, I apologize for my actions. I was out of line." He grabbed the door. "Now, please excuse me. I want to get out of these wet clothes." When she stepped away, he slammed the door again.

Zoie stared out the kitchen window and cried silently. She was furious. Furious at Silas for making his feelings known. Furious at his trying to kiss her. Furious at the fake apology and dismissal of what she said. More than that, she was livid with herself. Zoie prided herself on her honesty, loyalty, and kindness, and right then she was a vessel of none of those.

Her heart belonged to Hugh—yes. She wanted desperately to be next to him. But she was lying to herself about not wanting that kiss. She was angry at the storm for interrupting it. Her self-loathing was at a ten due to her lapse in loyalty to Hugh and their love and relationship. And the way she'd spoken to Silas—the bold-faced, italicized, 60-point font, all caps, underlined, highlighted in yellow—was the opposite of kind.

The thing Zoie hated most at the moment was herself. This always happened. She got comfortable in a relationship—let herself care about someone deeply—and then someone else would come along and capture her attention. She never, ever acted upon it. That would be hypocritical of her, at best. But the desire would drive a wedge between her and her partner. She would retreat into herself in self-disgust at her traitorous heart and brain, and the partner would get bored and move on or cheat.

Zoie detested cheating. But her mother's alternative was distasteful. Zoie knew how everyone in their small town saw Carol. She heard the things that they called her, and it was mortifying. Her mother was openly polyamorous, and everyone just saw her as promiscuous—a common whore.

Maybe Carol was what they said. She did things that warranted the title, such as sleeping with most of her daughter's supposedly monogamous partners.

But that was the thing—Zoie and Hugh had *consented* to a monogamous relationship, and until she was able to discuss any change to that part of their relationship, that's how it had to stay. She would have to muster up the courage to have a deeply honest conversation with him about it, when or if she ever saw him again.

—Hugh—

Hugh pulled his car over after almost blasting passed the small
floral shop. It was an unscheduled stop, but he felt that it was
necessary—it would be entirely improper to pick up a woman for
a date without flowers.

A bell rang as Hugh opened the door and stepped inside.
Dozens of different floral scents rushed him the moment he took
a breath. The tiny shop was big enough for two or three patrons in
addition to the shop owner. As soon as the door closed, the owner
was right next to Hugh.

"What's the occasion?" she asked.

Hugh shrugged. "Date." The owner went to grab some roses,
and Hugh objected. "She's not that kind, and it's not that serious
yet." Did he say yet? Hugh told himself to slow down.

"Well, tell me about her."

The truth was, Hugh didn't really know much about her. He
pondered and then smiled a little. "She's… she's really come to me
at a time that I needed someone, and she's fun and smart and very
driven. And really brave."

"Daffodils or daisies, then. They represent new beginnings."

She pointed to the flowers.

Hugh cringed at the sight of the daffodils. "Those are a waking nightmare. Creepy." He selected some white daisies and then grabbed a small box of chocolates—*not* a heart-shaped box—and thanked the florist for her help.

Rosalie lived downtown, above The Pizitz, an exclusive building. She either knew someone or had been on the waiting list a very, very long time to get in there. In the elevator, he saw she lived on the top floor. So, either she really did know someone in the leasing office and had gotten a deal or the business that she ran was extremely successful, to be able to afford this loft.

When the elevator opened, he walked directly to her door and lifted his hand to knock, then stopped himself. Hugh was second-guessing himself. He could feel Zoie in his heart, but he still had no real idea as to what she would want him to do. Would she approve of Rosalie, or would it be like Cade predicted?

Taking a deep breath, Hugh adjusted his shoulders and knocked. Through the door, he heard "Coming!", so he waited, taking another deep breath.

The sound of multiple locks clicked before the door opened slowly. "Hey!" Rosalie smiled, opening the door more. "Are those for me?!" She reached out for the flowers and candy, her fingers wiggling in a very gimme-gimme fashion. "These are so pretty." She put them on the kitchen counter and opened the chocolate immediately.

She popped one of the chocolates in her mouth, and grabbed Hugh's hand. "Let me give you a tour," she said around the chocolate.

She showed him from room to room—the apartment was immaculately clean and decorated with modern, expensive items. Her apartment could be used in a movie about pristine and over-the-top places.

As she slide the doors to her bedroom open, Rosalie bit her lip at Hugh. "This is my room." Her hands grazed his forearms and found their way to his shoulders. "Do we have anywhere urgent to be?"

He smiled at her but took a step back, holding her hands in his. "Rosalie, I want to talk to you about…" he pointed back and forth between them, "…us."

"Oh." A look of worry took over her face. She led him to the living room and they sat on the couch. While Hugh hesitated, trying to find a way to be as gentle as possible, Rosalie gathered courage and said, "Just tell me. Don't sugar coat it."

Hugh took her hand in his. "Rosalie, I want to get to know you, but I have to be up front with you. For me, our relationship will never move beyond what it is. I can't get close to someone like I was with…"

"…Your wife?" She had been looking down at their hands, but she looked up to make eye contact with him. Releasing her hand from his, she folded her arms across her chest.

Hugh shook his head and let out a sigh. "Zoie and I weren't married. Cade was just being protective. They've seen how hurt I was at the loss of…"

Her eyebrow rose as he trailed off. "Look, I'm used to there being another woman when I'm going on work dates. A lot of times, that woman is like a ghost on the date. The man that I'm playing girlfriend for usually has a wife, and she's metaphorically sitting there on his shoulders, weighing down the experience." She sighed. "I don't want that in my personal life."

A weight in Hugh's chest lifted at that. "Well, that's kind of what I wanted to talk to you about. When I'm with you, she's not in the corner of the room, or sitting on my shoulder, or whispering in my ear." Hugh reached out for her hand again. She cautiously placed her hand in his. "I just want to be open and honest with you." He rubbed his thumb over her knuckles. "I don't know that our relationship could ever be more than what it is right now, but I…" He hesitated.

Rosalie closed the space between them, kissing his cheek. "I agree to being your distraction." She quickly stood up and, more or less, danced down the hall to her bedroom.

Hugh stood there, unsure whether she intended for him to follow, but when she didn't come back, he stood at the windows and looked at her view of the city. When he heard heels on the wood floor, getting closer, he realized he'd been starting at nothing, not a thought in his head.

Rosalie wore a simple black dress with purple-and-green skull-motif heels. He closed the space between them. "Where do you think we're going tonight?"

She grinned. "I don't care if you take me to Waffle House. I just want to spend time with you." Rosalie pulled him close, kissing his cheek again. "But seriously, where are we going?"

"Waffle House." When Rosalie playfully swatted his arm, he laughed and asked, "Before we make any decisions on dinner, do you have any dietary restrictions?"

"Nope, and I promise to not order a really expensive salad and just eat three croutons." They went back and forth on places to eat as they walked out the door, but as soon as the lock was engaged, Rosalie excitedly said, "I'm in the mood for a really good burger. Not like a fancy, expensive burger, but more like the best burger in Birmingham."

Hugh thought about it for a moment, pondering a few different places. He pressed the button for the elevator. "So, we're dressed up, and you want to go to get a hamburger? I just want to be clear that this is what you want to do tonight." She nodded and grinned.

The doors to the elevator opened, and he took her hand. "Okay. We're going to Baha Burger in Hoover."

The 20-minute drive was more or less a straight shot. Rosalie talked nonstop the entire way about how excited she was to go somewhere that she had never gone before—especially since Hugh claimed it was the best burger in Birmingham.

When they got to the restaurant, it was packed, but Hugh had been several times before and knew that everything would move quickly. The pair of them looked completely out of place waiting in line in their fancy date-night outfits. Everyone else was in jeans and t-shirts. Kids had ketchup and mustard on their faces, and Hugh heard a sound that made the hair on the back of his neck stand up—a child slurping the end of their drink.

"Will you order for me?" Rosalie asked. "I don't know what's best."

He looked her in the eyes and, very seriously, asked, "And you'll eat whatever I order for you? No matter how weird it is? Promise?" She nodded enthusiastically, so when they got to the front of the line, Hugh ordered the Bacon Swiss Burger for himself and the signature Baha Burger—that included pineapple on it—for Rosalie. He ordered them both sweet potato fries with their secret sauce, which he had not figured out how to recreate at home, despite trying many times over the years. Just before they gave the total, he added, "Oh! And two pieces of key lime pie." He looked at Rosalie and smiled. "You're in for a treat because it's sooooo delicious."

After getting their drinks, they found a seat on the patio and waited for their food. Rosalie moved her seat closer to Hugh's and linked her arm in his, leaning her head on his shoulder. "I saw what was on that burger you ordered for me. Chipotle barbecue sauce. Pineapple. Pepperjack cheese. What if I don't like it?"

Hugh smiled and turned towards her a little. "It's really good, but if you don't like it, I'll switch with you."

When their food arrived, Rosalie cautiously took a bite, and her eyes grew wide. "Wow!" She put the burger down and actually clapped her hands like a child. "So yummy."

Hugh was telling her to try the sauce with the sweet potatoes when a random woman sat down at their table. He and Rosalie looked at each other.

Since it was obvious to each that neither of them knew this woman from a hole in the ground, Hugh asked, "Can we help you?"

The woman glared at Rosalie and uttered one angry word. "You."

Rosalie was visibly confused. "Do I know you? I'm sorry, I don't remember you. I'm, like, the literal worst with that."

The woman's face got so angry that she started to turn red. "You. How. Dare. You."

It was obvious from Rosalie's face that she was trying to place the woman. "Ma'am, I'm sorry. I think you may be confusing me with someone else. I can't place your face and I have no idea what I've done."

The woman slammed her hand on the table. "Last weekend, you attended a party. With my husband. We couldn't find a babysitter, so I stayed home. I guess he picked you up from the corner and took you." She grabbed a condiment bottle from the table. She squeezed it, and mustard shot out all over Rosalie's dress. "You two-bit whore!"

Rosalie jumped back in her chair, but it was too late for her outfit. "Look, I don't know your husband, and I think you're mistaken."

The woman was still squirting the mustard when Hugh took it from her. "You need to leave. Immediately."

"Your little girlfriend is a hooker." She turned back to Rosalie. "Those pictures are posted on our friend's Facebook page and you're in the background shoving your tongue down my husband's throat." She grabbed some napkins to wipe off her hands. "Who knows what was shoved down your throat later."

Hugh glared at her. "Listen, Karen. I think you're mistaken. And, on the off chance that you're not, don't you really think your husband is in the wrong? He's the one who made those wedding vows. He's the one who went outside his marriage. No one forced him to do that."

"My name is Natalie, and her face is etched into my mind. I looked at those photos for hours. For days. She's a gold digger, obviously."

"Whatever, Karen, oops, Natalie. Your anger is misdirected. You'd better leave before the police come and hold you responsible for the cleaning of her clothes and, worse, take you to the police station because you assaulted my girlfriend."

"She assaulted my marriage!"

Rosalie started laughing. "Assaulted your marriage? Get the fuck outta here! You're too much." She grabbed some napkins and tried to clean off her dress, shaking her head and chuckling the entire time.

The woman started shrieking, and the manager of the restaurant came over and asked her to leave. She kept yelling—climbing in pitch with every word—as they tried to get her to leave.

Rosalie, however, just sat in her chair and started to eat her fries. She looked over at Hugh. "You're right, this sauce is really good." This sent the woman into a frenzy. She tried to flip the table, but Hugh's hand was on it, holding it down. Instead, she threw the rest of the napkins like confetti.

Finally, the police came and escorted the woman away. Some people at other tables clapped. While another officer asked them questions, Rosalie kept eating, keeping as calm as possible.

When the officers left—with Karen/Natalie in tow—the manager came back over and apologized, handing Rosalie one of the t-shirts that they sold to put on over her dress and also refunding all of the money for their meal, even after Hugh had said that wasn't necessary.

As they walked to the car, Hugh chuckled. "First of all, you're incredible. How did you remain so calm while she was yelling at you?"

Rosalie shrugged. "It's not the first time that this sort of thing has happened to me. It's one of the hazards of the job. Momentarily, I considered telling her what kind of evil man her husband is, but I know she would have never believed me."

Hugh nodded in agreement. "She would have blamed you, in the very best of circumstances."

Rosalie asked, "Was there a 'second of all'?"

"Secondly," he laughed, "it looks like you murdered someone with yellow blood." He shook his head. "It's in your hair, Rosalie." He paused. "I think it's in your ear!" He started laughing again.

She shook her head. "This is why I avoid jobs in the Magic City. Can you take me home? I think this evening is kind of ruined."

As much as he didn't want the evening to end, Hugh knew that Rosalie was right. Still, he stayed with her until she was done showering, in case she needed assistance with eliminating the evidence of the Great Mustard Massacre, as it came to be known.

Rosalie came out of the bathroom, towel drying her hair. "Are you going to stay the night?"

Despite hearing the hopeful tone in her voice, Hugh shook his head. "Not tonight." She didn't fight him, and he respected that about her. It wasn't that he didn't want to stay. The truth was, he wasn't sure that wolf part of him could stay hidden that night.

—Zoie—

Rotating her hand ever-so-slightly counter-clockwise, Zoie erased the etching of the X in the tree bark. She focused her attention on some vines growing nearby, turning her hand rapidly clockwise, willing the vines to grow up the tree. It was slow going. Zoie felt as if her heart was racing at 150 beats per minute, and she was concerned that she was sweating.

From behind her, she heard, "You are getting better at controlling where things grow." He was no longer able to sneak up on her; Silas hadn't caught Zoie off-guard. Since she had started reading his thoughts, his current thoughts would sometimes be very loud in her head, depending on how much she was focusing or how loudly he was thinking. Still, Zoie wasn't privy to all of his thoughts, or perhaps Silas was working harder at hiding them. When he didn't know she was zeroing in on his thoughts and feelings, she could feel that he was full of worry. She didn't know the reason for such worry. She couldn't find the source in his mind.

Zoie dropped her arm and the vines crawled back to their previous form. She nodded at Silas in appreciation. "I'm still not able to change what large animals or people are actually doing, though. I'm not sure how much help making a plant grow is going to be. And I know that my Moon and Earth magics are supposed to be weaker, but they seem to barely exist."

"Correct me if I'm wrong, but doesn't the moon reflect sunlight?" He was eating some trail mix that they had made together a few nights prior, and the crunching began to annoy her.

She rolled her eyes. Everyone knew that about the moon reflecting the sun's light. "Yeah, so?"

Silas suggested. "Try thinking about it like that. Sure, it's a reflection, so it's a little less pure, but it's still sunlight. And everything on Earth—the dirt, the rocks, whatever—it all changes with time. Use your strong magics to influence the other magics."

She hadn't thought about it that way before. She smiled. "That makes sense. If we've been working on this for a weeks, why are you just now suggesting it?"

He shrugged. "Just thought of it." He smirked and popped another handful of trail mix in his mouth.

"Suuuuuure." Sometimes Zoie could swear that he just wanted to make things more difficult for her for as long as he possibly could.

"Fine, don't believe me. We don't have time to argue right now. You need to get ready to go. You have an appointment." He started walking back to the cabin.

She called out, "What kind of appointment?" He ignored her, so she tried again. When he ignored her that time, she reached out, focused on the leaves near the path, and created some wind—or maybe she fast-forwarded time to when there would be a big gust of wind; she just wasn't sure how her own magic worked yet—that kicked the leaves up into a wall in front of Silas, and she held them there. When he turned around, she asked again. "What kind of appointment?"

"You're going to NightBrooke to be registered, and then…"

he pressed his lips together. "Then, against my better judgment, might I add, I'm going to take you to Birmingham." There was something more to this—some reason that he was taking her back to Hugh—and it wasn't that she was ready. She knew that she wasn't ready—she was barely cracking the surface of most of her skills. She couldn't figure out what kind of game he was playing.

It didn't matter to her, though, when she was honest with herself. Zoie wanted to get back to Hugh. She lost all focus on everything that she was practicing and ran to Silas, allowing the leaves to succumb to gravity and fall to the ground. "Really?" She gave him a hug. "Thank you!"

"Zoie…" She was already heading towards the cabin. "Zoie!" He growled to himself as she ignored him. Pulling the vines he used as rope from his side, he threw one end at her, causing it to lasso her. "Zoie," he repeated as the vine pulled her closer, despite her struggle. "I don't know if Hugh is still in Birmingham. He could have left."

"Get on Google and see if he's still a professor at UAB," she suggested. It seemed obvious to her. She was too excited to care about Silas and his negativity.

Silas twirled around in a circle. "Ah, yes, why didn't I think of that, especially since we don't have internet access here." He had a point, and Zoie felt silly for suggesting it. If they had cell phone or internet access, she would have used it ages ago.

Zoie tried using her magic to reverse the knots in the vines, in hopes of releasing herself from Silas's control. "Let me go!"

"The magic won't work, remember?" he stated, pointing out the obvious. He pulled her closer. "Zoie, I…" He stumbled over his words. Silas changed gears. "Zoie, I'm worried about Lettie." He released Zoie from the vines. "She has been gone too long." So this was the reason for his worry—and possibly the reason that he was taking her back to Hugh.

Zoie shrugged. "I'm used to her disappearing from my life, so I guess I didn't even notice that she hadn't returned like she said she would." She did find it odd that Silas was worried, so perhaps he was going to attempt to track her. That being said, Zoie didn't know how often Lettie typically checked in. "What makes this different from usual?"

Silas closed himself off, but Zoie worried that this was more than just not checking in. She placed her hand on his forearm, and he admitted, "A hit was put out on Lettie a couple weeks ago."

"What exactly do you mean?" Zoie was appalled that he hadn't mentioned this at all.

He frowned. "Remember when you and Hugh were in trouble? It's like that."

Zoie's mouth dropped. "Why didn't you go and find her? You're supposed to be the best in the business. Do you think she's been captured?"

He scoffed. "I am tasked with taking care of you. I wasn't going to leave you here, defenseless." Silas then answered the other question with what Zoie believed to be a lie. "I think she's probably just hiding out."

"Why didn't you tell me about this?" She folded her arms across her chest. Her eyes narrowed and her jaw tightened.

"There's nothing you could have done. I didn't want to worry you." His voice fell soft, trying to hide his concern.

It was her turn to scoff. "I could tell something was off. I thought we were friends. Friends don't keep secrets like this."

He turned to her. "Friends? Friends?! It's so hard being friends with you. It's impossible, really."

She was taken aback at this unexpected turn. "What did I do? What makes it difficult?"

"Your constant whining about missing Hugh. Your pining for him. It's miserable. It's pointless." He shook his head. "What are the odds that he waited for your return, Zoie? He thinks you're dead."

Unprepared for this conversation, her lip started to shake. "He would know." She wanted to believe it. Zoie had to believe that Hugh would know that she wasn't really dead.

Silas shook his head. "Pathetic, really." He started walking away but stopped and came back to her. "He has no clue. At best, he just thinks he's going to feel heartbreak forever. But he's probably moved on. I mean, if for nothing else, he probably just wants the physical contact."

"You're awful!" She was so angry that she started to cry.

"Don't be naive. You want it too! You feel the same way. Starved for the attention that you gave each other. That's why you wanted that kiss, remember? You would have been using me for the attention." He started walking away again.

She followed him, anger in every step. "You know nothing! I know that he knows I'm still out here, alive."

He turned and came back to her. "Then why hasn't he fucking found you yet? If the mating bond is that fucking strong, why hasn't he found you?" His eyes met hers and locked on them. "I mean, it's realistic to believe that he hasn't even looked for you whatsoever." He laughed. "Maybe it's because he lied to you about your stupid fucking bond, just so he could have you. To lure you in."

She slapped him. "I felt it, too, you asshole."

He didn't flinch or turn his head; he just took it. "Did you? Are you sure?" He scoffed. "You didn't even know you were a witch until a few months ago, so you had no damn clue. He probably just manipulated you…"

She went to slap him again, but he grabbed her wrist. "I wouldn't do that again, if I were you."

"Why? Should I be afraid that you'll hit me back?" She fake pouted and then glared at him.

He smirked, "You should be afraid that I'd enjoy it." He winked at her and turned away, letting her wrist free.

Her blood was boiling. His behavior didn't make sense to her. She had thought that they were beyond the hot-and-cold whiplash from the beginning of their friendship. "What game are you playing, Silas?"

He stopped and turned yet again. "This isn't a game for me, Zoie. I didn't keep the information about Lettie a secret to purely keep you in the dark. It was to protect you. I didn't want you running off to try and find her or something unhinged like that."

"That's not what I'm talking about, and you know it." She stood firm, motionless, still glaring at him. "You know exactly what I mean."

"Oh, you mean this?" He pointed back and forth between the two of them. "There's no game there. I am tasked with protecting you, and I have watched you pine over Hugh the entire time you've been here, and before that, I watched you fall in love with him because he pulled out all the stops to make it happen. Who the fuck knows who he repeated that process with since you've been gone. He's going to break your heart. Crush it."

She inched closer to him. "What do you even care for? Why do you care?"

"Because I'm the better choice!" He yelled.

She stepped back. "What do you mean?"

"With me, you wouldn't have to worry that if we got into an argument I would lose control and change into an animal and shred you to pieces. You wouldn't have to worry that I would hurt you when I hold you tightly. I wouldn't have the strength to crush you." When she glared at him silently, he finally said, "You're going to make me say it to you, aren't you?" He shook his head and growled a little to himself. Then he sighed and admitted, "I'm in love with you, and I want you to choose me."

Deep down, Zoie had already known—it was more than the near-kiss out by the tree. More than him saying that he had feelings. He didn't want to return her to Hugh because he had wanted a life with her, free from everything else. "I will always choose him."

Silas shook his head. "You're choosing wrong." Then he said something that tugged at Zoie's heartstrings, though he couldn't have known. Quietly, almost as if it was a thought in his head rather than spoken words, he offered, "I mean, I know that you'll always choose him first, but I would… I would be willing to be second. To be there in the ways that he cannot." His eyes focused on the dirt at his feet, and that offer was an admission of defeat.

She closed her eyes and shook her head. He had just given her what she'd wished she had the courage to ask for in every relationship. "Hugh and I are in a committed, monogamous relationship. I'm sorry." Zoie turned and ran into the cabin. This was too much for her to navigate.

She needed to concentrate on getting back to Hugh. That was the most important thing to her at this moment. Plus, maybe being away from Silas would erase the feelings she had for him. Maybe the distance would help him, as well. Perhaps they could both move forward.

Zoie went into the bathroom and turned on the shower. She heard a faint knock at the door. "It's Silas." Who the Hell else would it be? "Can I come in? I promise I won't look. I'll face out the door."

"Whatever." She was already rinsing her hair. She didn't want to have the conversation she assumed was coming, but Zoie also knew that she couldn't stop Silas from doing whatever he wanted. He was, at times, even more stubborn than Hugh.

He covered his eyes and came in the room, then turned around and leaned on the door frame. "I shouldn't have said anything. I should just have taken you back." He continued, "Things escalated, and I don't know why." He paused. "No, I do know why. You're leaving, and I don't want you to go."

"You're the one that is making me leave—not that I haven't wanted to go the entire time." Even though he was facing away, she could tell that he was hurting. "How long have you known?"

He went to turn, almost involuntarily, but Zoie made a little eh-eh-eh sound, and Silas caught himself. "I knew for sure in Romania." His shoulders slumped. "I always watched from afar, but it was the day… the morning of…"

"…when I died."

"Yeah…" He sighed. "Like I said, I usually watched from afar, but I knew that Hugh was going to be leaving you, so I stayed closer that day. I heard you crying when you were saying goodbye to him." He placed his hand on the sink and started to turn again but stopped himself. It was almost as if he was holding onto the sink to keep him in place. "I heard you start to tell him that you love him, and he declined for some idiotic reason—typical Hugh…"

"Hey now!" This jerk just couldn't stop insulting the man she loved. If he thought that continuing down that path was going to win her heart, he had another thing coming.

"Sorry." He ran his free hand through his hair. "I remember thinking that, well, he's a fucking idiot, y'know? Why wouldn't he want to hear that? He had told you loads of times." He shrugged. "I wanted to come in the room and tell you how loved you are. I don't think he did a very good job of reassuring you that day. I felt like he didn't want to hear that you loved him because he didn't feel it himself, and he…"

Silence.

And, whether Silas knew it or not, it was a furious silence.

"So… anyways, that's the day I realized it, but I actually think it started sometime prior, like the night in the tree when you ended things with that real fuckhead of a fiancé, because, well, that's how love works. It grows. It isn't instant. It just isn't touch-my-hand-and-feel-electricity instant. It's not. It's just not." He stood there for a moment, looking at the floor on the other side of the threshold. "Whenever you are ready, I will take you to get registered, and then I will take you to Birmingham. But I can't take you to his house. I'd rather die than deliver you directly to him."

Zoie wanted to reply that she hoped he would die. But it wasn't true. Silas had been right the entire time—she had feelings for him, too. She didn't know exactly what they were or how powerful they would grow to be, given the chance, but they were there.

"Why did you sometimes act like you hated me?" This was always her biggest question. It was so elementary of him. It was the thing about him that she hated the most—the biggest concern she had about him.

Silas scoffed. "I told you outside. Your constant whining about him."

"You say you love me…"

"I do…"

"Then why wouldn't you want to see me happy with him?" Zoie always saw Hugh's love for her as selfless; he would give his life for her. She had no doubt about his loyalty or his willingness to do anything to protect her—physically, mentally, or emotionally. Knowing this about Hugh's love, Zoie couldn't understand why Silas wouldn't do something that was giving far less than everything.

He answered the question with a question. "Would you like to see him in the arms of someone else? Wouldn't that fucking hurt like hell?"

"Fair." No matter how much Zoie wanted to have the freedom to be with more than one partner, she still knew that she harbored jealousy within her heart.

Silas waited for a few seconds and then stepped out of the bathroom and shut the door.

This wasn't right. Something weird was going on. This couldn't be right. "Why is he telling me this now?" She finished up and wrapped a towel around herself and walked out to the main room. "Why now?"

Silas was seated on the couch. He paused the television and turned around. "What now?"

She stepped closer. "Why did you tell me this now? When I'm getting ready to go back to him?"

He stood up. "I didn't mean to."

"This… it complicates things. I don't like hurting people." She looked down at the floorboards, trying to concentrate on the different knots in the wood.

"Then…" he swallowed. "Then, I lied." He shrugged. "I lied. I lied to piss you off." Silas lied harder, "I hate Hugh so deeply that I lied so you wouldn't go back to him, and he would lose."

She shook her head. "You're such a piece of work." She turned and went back in the room to change clothes and gather anything she needed for her appointment—what does one need for registering in the supernatural realm?—and her return to Birmingham. Just as she was pulling her shirt over her head, the door swung open. "Hey! We always knock first!" What happened to boundaries, Silas?

"What do you want from me, Zoie? Do you want me to tell you the truth or to lie or what? What would make this convenient for you?" Silas's eyes started to fill with tears. "What would make leaving the easiest path for you?"

"You've wanted me gone since the ..."

"No! No! You don't get to do that!" He took a couple deep breaths. "You're... you're leaving, and, cool, I get it. You get to go back to the love of your life. But, I..." He took a couple more breaths. "But, I have to take you back, and watch you—someone I am wildly in love with—leave. And I will never see you again." He pinched the bridge of his nose and turned around. "Because, as much as I want it to be true that he's moved on with his life, you know that motherfucker is perfect and he's waited for you, wishing every night that you would come back to him." He turned back around and coldly ordered, "Get your shit. We're leaving. Now."

Zoie grabbed her bag and put on her shoes and followed him out the front door. He closed his eyes for a moment to concentrate, and then placed his hand on her shoulder, preparing to transport them to a portal. "Let's go. It's time to get you all registered. Did you finally pick a new last name?"

She shook her head. "Nothing sounds good with Zoie really."

"Who's your favorite character from a book?" He quickly added, "NoonefromTwilight."

She laughed. "Jo March."

"She married that professor, right? Use his last name." He turned towards her and moved his hand from her shoulder, taking her free hand in his. "Don't let go." They were sucked into the darkness in an instant, and, just as fast, they were in the middle of a different forest.

As they started walking, Zoie asked, "Will you go back to bounty hunting now?"

"Yes." He somehow made the word seem even shorter than it was.

He didn't seem to want to talk about that, so she thought of another question to ask. She went with the most obvious. "Where are we?"

He smiled at her. "Forks, Washington."

"No way!" She started to look around. For what? She wasn't sure. But she knew that there had to be something cool around there.

"Zoie, Edward and Bella aren't here." He teased. "But over here, near this particularly mossy tree—there's a portal to Nightbrooke."

As they approached the tree, Zoie saw the glowing tree symbol. "What do I do?"

Silas shrugged. "I don't know what the sun witches do to open a portal." He started walking towards the portal, leaving her behind. "See ya, wouldn't wanna be ya!" He teased.

She grabbed his arm so he wouldn't go any farther. "Jerk." She decided to hold her hand out and turn it clockwise. The moss started to roll away but then returned to its place.

"Zoie, you have to believe that you can do it." He said, "Remember when Yondu says that he doesn't guide the arrow with his head—he uses his heart."

She turned to him and busted out laughing. "Did you just use *Guardians of the Galaxy* to try to coach me in magic?"

He shrugged. "It was relevant." Silas snuck a smile at her. He tried to hide it, but she saw it. *Guardians of the Galaxy*, Volumes 1 and 2, had been something that they'd thoroughly enjoyed together—

poorly singing along to the music, not caring in the slightest if they were off-key.

She shook her head, still lacking confidence. "Today with those vines… that was the first time that I really could direct them."

"So, you couldn't do it before?" She nodded, so he continued, "Then you improved, which means that you can always improve more, if you believe in yourself." Omigosh, he was a motivational speaker now.

He walked up behind her. "Take your stance." When she did, he touched her shoulder. "Relax." Silas whispered in her ear. "You can do this." He put one hand on her left hip and reached the other out with her extended arm, placing his hand against hers.

Zoie felt her heart flutter, but she took a deep breath, attempting to get it back into a normal rhythm.

Pulling her closer, he explained, "I'll share some of the magic in my hands with you." She turned to look at him. "Concentrate. You just do your thing, and I will send magic through my hand to yours." He added, "You already know that it's a clockwise turn."

She closed her eyes and concentrated a little, then focused on the moss, turning her hand with his. The moss rolled away, revealing a door in the trunk of the tree. "We did it!"

As soon as they passed through the door, Silas looked at her. "Yeah, so back there, I didn't do anything. I just lied so you would think you had help." He grinned at her, proudly.

"You just wanted to touch me!" She shoved him playfully.

"Yeah, that didn't hurt as motivation." He winked at her. "But, seriously, you did that all yourself, and now you know that you can. You can do anything."

She frowned at him, trying to be angry. "You're crafty."

The truth was that he was a good teacher. It wasn't because he could do the same things that she could—he pulled from the dark, whereas she pulled from the light—but because he knew how to get her to do things. He knew how to motivate her, and, if that wasn't working on a particular day, he knew how to trick her.

He smiled and nudged her with his elbow. "It worked." Silas led her to the registration line and they queued. "Hang out here for a second. I'm going to go talk to someone to get us pushed up."

"I thought we had an appointment? Or was that a lie?" She asked.

He made a pfft sound. "Zoie, you're a writer and you've never heard of a figure of speech? Do they actually teach you anything in school? I would love to blame Hugh's piss-poor educating efforts, but you should have known about them ages before then."

She playfully shoved him. "Get away." He laughed and headed towards his destination.

The line stretched for what felt like miles. There were hundreds of new supernatural beings surrounding her, waiting to have the right to walk freely in their little world.

She watched as Silas went over to a security person and had a short conversation. Zoie was impressed that he looked as if he knew how to be friendly in public. Fun, even. He and the security guard laughed about something and then shook hands. Silas, returned part of the way to Zoie, then waved her up to where he was.

Someone in the line—a lumberjack-looking man in red-and-black plaid with jean overalls and giant, pink butterfly wings that sprinkled silver glitter every time they moved—grumbled about her getting to cut line, but she ignored it. Zoie wanted to draw as little attention to herself as possible.

Once they got into the building proper, the pair of them waited in yet another, albeit shorter, line. This one was one of those roped-off maze-like lines. There had been hundreds upon hundreds of people outside, but probably fewer than 100 people in front of Zoie and Silas now, and this line was moving quickly.

At the start of the maze-line stood a tiny security guard—maybe three feet tall—at a security station. As each person reached the station, the guard pointed unenthusiastically towards a table. Their voice was unexpectedly deep, and with each word, their clear wings moved gently. "Take a pen, clipboard, and form." Zoie picked up one of each and would have said thank you, but they spoke over her. "These need to be completed before you reach your case manager."

Zoie got to work quickly, trying to write as neatly as possible while walking. The form was one sheet, about 5 by 7 inches, one side only, and requested only basic information. Name—first name only, oddly; contact information—just phone number, species, true date of birth, and so on. She got down to two whose answers she didn't know.

She whispered to Silas. "What should I put for first moment of transition and cause?"

He took a deep breath in, obviously trying to decide between the truth and some version that wouldn't implicate her. After holding his breath for a few seconds, he slowly exhaled. "You need to tell as close to the truth as possible because the Shrews know. Ha knows everything. You don't want to give yourself away, but in the event that you are found out, you need to be as honest as possible. Put the year your dad died—or maybe one of the years around it. The cause could simply be accident."

Zoie nodded and chose two years after her father's death. When she showed Silas, he nodded with approval. She clicked the pen shut so that the ink wouldn't dry out, and the two of them in line in silence for a few minutes.

As they neared the front of that line, Silas took Zoie's hand. She tried to get free, but he held tighter. Not even a second later, she discovered why.

"But I'm with him," pleaded a woman who appeared to have tree branches as fingers for one of her hands. As she pointed at the person she was allegedly with, Zoie noticed a small golden circle around one of her fingers—perhaps it was a wedding or commitment ring of sorts. She smiled, thinking about how people so different from one another could possibly be committed, despite being, in a way, different species.

The huge security guard looked at them—Ms. Tree Branch Fingers and, from the look of his torn clothes, a were-wolf or were-bear—and it was obvious that he was apprehensive. "Are you both registering today?" When they both nodded, the security guard scratched his head next to one of his horns, for a moment, and then replied, "Then you can stay as you are now." The woman tried to protest again, but the glare from the buffalo-sized security guard made her cower. She got into her assigned line, shoulders slumped in defeat. Zoie could swear that she had heard a sniffle from the woman, who then reached up and wipe her cheek.

When Zoie and Silas got to the stopping point, Zoie prepared to stand up to the security guard; she didn't want to not be next to Silas. The security guard looked at their hands and then smiled at Silas, greeting him with an actual fist bump—did adults actually fist bump? Zoie hadn't know that was a real thing that happened outside of movies until that moment.

"It's been ages since I've seen you." The security guard looked back and forth between Zoie and Silas. "I guess you've been preoccupied."

Silas smiled. "Zoie, this is Ben. Ben and I used to be competitors in the industry."

It took Zoie a second, but she realized that Silas meant his work—bounty hunting. She whispered, "Oh," and nodded.

"Friendly competitors," Ben clarified. "Sometimes we would help each other. Sometimes we would see who could bring in the most marks in a month. Whichever felt right at the time." He chuckled. "There was a time when everyone was wondering if it was going to be the strong guy or the puny guy who delivered the next shipment."

Chuckling, Silas nodded, "Yeah, I still can't believe you didn't kill everyone that was calling you puny." They both laughed, and it was obvious that they really did have a camaraderie between them. Silas teased, "Ben had to get a real job when he met his wife, who asked him to step back from all the alleged danger."

Ben stood up, towering over the two of them. He was even bigger than Zoie had thought. Terrified, she pulled herself more tightly to Silas, as Ben reached around as if he were going to draw a hidden weapon. To her surprise and delight, it was actually his wallet that he was getting and, as he opened it, Zoie couldn't help but giggle at the way a big set of pictures unfolded, pooling at the floor. It was almost as if they were living a moment in a comedic performance when someone would, to the protagonist's dismay, start telling the life story of each child, grandchild, great grandchild, and family pet in their life, no matter how obvious it was that the main character did not care. "Silas, you flat out know that isn't true. It was at the request of my children." He pointed each one of them out to Zoie. "This is Ella, Celine, Gerard, Danzig, Ramone, Rollins, Sid, and Bette."

As someone who actually feared dying during childbirth—

despite never wanting children to begin with—Zoie was shocked that anyone would go through the pain of having one child, let alone eight. Not wanting to be rude, and truly clueless as how to respond, Zoie politely said, "You have such a beautiful family."

Ben's gruff expression softened, and his eyes lit up as he spoke about his children. "Yes, little Celine was crying one day, worried that I wouldn't come home from work because it had taken me a day or so extra to…" He thought of a way to not give away what he used to do. "…collect the goods and deliver them." Ben looked at Zoie. "It was then that I knew I had to get out of the business and do something that would keep me close to home."

The whispering from the line behind them had been growing and was now almost a soft roar. When Ben opened his mouth to ask everyone to quiet down, some bold person in line loudly groaned and fake-mumbled, "Keep the line moving! Stupid guard. Pfft."

Ben looked at Zoie and Silas. "Excuse me, I do have to get back to work, but it was great seeing you, Silas." He smiled, "Hopefully we can catch up some other time. I'm sure my wife would love a night out without the kids, and maybe we can share how we met our sweethearts."

Silas handed Ben what appeared to be a business card and agreed that they needed to catch up, and then he led Zoie in the direction they needed to go.

As the two of them caught up with the rest of the line, Zoie heard Ben ask someone to "repeat that" and then heard a ruckus followed by Ben asking if anyone else was "willing to challenge" his authority.

The walls were a ridiculously clean white, and it was cold in the long hallway. Perhaps it was because there were fewer people in the line. Or maybe it was that Zoie was still reacting to the fact that the security guard might snap someone in half for catching an attitude.

She didn't have much time to think about it, though, because they were called into a room, and the woman at the desk smiled and loudly greeted them with a high-pitched, "Helloooo!" She had a blue beehive hairstyle with black cat-eye glasses with gems on the arms balancing on the tip of her nose. Her glasses barely hid the bright blue eyeshadow that went up to her black penciled in eyebrows—which were not even close to being mirror images of each other, instead causing her to look as if she was always suspicious. Her light-pink blouse had a couple drips of tea on it, and her pearls were neatly lying under her collar. "I'm Dolores. You must be…" she glanced at a folder, "Zoo-i-ee."

"Zoie." Zoie sat down. Manilla envelopes? The Supernatural Realm didn't have have something a little more modern. She smiled at Dolores. "Okay, what do I do?"

"Well, m'dear, we're going to assign you a number and everything. Just a couple questions." Dolores nodded at her, requesting permission to continue.

"Okay."

"Species?"

"Witch."

"Subset?"

"Um… Sun."

"Ooooh, Sun Witch. That's lovely, m'dear. I always wanted to be a Sun Witch. I'm an elf myself." She pointed at her ear. She then asked, "First name… I have here as Z-O-I-E. Is that the correct spelling, m'dear?"

"Yes." Zoie didn't mean to be short with Dolores, but she felt like efficiency needed some assistance, with the line being so long.

"Perfect. And if you ever want to add an alias, we'll just give ya a card when we're done, m'dear. You must add any aliases you use to the registry." She typed a little bit. "Now, I don't have a surname for you."

Quickly, Zoie spat out the first thing that she could think of. "LaForge."

"Oh, that's lovely. French? Is that L-E-F-O-R-G-E?"

Zoie shook her head. "L-A-Capital F-O-R-G-E." Silas looked at her and chuckled, realizing that she had chosen a last name from a show they often watched together.

"Lovely. Lovely, m'dear." She typed a little more. Then her eyebrow—not the suspicious looking one—raised slightly, making the pair match. Before Zoie could ask if something was wrong, Dolores asked, "Is the information here about your initial time of transition correct? It seems a bit vague, and, m'dear, it's more than 20 years ago."

Zoie nodded innocently and decided to go with the truth. "You see, ma'am, I didn't realize what had happened when it, well, happened. It wasn't until very, very recently that I found out what I was." She looked at Silas but didn't wait for his reassurance to continue with the explanation. "I was talking to my partner when we realized what had happened. I was telling him the story of how my father died…" She trailed off.

Dolores frowned empathetically. "Oh, m'dear, that's so sad. You had to live with such pain and you also didn't know who you really were." Then she smiled and looked at Silas, "And, there you were, to help her find her way. How wonderful!" She noted some things in the computer. "Hold out your arm. I'm going to do the little implant of your symbol in your forearm."

Nervously, Zoie asked, "Which arm?"

"Most use the left, m'dear." She smiled, pulling out a handheld apparatus with a green tree label on it.

Silas took her right hand. "It doesn't hurt." He looked in her eyes. "I promise."

Dolores sighed. "Young love. How sweet." She placed her hand over her heart. "He's telling the truth. It doesn't hurt." She looked at his arm, and then scanned him really quickly. "Ooh, Silas Smith. You come from a time before these were perfected and they did hurt—it was a teeny tiny bit, but still did." She glanced back to Zoie. "If he's saying they didn't hurt then, then they definitely don't hurt now."

Zoie definitely didn't trust them now. She held out her arm.

Dolores pointed to Zoie's mustache tattoo on her finger. "That's a lovely little tattoo there. If you got one of those, this will be nothing." She didn't respond. Instead, Zoie closed her eyes tightly. She felt something cool touch her arm and then she heard Dolores' voice. "All done!"

Zoie looked down at her arm and saw the little green tree symbol glowing. "Oh, that's kind of cool."

Dolores smiled. "Well, m'dear, that's all there is to it. Best of luck to you, and welcome to the Supernatural Realm. Hopefully I'll see you two out and about. You really do make a lovely couple." She handed her a business card. "Remember, if you change your name, you need to let us know here in the registrar."

Silas smiled at her. "Thanks, Dolores. I appreciate you taking the time with us today."

"Of course." She clicked another button and then the printer kicked into life, loudly. Zoie was certain it had to be one of those printers that used carbon paper and had the bits on the sides with the perforations.

Silas took Zoie's hand and led her out of the building. "Okay. Now, it's off to Birmingham."

"Smith?!" She grumbled. "Why didn't you tell me I could pick a last name like Jones?"

He chuckled. "I did. I said you could pick any name you wanted." He admitted, "My birth name is Kekoa Māhoe, but I changed it to disconnect from my family and previous life entirely."

"Really?!"

He smiled softly. "I haven't said, heard, or thought of that name since I was in my teens." Silas looked over at her. "You are the only being alive that knows my birth name. I go by Silas exclusively, and it should go without saying that, no, Zoie LaForge, you cannot call me Kekoa."

Zoie was about to tease him, but her attention was pulled elsewhere as they tried to walk through the square and she nearly collided with someone. A large crowd was gathering. "What's going on?"

"Shit." Silas pulled her close. "No matter what happens right now, you cannot react. At all." He looked at her in the eyes. "Do not react. Promise me."

Even though she was confused, she could feel from Silas's reaction that something intense was about to transpire. "I'd do my best."

"Your best isn't going to be good enough right now." He pulled her closer. "You aren't going to like this, and you can't draw attention to yourself right now."

"Why?" This was the most serious that she had ever seen Silas—even compared to their earlier fight. Zoie needed more information.

He wasn't giving anything away. "It's your first day back. Shhh."

Suddenly, there were people on the stage. Zoie recognized some of them. The King of the Abyss was front and center, his wife just off behind his shoulder. Next to her, Alvin. Then, just off the stage, someone she didn't recognize, and then three women. On the other side of the King was someone in chains on their knees and a hooded figure held those chains.

The person in the chains had a mess of red hair, pulled back into a ponytail. They reminded her of Lettie, and Zoie got distracted, hoping that Lettie was safe in hiding.

"Welcome to the public trial of…" he looked down at a scroll. "Lettie Seavers, of the Witches community. Lettie is on trial for sharing our world's secrets with those outside of it."

Zoie gasped a little. It had never occurred to her that the person on that stage would have been Lettie. She couldn't believe that her aunt would have been caught.

Lucky for Zoie, others had let out a gasp as well. Still, Silas still shot her a look. "Don't react," he whispered, taking her arm when she had involuntarily taken a step forward.

"Lettie, do you deny the claims against you?" She must have replied, but Zoie couldn't hear her. The King said, "Project, Lettie. The jury of your peers cannot hear you."

She spat. "No. Just do with me what you will. You always were going to anyways."

"What are they going to do to her?" Zoie asked quietly.

Silas pressed his lips together and then quietly and cautiously replied, "Turn her into a gargoyle."

Zoie's eyes grew wide. "She'll have to be in gargoyle form forever?"

Before Silas could explain, the King started. "The punishment for this crime is lifetime imprisonment in gargoyle form, unless evidence comes forth to exonerate you."

"Never does." Lettie stood up, almost proud that she was going to be imprisoned for eternity. She was ready for her punishment.

The king nodded in the direction of the witches and the one in the middle spun her hands, kicking up some dust. Once the dust settled, Lettie was a stone gargoyle—horns and all. She somehow still looked like Lettie, just different.

Zoie gasped again. "This is terrifying. That was a trial? No one even said if they felt she was guilty or not…"

"They are always guilty." Silas sighed. "We need to leave." He started to look around for a path to an exit.

"That's Lettie! I can't… we have to save her." She started walking towards the stage.

"We can't." Blocking her path, he placed his hands on her arms, pinning her. "We have to leave."

Zoie was still watching the stage. "Who is that? Taking the chains off?"

"Not sure." His jaw tightened. Zoie could tell he was withholding information, so she just stared at him. Hesitantly, Silas responded, "A Bounty Hunter."

Zoie's jaw dropped. "This? This is…"

Silas looked her in the eyes and held her hands. "Don't react right now. Please." He whispered, "No one can know what I do, or it will compromise me."

"This isn't about you! I mean, what you do is evil. You bring people to their death!" She whispered, angrily.

He closed his eyes, took a breath, and then looked in Zoie's eyes. "Not all of them."

She pointed to herself. "And this should absolve you?"

"Zoie, don't do this here, please." He glanced off to the other side of the square. "We only have from here to that door over there. Please, don't do this right now."

She shook her head. "Fine. But I need to find a way to save her."

Ignoring everything besides the path to the portal they needed to use, Silas took her hand. "Let's go." They walked towards the square to the door that led to Birmingham as if they were on a mission from God. He opened the door, exiting into the alleyway that led them to the fountain that Zoie recognized.

She nearly started to cry in relief, momentarily forgetting what she just witnessed, and then she took a moment to collect herself. Then it hit her. "What if he's left?"

Silas put his hands on her shoulders and then ran them up and down her arms. "Listen, Zoie. I'm going to wait there..." He pointed to a nearby bar, "...until midnight. That should give you plenty of time to check where he lives and works and to check the places that he hangs out to find out if he's still here." He looked deeply into her eyes, placing a compass in her hand.

"What's this?"

He squeezed her hand. "My grandmother, who was an evil bitch, if you recall correctly, had a neighbor. He was really old, but really cool. He was probably the only thing that kept me from running away. He gave me this before he passed away, so that I could always find my way."

"Silas, I can't accept this..."

"Yes," he said firmly. "Yes, you can." He added, pushing a curl behind her ear, "You, Zoie, are my true North. The light to my dark. I think I'll be able to find you wherever you are." He hugged her. It was in that moment that she realized how much he truly cared about her. "Get your Lyft or Uber or whatever you kids call taxis these days. Go. Just go." He looked away from her and exhaled shakily.

Zoie said nothing while they waited. When the car arrived, she turned to Silas. "You'll wait until midnight?"

He nodded. "Yes. But, you won't need me to." He hugged her

again, tightly. "I hope you'll be happy, Zoie."

She kissed his cheek and got in the car. She didn't look back; she couldn't have born it. Zoie knew that she belonged with Hugh. Silas would distract her from what she wanted to build with Hugh, so she needed to move forward and forget that he even existed.

—Hugh—

Hugh wrapped his hands around the metal railing and looked out over Birmingham. It was a weekday, so most people were at work, and the weather was cool, so those not working were unlikely to be hanging out at Vulcan Statue. He had the place mostly to himself.

He had gone through the museum dozens of times, but he walked through again, then headed back outside. There were plenty of lookout spots at the Vulcan, but one was best: the walkway toward the top of the statue. He could see all of Birmingham. He took in the view for a minute, the wind swirling around him. He took the elevator back down and walked around, making his way to the lookout point where he'd brought Zoie to see fireworks.

Hugh had planned to bring Zoie back to this very spot once they had taken care of Alvin. He was going to rent the entire place for a private event, set up a table next to that very lookout point, and propose to her before the end of the evening.

He had been robbed of that—because he had been robbed of her. Still, in a way, she was right there with him. Zoie haunted Hugh's every breath, every painful beat of his heart. Closing his eyes barely helped. Zoie was there, behind his eyelids, just like in his dreams each night. Her red hair, green eyes, and freckles. Her smile. The way she laughed. Her soft skin under his rough hands. It was as if she was right there with him always.

His phone buzzed. A message from Rosalie: *Can't wait to see you tonite! xx!*

He swiped the message away without opening it. Hugh felt lucky that she was patient with him about Zoie, but how long would that last? Every time they were together, Rosalie was hoping to get closer to being the only two in the relationship, but that wasn't happening at all. The band-aid that Rosalie acted as—it worked, but it was tearing and becoming weaker. Zoie occupied his thoughts sooner and sooner when he left Rosalie's side.

He stared at his phone even after swiping the message. The background picture was still Zoie, a picture he had taken of her wearing one of his shirts. He closed his eyes and remembered the moment. It was morning on the island, and he could smell the salt in the air. She had buttoned all of the buttons, so he had undone a few. Her curls were loose, and he moved them out of the way to kiss her neck—she would softly moan and then say his name when his lips touched her skin.

I still love you. I will always love you. He ran his thumb next to her face in the photo. But I think I need to let you go. He felt a tear escape and wiped it away. To try to eliminate the sadness, he told himself that he was doing the right thing; she wasn't coming back, and he needed to find a way to move forward. He knew that he didn't know how to do that. His heart was still beating in the past, a place in time where she was still alive and with him.

He shoved his phone back in his pocket and looked out over the city again, hoping that the answer would appear to him. He took a deep breath, filling his lungs to capacity, and held it for five seconds before emptying his lungs entirely.

Some orange and yellow leaves danced in the wind in front of him, then stopped mid-air and held still in front of him before dropping—defying everything he knew of physics.

Magic. He felt his body heat up to defend himself. If his eyes weren't already glowing, they would be soon.

He took another breath, preparing to face whatever enemy had come. And that's when he caught the scent of Prada CandyPop perfume—something he was very familiar with. A scent tied to some of his best memories.

He turned slowly, knowing that his brain was playing tricks on him. "Hugh…"

The glow in his eyes subsided and the defensive pieces of him retreated. "Zoie?" He stood, frozen, unsure if this was a dream.

She nodded. "I'm here."

He took two large, cautious steps towards her, not convinced that this wasn't another one of his dreams. He reached his hand out, shaking and afraid to actually touch her, in case she wasn't really there. "How?" He took another step and slid his hand to her cheek. The moment his fingertips touched her skin, electricity shot through his entire body, confirming that this wasn't a fantasy. Hugh couldn't stop the tears from streaming out of his eyes. He didn't care—the entire rest of the world had disappeared at this point.

She reached her hand up to his cheek and wiped the tears following the trail of his scar. Before she could answer, he pulled her close, put his hand in her hair, and just held her as he cried.

He broke the embrace just enough so that he could look at her face. "I saw you… I saw that you were… I held you." He searched her face for some sort of explanation. "Zoie, how?"

She wasn't letting go of him either; his shirt was balled up in her fists. "There's a lot to talk about."

He looked around. "Let's not talk about this here." Hugh took one of her hands in his. "Let's go home and talk there. Tea?"

Zoie smiled and squeezed his hand. "I would love that."

Hugh's heart pounded in his ribcage. It was the first time that he'd felt like he had a heart since Zoie had died—well, appeared to have died. He didn't care if he had fallen asleep, resulting in this wonderful dream. He didn't care if he'd died and she was with him in the afterlife. It didn't matter to him what this was. He was going to ride it out. He hoped it was real.

He turned the ignition to the bike and Zoie's arms tightened around his waist. He could finally feel the life circulating through his body again. Hugh placed one hand over Zoie's and then turned his head to glance at her, just to make sure that she was there.

They got back to his house quickly. When he opened the door, he remembered he hadn't made his bed that morning. "I'll be right back." He hoped the panic wasn't evident. Before leaving the room, he asked, "You'll be here when I get back? You're not going anywhere, right?"

She smiled softly at him. "I'm staying for as long as you want me."

He came close enough to touch her cheek and look into her eyes. "Then you're staying forever." Then, he cleaned his room as fast as he could. He was gone less than a minute, but it felt like an hour to him.

When he got back to the living room, he handed Judy to Zoie.

"My mom let you keep Judy?"

He shook his head. "No." He looked at the floor. "The night you… you died… or whatever that was… I took some stuff from your apartment. I stole her."

He felt her hand on his arm. "I missed you, too, Hugh." He loved that he didn't have to ever say the specific words for what he meant. Zoie always knew.

"What happened? Why did you take so long to come back to me?" He pushed some hair behind her ear. He wanted to lean in and kiss her, but hesitated. It seemed like a long time—like forever—since they had been together, and a lot could have happened in that time. A lot could have changed for her. For them.

She gnawed on her lower lip. "I was told it wasn't safe."

Confused, Hugh took a step back. He started water for the promised tea. "Not safe? I could have protected you."

"I was told it wasn't safe for you when I woke up. Things needed to quiet down. So I waited as long as I could, and then I was told that I had to wait longer." She walked over to him. As he poured the hot water over their tea bags, she put her arms around him from behind. "I wanted to come back right away."

He turned in her arms so that he was facing her, then drew back a little bit. "I didn't want to live without you, Zoie." He felt his heart break all over again. "Why didn't you send me a sign, some sort of communication? Something? Anything, Zoie?"

She started to cry. "I'm sorry. I was told it wasn't safe. I didn't want to put you at risk."

"How could you live months without me? I could barely live five minutes."

"First of all, I was asleep for four of those months after some witch—Claudette, I think was her name—reversed much of the damage done by the water, but I still had some healing to do. Secondly, do you think that what I was doing while we were separated was actually living?"

She pushed away from him a little farther. "I was training

and learning and…" she scoffed. "I was living in a cabin out in the middle of the woods, in God knows where in the middle of nowhere Canada… living off the land, with minimal fucking electricity and no internet or cell service!"

He slammed his hand on the counter. "Well, I spent my time sitting in this house, barely fucking eating or sleeping, wondering why in the hell I could still feel you as a part of me when you were gone. I mourned you, Zoie. I never stopped." He ran his hand through his hair. "I still don't even know if this is real."

"Do you think I stopped caring for you because we were apart? Do you think that I didn't wonder every second of every day if you were okay?" She shook her head in disbelief.

He growled a little. "You said you were training. Someone was training you. Why didn't you have them reach out, Zoie? Why?"

She groaned. "I have told you at least three times now. I was told that it wasn't safe. It. Wasn't. Safe. I didn't want to risk your life." She let out an annoyed breath and turned away from him, taking a few steps back into the living room. "You're so damn stubborn."

He closed the space between them, placed his hand on her shoulder, and spun her around so they were facing again. "I'm sorry." He looked in her eyes. "I'm sorry. I think I'm just…" He took a deep breath. He needed to know if she was really, truly there, so he leaned over and pressed his lips to hers.

Their bond shot electricity through him, and the voltage increased as she put her fingers through his belt loops and pulled him closer. One of his hands tangled in her hair, and the other slid up the back of her shirt. He quickly retracted his hand, realizing he might have crossed a line.

He felt her hands slide to his belt buckle, and she whispered, with their lips still touching, "Why did you stop?"

"I am still in love with you, Zoie." His eyes searched hers. "Just say it. Tell me that you still…"

She didn't even wait for him to finish his sentence. "My feelings for you have never wavered. Not for one second." She placed her hand on his chest and pushed him back onto the couch, then straddled his lap. "I have desperately wanted you the entire time that we've been apart."

He grabbed the hem of her shirt and lifted it over her head, then took off his own. Hugh put his hand on her back, pushing their bodies closer together. He moaned at the soft feel of her skin against his.

Just as they pressed their lips together again, the front door opened. "I hope that you are okay with steaks to—What's going on here?"

Hugh stood up quickly, nearly knocking Zoie off of him. "Rosalie!"

Zoie grabbed her shirt and turned around and mouthed to Hugh as she put it on. Rosalie? Hmm?

"Who is this?" Rosalie placed the bags on the table with a little bit of force.

"Rosalie, this is Zoie," Hugh said with some emphasis.

"Oh," Rosalie said. "I'm sorry; I thought you told me that she had died." She whispered the word died as if it were a secret.

"It seems I was incorrect."

Zoie let out an angry sigh. "Apparently, I was incorrect as well." She grabbed her purse and looked Hugh straight in the eyes. "Mourned me, hmm?"

"Zoie, c'mon… It's not like that." He reached out to her.

She yanked her arm away. "Sure. It's nothing. She just walks right into your house. Seems pretty cozy to me." She turned towards the door. "Lovely meeting you, Rosalie. Enjoy your romantic dinner with Hugh." She grabbed Judy and exited, running down the street.

Rosalie looked at Hugh. "I'm so sorry. I didn't know she was here…"

Hugh shook his head. "There's no way you could have."

"I—I'm sorry about my reaction. You've been clear that we're not serious and that given the opportunity to have her back, you would take it." She looked down. "I didn't realize my feelings for you were strong enough that I would be jealous…"

She stepped closer to him and put her hand on his arm. He pulled back. "I'm sorry, Rosalie. I have to—I have to go after her." Knowing that it would hurt her, he still requested, "Please, don't be here when we return."

"Hugh, this isn't fair." She reached for him again, desperate to keep him.

"Rosalie, have I not been clear about what our relationship is for me?" He put his shirt back on. He knew that he had no choice but to be direct with her. Perhaps even very harsh. "You, Rosalie, are a band-aid. A suture that holds the pieces of my heart together, knowing that I would never heal to be as whole as I was before. Zoie, on the other hand, is the love of my life, Rosalie, and I am going to choose her. Every time." He repeated, "Every single time."

Rosalie's voice started to shake. "She was alive and didn't tell you." She begged, "She stayed away from you, while I picked up the pieces. She let you hurt. I know you could have grown to love me, Hugh."

He rubbed his temples. "You don't understand. There isn't a true life for me without Zoie. She and I… we're bonded mates."

Rosalie repeated herself. "She allowed you to suffer and mourn her while she was still alive, in hiding. You didn't leave your house for ages, Hugh. You didn't want to live. She let you go through that. That's not how soul mates treat each other."

"Rosalie, I appreciate what you're trying to do here, but I have to go after her." He couldn't entertain this any further or he risked losing Zoie again. "Just lock up when you leave." He ran out the door and got on his motorcycle, hoping that his bond with Zoie could help him find her.

Running down the street, Zoie started to sob. Her heart was breaking. After trying to get back to him—training to be strong enough to fight whatever came at them; learning the laws and rules; missing him; desperately wanting him and wishing to be next to him day and night—Hugh had moved on as if she had never been in his life.

She stopped at a street corner and closed her eyes for a moment, allowing her mind to move her to the Storyteller Fountain was in Five Points South. Her eyelids shot open once she saw the path in her mind, and she started on the fastest route.

She needed to find Silas. He would help her escape this hell. He would help, and he would be happy about it. Zoie knew that he would protect her and help mend her broken heart. While her heart would never fully heal from this disaster, Zoie knew that Silas would do everything in his power to get it as close to complete as he could.

There were no streetlights, so she lit a ball of fire in her palm and used it as a flashlight while she ran. It didn't illuminate as much as she needed, but Zoie would make do. She took a shortcut through the woods, almost running directly through a figure who stood in front of her.

"Zoie."

She fell into his arms and sobbed. "Silas."

"What happened?" He held her close, and she felt safe in his arms. "Are you hurt?"

She shook her head. "He—he's met someone, who walked in while I was there…" She sobbed again. "He's moved on. Just like you said. He's moved on." She pushed away a little bit. As she wiped her tears with her sleeves she asked, "How did you know where I was?"

"Zoie." He smiled very gently—almost cautiously—at her. "It's my job to find people. Plus, I told you that I could always find you." Silas pulled her closer. "I felt as if you needed me."

She sobbed into his shoulder. "I wanted to get away from here. There's nothing left for me in Birmingham. Take me somewhere."

He kissed her hair and then asked, "Are you sure?"

"Just take me anywhere. Anywhere but here." She wrapped her arms around him even more tightly.

"Keep holding on." He held onto her, as well.

The sentence was barely uttered when they went swirling into the darkness, then reappeared on a beach. Zoie looked around and up. The wooden pillars, covered in barnacles, led her to believe that they were under a pier.

Before she could open her mouth, Silas spoke as if she had asked him a question. "We're in Destin."

"How did you…"

"I just know. You ask 8,000 questions, but you always start with the most basic ones." He smiled at her and took her hand, started walking down the beach. "I noticed that some nights, you put ocean sounds and pictures on the TV. I thought you would maybe be comfortable here." There was sadness in his eyes. "Those are the nights that you slept the best, and I think that's because of the safe house off the coast of Hawaii. With the exception of the times that I had to chase off Miles, you slept really well there. I have a place here, and I thought you might find it relaxing. A place to let the outside world do its own thing while you... decide what you really want to do."

He admitted, "The walk from the pier to my place is quite far. Almost a mile. But I thought it would be..." Silas trailed off when he realized that Zoie had stopped walking. She didn't let go of Silas' hand. He turned and looked back at her. "Something wrong?"

She closed the gap between them and hooked the fingers of her free hand in the front pocket of his jeans, pulling him closer.

"Don't do this." He looked in her eyes.

She moved even closer to him, putting her arms around his neck. "Why not?"

He placed his forehead to hers. "For starters, I'm not entirely sure that it's safe to be out here in the open like this, especially at night."

She placed a small kiss at the corner of his mouth. "So?"

Zoie felt his hands squeeze at her waist as he pulled her closer. His lips were still close to hers, and he moved so that his lips were on hers as he spoke. "You'll regret this."

"Why?"

She heard him swallow hard. "He loves you, Zoie." He pulled away just a little bit, and his voice cracked. "You love him."

"Does he?" She asked, despite knowing deep, deep down that Hugh did love her. Suddenly she felt Silas's thumb grazing her cheek; she hadn't realized that she was still crying.

He nodded slowly. "He does."

"And you?"

Silas chuckled. "I'm pretty sure he's going to hate me when we actually meet."

"You know what's not what I meant."

He dropped his hands from her and went to move away, but she pulled him back by his shirt. He protested, "Zoie, do not do this."

She finally realized that he was telling her no, and she needed to stop trying to force this. "Oh." Dropping her hands away from him and looking down, Zoie realized how awful she truly was and how disgusted she would be if the roles were reversed.

When she started walking again, Silas grabbed her wrist and turned her around. "It's not like that, Zoie."

Zoie was so confused by this back and forth. It was just like when they were in Canada again—hot and cold, and then hot and cold again. Between that and the idea of Hugh being with someone else, she was mentally drained and couldn't begin to figure out what he meant.

Silas held her hand in both of his. "Zoie, I won't do this tonight because you're emotional, and if something happens between us, I don't want it to be something you grow to regret." He put her hand to his heart. "Zoie, I'm… I respect you so much, and if we're going to be together, I want it to be because you want to be with me. Not because you're hurt due to someone else's actions."

"You think I would be thinking of him?" She shook her head. "I want to forget him."

They started walking again and Silas slid his hand into hers as they turned onto an actual street. "You don't want to forget him. You never would forget him." Looking straight ahead, he admitted, "I would be okay with that, just so you know." When Zoie didn't respond, he began to explain, "I know that…"

The hair on the back of her neck stood up. "Shhh…"

"Geez, sorry."

"No." The quiet street gave Zoie a strong feeling of déjà vu. "I've been here before…"

"Oh? On vacation?"

"In this moment." Her heart started to race. She did the only thing she could think of, and manifested flames in her palms. "Someone's here."

Out of the shadows came a familiar figure: model-perfect body, bouncing black curls, and bright geometric earrings. Zoie lifted her hands and made the flames bigger, casting some light on the deep scars down the side of their stalker's face. Zoie growled. "Stevie."

"You look well, Zoie. Much better than the last time I saw you." She smirked.

Zoie narrowed her eyes. "No thanks to you." Stevie chuckled.

Stevie didn't waste a moment—she pulled water from the Gulf and surrounded Zoie's head, attempting to finish what Miles had started. She felt her feet lift off the ground.

Things were different this time, though. Zoie knew that she could change the outcome if she focused enough. Zoie calmed herself and focused on reversing the course of the water, but she didn't want to fall to the ground and get injured—she didn't know how far she had been lifted.

She concentrated, picturing what she truly wanted to have happen—the water to just reverse its exact course. Zoie felt her feet gently touch the ground and then, knowing that she could create the result she wanted, she sped up the process because she felt herself getting lightheaded.

Once the water was retreating back into the Gulf, Zoie turned to Stevie and smirked. "C'mon, Stevie. Do you really think the same trick Miles played was going to get me?"

Stevie chuckled. "No. It was a distraction and a way to kill some time."

Out of the shadows came two more figures, flanking Stevie's sides. "Who's your friend, Zoie?" Three more behind them. "He's cute." Silas went to touch Zoie, but a strong stream of water ripped up from the Gulf and splashed in between them, causing him to jump back. "Don't even think of trying to transport out of here. We'll just follow."

"Why did you betray us?" It was the one question Zoie had had for the last several months. The one answer she needed to know whether she could ever forgive Stevie.

Stevie frowned. "Well, I needed to get back on my parents' good side. It isn't what I wanted to do. I love you; I really do. You're one of the first true girlfriends I ever really had. You had all the wonderful qualities of a true friend. A chosen sister." She smiled gently at Zoie. "I didn't want to betray you, but I had a small piece of hope that…" Her face turned to disgust. "I thought that Hugh, or at least Cayden, would forgive me. Would understand…"

Zoie scoffed. "You thought Hugh would forgive you? For killing me?"

She waved her hand dismissively. "You seem no worse for wear." She stepped closer to the light. "I, on the other hand…"

The scars were deeper than Zoie had thought—green and yellow at the deepest parts, as if they were still manifesting an infection. Her eye was no longer the dark brown that it was before. There was a scratch down the center—but no pupil or iris. Her hair hadn't been pinned back on the side—it was unable to grow through the scars.

Zoie's concern grew for Stevie. "What… what happened?"

She stepped closer, scaring Zoie and forcing her to take a step back. "Hugh." She repeated, "Hugh happened. And, it's the reason that I have to do what I really don't want to. Hugh took from me the one thing that I truly loved—my perfection, my beauty. It's so hard to love myself when I look like a nightmare."

Zoie spoke to disagree, but Stevie continued, speaking over her. "So, now, I'm going to take the one thing he truly loves." She smiled, sickly evil. "That would be you, Zoie. You." She frowned. "I'm so sorry. You have to die."

Silas grabbed Zoie's bicep. At just above a whisper, he said. "We should go. They have at least one vampire."

"Do you think you can travel out of here faster than a vampire can fly to you?" Stevie fake pouted. "Let's see you try."

"Quit fucking around! Let's get this over with." Another voice that Zoie recognized.

She searched her memories; it was just vaguely familiar. She didn't have time to figure it out, because out from the shadows came a circle of people, surrounding them. She recognized one of them: Rosalie.

Zoie wanted to attack. She felt like she needed to attack, but of course, her natural tendencies to ask questions took over. There was no way Hugh knew that Rosalie was in league with Stevie; he wouldn't risk it. It seemed likely he didn't know she was a supernatural being. "How did Hugh not know what you were?"

Rosalie groaned. "Oh my god, you ask so many fucking questions." She acted dramatically as if she was thinking. "It's probably because he really doesn't know anything when we're together, if you know what I mean." She winked. The balls of fire from Zoie's palms grew, and Rosalie announced to everyone, "She's jealous."

"How did he not know? How did Cayden not know?"

The light from the flames made it much easier for Zoie to see how dramatically Rosalie was rolling her eyes. "How in the hell does he love you? You're so fucking annoying!" She stomped her feet. "Let me kill her, Stevie. Please, let me do it."

"How…"

"Oh my fucking god!" She waved her hands in arches over her head, raining down black smoke. Her entire appearance changed, melting away anything that allowed her to resemble the person she was—her hair went from the straight black to waves of lavender. Her eyes changed from brown to a nearly clear blue. She no longer towered over Zoie in height, but was taller by only two or three inches. Even her voice changed, from a bright soprano to a low alto. "I'm a witch and I used a fucking masking spell. Are you happy, now? I can give you the directions on how to mimic the spell, since you probably need it now, since he's had me. I'll even include some tips for in the boudoir." She winked at Zoie, dramatically.

The circle drew closer, not allowing Zoie time to react to Rosalie—if that was actually her name. Furious, she decided to try something that wouldn't really help them to fight, but would perhaps help in another, defensive way. She tried to read Stevie's thoughts. She searched for anything that could help them get out of this situation.

All she could find was the memory of Cade holding Stevie to a wall and then wolf-Hugh tearing her skin apart. That had to be all that Stevie was thinking about in this moment, all she could focus on—revenge for what was stolen from her.

The sound of bones cracking took Zoie out of her efforts. She looked behind Stevie and Rosalie to see two pairs of glowing yellow eyes, with mangled bodies lying on the ground below them—and everyone turning in slow motion to look at them.

This was her opportunity—Zoie shot a fireball straight at Rosalie, catching the hem of her sleeve on fire. Rosalie raised her hand up in the air and some large, hairy spiders came crawling out of the bushes nearby, while Stevie drew some water from the gulf and put out the fire.

Terrified and inexperienced in battle, Zoie went to shoot fire at the spiders, but Silas put his hand on her arm. "No. I've got this." He pulled from the darkness that surrounded them and made it vibrate the ground, almost like a small earthquake, sending the spiders running in the opposite direction.

Stevie and Rosalie fled the scene almost immediately after that, carried away by one of the unnamed vampires, but the others in her ranks weren't so lucky. It didn't take long for the owners of the two pairs of yellow eyes—Hugh and Cayden—to rip through them. One victim, however, lay on the ground, shaking and crying.

Hugh put his foot on the victim's chest, not crushing their ribs, but definitely making it known that he could. "What is their plan?"

"I… I don't know anything." Hugh took his foot off of her chest and slammed it down on her arm, shattering the bones. "You know something. Where they are working from, what their goal is. You know something."

The victim cried, unable to speak at first. Another angry growl from Hugh, and she replied, "The only thing I know is that she's after the redhead."

"Why would you help if you don't believe in the cause?" He growled again and placed his foot back on the young girl's chest.

She sobbed. "I've been homeless; she took me in. Fed me. Please don't hurt me anymore. I'll tell you anything I know. Anything. I swear."

Zoie approached her. "She's just a teenager. She's more or less a child."

Hugh turned to Zoie and growled, "Stand back. She came here to hurt you."

Zoie ignored him. "What's your name?"

"Zar... Zar..." She stuttered, her eyes bouncing back and forth between Hugh and Zoie.

"Zarzar?" Hugh growled.

The girl shook her head. "Xariella." She tried to be brave, but her voice shook. Turning towards Zoie, she begged, "Please don't let him hurt me anymore."

Zoie looked her in the eyes and sincerely said, "I can only help you if you promise to help us."

"I promise!" She cried, "I promise."

Zoie touched Hugh's arm. "Hugh."

As Hugh returned to his human form, Zoie turned to Silas. "Give them one of your socks, a shoe, anything! Give them clothes!" She motioned towards Cade.

"We need to get her some care." Silas said, handing his shoe to Cayden.

Zoie knelt down on the road next to Xariella. "I'm going to try something, and I can't promise that it won't hurt. I can't even promise that it will work. Will you trust me?"

Xariella nodded slowly, her eyes terrified. She didn't trust Zoie, and Zoie didn't blame her. What was stopping Zoie from taking advantage of her? She had all the control at the moment. She needed to prove to Xariella that she—the lot of them—could be trusted, so she was about to do her best. Her very, very best.

Zoie gingerly placed her hands on Xariella's arm, concentrating everything on her efforts. Closing her eyes, she thought of Hugh slamming his foot onto Xariella's arm and then willed her mind to reverse it. It happened in slow motion, but as she worked, she could hear Xariella cry out in pain.

She pushed that distraction from her mind, laser focused on what she was doing. Everything other than her and Xariella became foggy; sound came through as if they were underwater.

Silas knelt beside Zoie and put his hand on her back, entering her area of concentration with his encouragement. "Don't stop. It's working." He yanked his belt off and folded it a few times. Handing it to Xariella, he suggested, "Bite down on this so you don't bite your tongue or break your teeth."

Zoie continued to concentrate, and, after a few minutes, opened her eyes, exhausted and silently praying that it had worked.

Silas assisted Xariella to a seated position and then used his belt again, this time to act as a sling. He quickly turned to Hugh. "Your belt? I want to better secure her arm."

Hugh removed his belt, but not without asking, "Who the fuck are you, pal?"

Silas ignored him and further secured Xariella's arm. "You are going to want to not use that for a bit, even though you'll heal much faster than you ever would have as a human."

Hugh put his hand on Silas's shoulder and yanked him so that he would turn around. He glared at him. "Who the fuck are you? When did you get the permission to touch Zoie?"

Silas pretended to think for a moment. "I don't know, probably around the time you forgot to tell your mistress to not come home tonight."

Hugh growled. "It's not like that. I thought Zoie was dead." It was obvious that Hugh was battling not only thoughts of regret, but also the tendency to be quite territorial.

Silas laughed unhappily. He stirred the pot further. "Not sure when you arrived, Hugh, but perhaps you heard that your replacement girlfriend…"

Hugh, nearly a foot taller than Silas, stepped closer to him and poked two fingers into Silas's chest. "I appreciate that you took care of Zoie, but I can take it from here."

"Can you now?" Three words had never been so heavy with distaste.

"Guys, stop." Zoie stepped closer to them, trying to put an end to this little pissing contest.

Hugh stepped closer to him. "I'm more than capable."

"Capable like when you let her drown in a pool in Romania?"

Hugh grabbed him by the shirt. "You have no idea what happened that day." He lifted Silas enough that Silas's heels came off the ground.

"Stop!" Zoie yelled, stepping up beside them like a referee.

Hugh put Silas down with a little throw. He turned to Zoie. "Are you okay?"

Silas mumbled, "She wouldn't be in this situation if you could keep it in your pants."

Zoie's head snapped in his direction. "Enough." Turning her attention back to Hugh, she placed her hand on his forearm. "How did you find me?"

All of the anger and annoyance towards Silas on his face melted away. "I've told you before—nothing could keep me from you." Hugh placed his hand on Zoie's waist. "If you think for a moment that I would simply let you go after just getting you back, you don't know how deep my love is for you." He smiled softly at her. "Since I knew you were alive, I trusted our mating bond to show me how to find you. I nearly lost you at one point, but Cade… I had asked

Cade to make sure that Rosalie left the house, and they overheard her conversation with someone on the phone. Cade and I got in my car and drove." He turned to Silas and growled, "Your transportive powers leave a trace."

Silas rolled his eyes. "Perhaps, it's your alleged bond with her." He waved his hand dismissively.

Hugh looked back into Zoie's eyes. "I am so sorry. I am so sorry that I broke your trust in me."

Cade interjected, "To be fair, Zoie, Hugh really did think you were dead. And that chick just came in the picture…"

Zoie smiled at Cade, simultaneously irritated that they would interject themself into her relationship with Hugh and also thankful that they cared enough to do so. "I understand." She looked back at Hugh. "I think we have a lot of catching up to do."

Silas slammed his hand on the trunk of a palm tree. "Are you fucking kidding me? You're just going to forgive him? He was fucking that witch. If you really were dead, your grave wouldn't even be cold."

Stepping in front of Silas, Cayden said, "I know we arrived late, but we all heard that she used an enchantment."

"Fucking excuses. If your mating bond is so strong, you would have known. You would have felt that she was alive." He walked around Cayden and then put his hand on Zoie's arm, turning her slightly. He didn't pay any attention to the angry look on Hugh's face. "You deserve better than this. You can't take him back just like that."

Reaching over and putting his hand around Silas's arm, Hugh suggested, "I wouldn't touch my mate, if I were you."

Zoie saw the moment when Silas decided that he just didn't care anymore. It was written all over his face. "You won't hurt me,

Hugh. She'll never forgive you if you do." His eyes flicked to Zoie's hand in Hugh's and her other on his forearm, holding him back with just a touch. "What's it like knowing that all she has to do is say your name and you'll yield? Does it make you feel powerless? Like a child?"

"Silas, please," Zoie begged.

He shook his head. "Fine." He released Zoie and started walking away.

—Hugh—

The blood was boiling within Hugh's veins. He knew, though, that Silas was intentionally egging him on. Silas wanted this fight. It didn't matter who won the fight, Silas was right that Hugh would lose overall. He did his best to not react, but the beast within him wanted to rip this arrogant asshole to shreds.

He consciously focused on Zoie, who he could feel was confused and conflicted. "Let's all find a place to stay and get some rest."

Xariella looked over at Zoie, frightened. Hugh didn't want to let her stay close, but he also didn't want her to run back to Stevie. Hugh suggested, "You, too. But give up your phone."

"Fine." She pulled it out of her pocket, holding it up to display how it had been broken into several pieces, likely by Hugh's foot. "Here ya go."

"Throw it in that creek and leave it there." Cayden ordered. They looked at everyone else. "Does anyone know a place we can stay?"

Silas raised his hand. "I do."

Of course. Hugh rolled his eyes. He felt the gentle squeeze of Zoie's hand in his, and his heart started beating again, sending warmth throughout his body for what felt like the first time in ages.

He lifted her hand to his mouth and kissed it.

She tried to hide the smile on her face, but her blushing gave it away: she was happy to be near him again. In that moment, Hugh felt like he still had a chance to fix what he had broken.

Hugh slowed his pace so that Zoie didn't feel like she had to run, which also allowed Cayden, Silas, and Xariella to get a bit ahead, giving him some privacy with Zoie.

Glancing her way, Hugh told Zoie, "I love you."

She pulled herself closer to him, basically hugging his arm.

"Do you love him?" He immediately regretted the question. Just shut up, Hugh. Why did you do that? "I mean, he seems…"

Zoie sighed in annoyance. "Why? Why right now, Hugh?"

"Jealousy." His jaw tightened. "He had all that time with you, and I had a few weeks, tops. It's not unreasonable to think that you may… return his feelings." Stop pushing.

She shook her head in disbelief. "Wow."

Hugh stopped walking and pulled her close. "I'm stubborn, remember? I get stuck on this one thing, and until I feel like I've gotten adequate…"

She cut him off. "Yes, Silas and I are extremely close. And…" she paused, obviously trying to make a decision. "Yes, I was upset and hurt, and I ran to him and…"

Hugh put his finger to her lips. "Come to think of it, I don't want to know." His heart broke a little, images of her in Silas's arms running through his head like clips from a movie. "When we get to this house or apartment—whatever, you're with me, right?"

She nodded. "Of course." She grabbed his belt loops and pulled him closer. "That is, if you want me to be."

Was she out of her mind? Of course he wanted her with him. "Never, ever leave my side again." He placed a gentle kiss on her lips, and he felt her nod ever so slightly. Out of the corner of his eye, he saw that the rest of the group was getting farther away than he would have liked. He picked Zoie up and cradled her in his arms while he caught up with the group. She let out a shrieking laugh, and Hugh's heart felt as if it was lifting in his chest.

When they caught up, he put her down. Xariella teased, "Thanks for joining us." Bold of her to assume that she could joke around with anyone. She was still the enemy in Hugh's mind.

Zoie smiled. "Xariella, you'll tell us all about you tomorrow?"

"I can tell you now." She shrugged. "There's just not much to tell. I'm 19. I was a runaway since I was about 14—I had been in and out of foster care…"

"What are you?" Zoie asked.

"Vampire," Hugh and Cayden answered at once, both of their voices disapproving of her mere existence.

Remembering when they were building the initial plan to end Alvin's reign of terror, Zoie asked, "I thought that you didn't like…"

Hugh nodded. "We don't. But you wanted to help her, so we are going to help her."

"Who made you into a vampire? Was it one of the ones with Stevie?" Zoie asked.

Xariella looked at her feet as they continued to walk. "No. It was my boyfriend. He was turned into a gargoyle. Something about making an immortal child—but I'm not a child! I'm 19!"

"Sometimes they play it fast and loose with the rules." Silas led them up the stairs to the entrance of a beach house. He turned on the lights. "Welcome to my humble abode." He pointed to some stairs. "The master suite is up there. Down here, there's a room with two twin beds, and there's a sofa in the living room." Glancing at Xariella, he said, "No offense, but I don't think you should be left alone tonight. None of us trust you right now."

"Do you want me to stay with her?" Zoie asked. It was obvious that she felt obligated to take care of their prisoner because she was the one who decided to take her in.

Hugh looked at Silas, to see what kind of game this guy was playing. Silas looked Hugh in the eyes and coldly said, "No." He looked back to Zoie, and Hugh could hear Silas' heart speed up; he could actually see the man's pupils dilate to take in more of Zoie when he looked at her. "You stay with Hugh. Cade and I can take turns watching the vampire."

Cade scoffed. "Okay, Boss." Hugh looked at Cade, silently asking him to keep an eye on the situation.

Zoie suggested, "Why don't you use your ropes to cuff one of her ankles to the bed and she can just wake you up if she needs to use the bathroom or something?"

"Ropes?" Hugh asked, skeptically.

Silas smirked. "Oh, yeah, I have these magical vines that only I can release someone from. Zoie knows all about those." He winked at Zoie, and Hugh let out a small growl. He was going to kill this guy at the first available chance.

Zoie sighed. She held her hand up as a stop sign, and with each word, pulsated it in the air. "Please, just give it a rest for the night. Just… please." She looked exhausted. Suddenly, she asked with urgency, "Wait! What about the bodies?"

Cayden replied, "While you were healing Xariella —which kind of took forever but was really, really cool, by the way—I took care of them. Tide's headed out and it seemed pretty strong; I ran to the end of the pier and threw them in the Gulf. I think a storm is coming." They shrugged. "Hopefully they will get pulled out further into the Gulf or even the ocean."

Hugh put his hand on Zoie's waist. "Let's get some rest."

She nodded. "I'm going to get some water first, and then I'll be right up."

Looking in her eyes and smiling softly, he replied, "I'm not letting you out of my sight."

She smiled and stepped away to get a bottle of water from the refrigerator. Cayden was seated on a barstool at the kitchen island, and Zoie reached out across the granite and took their hand. "Don't think I didn't miss you, too."

They got out of their seat and walked around to give her a hug. "I missed you." The pair of them kissed each other on the cheek at the same time. "And I'm very sorry that Stevie betrayed you."

She shook her head—Zoie didn't blame Cade. "She betrayed all of us, not just me. She betrayed your amazing heart." She squeezed them a little tighter and then told Xariella, "I know this isn't ideal right now, but please, understand…"

"I do. I really appreciate that you healed me and also are trusting me. After some sleep, I hope that I can be of more help." Hugh was very skeptical of this girl, and his face must have shown it, because whenever Xariella glanced at him, she looked away and retreated into herself after.

Zoie gave Silas a hug. Hugh's muscles tensed. Between his shoulder blades, he felt his back tighten to a point that almost caused him pain. He wanted to see how Silas would use this to his advantage.

"You did really well tonight," Silas told Zoie. "You stood your ground. You were ready to fight." His arms were still around her when he said, "And you used your abilities to manipulate time to help Xariella." They hugged each other a little tighter. "I'm proud of you."

"Goodnight, Silas." She kissed his cheek, and Hugh's blood started to boil.

They hugged again, and with their arms still around each other, Silas glared at Hugh as he said, "It won't be the same without you waking me up in the middle of the night." He and Zoie both chuckled, as she was oblivious to that guy's games. Breaking the hug and looking into Zoie's eyes, Silas smiled. "Sleep well, Zoie."

In order to both make Zoie smile and because it was a complete power move, Hugh cradled Zoie in his arms as he walked up the stairs, looking in her eyes the entire time rather than where he was going. Still, he was careful not knock her head or feet on the walls or door frame.

As soon as her feet hit the floor, Zoie turned to Hugh. "Did you love her?"

Hugh didn't hesitate. "No." He watched as she processed whether that was better or worse than the alternative. "It's always been you, Zo. Even before I knew you, you were the one I was waiting for."

She took a couple shaky breaths. "Did you, um… did you…"

He figured that honesty was just the best way to go in this conversation, and Hugh knew what she was asking. "Yes."

He watched her try to maintain the tough image that she was trying to present, but her chin started to shake. "Was it…"

He shook his head. "Zoie, the moment I saw you, I forgot she even existed." Hugh took her hand in his and ran his thumb over her knuckles. "I don't know if this makes things better or worse, but she was just a placeholder."

She started crying. "It makes sense to me. Please, don't think it doesn't. But the entire time we were apart, I hoped that you knew I was still alive and were trying to find me or waiting for me to come back. That you wouldn't even dream of…"

Hugh pulled her into a hug. "I did feel like you were still with me, but I thought I was mistaken. I thought I just wanted you back with me so badly that I was forcing a feeling that didn't exist anymore." He took in a deep, shaky breath, which made him aware that his lungs hadn't functioned in a while. "Zoie, please, don't end this because of…"

She looked up at him. "End this? End us?" Zoie shook her head. "I would never. I just need to wrap my head around your being with someone else."

Before Hugh could stop himself, he said, "As long as you give me time to accept that you've obviously got an entire relationship with Silas, backed with something real." As soon as it came out of his mouth, he regretted it.

She wiggled out of his arms. "Seriously?"

He closed his eyes. "I'm sorry. I shouldn't have said that." When he opened them, she was sitting on the bed, crying. He knelt in front of her. "I'm sorry."

"Are we broken?"

He wiped her tears. "No, Zoie. Today's just been a very long, very emotional day." His heart was breaking all over, fearing that she was going to end things.

She put her hands on his biceps. "I just want to know that you still want me."

Heartbroken that she would even think anything else, he immediately replied, "Of course I do." Hugh looked in her eyes. "You are the fire in my blood, Zoie. The very thing that makes me everything that I am." He tucked some hair behind her ear. "Part of me believes that the entire reason I'm a werewolf is so that I could live long enough to find you. I love you. I will always want you." As he stood, he lifted her with him and kissed her. He sat her on the top of a chest of drawers, knocking a lamp to the floor.

Instead of stopping to pick it up, he tore Zoie's shirt off of her and threw it across the room. "Let's get back to where we were earlier." Hugh took his own shirt off and tossed it somewhere else. "That is, if you want to."

She bit her lip and nodded. "Yes." Zoie hopped down from the dresser and slid her jeans down slowly while looking in his eyes.

He led her over to the bed again and sat down. She stood between his knees and unbuttoned his jeans while kissing him.

Hugh immediately pulled her closer, sliding one hand over her lace underwear. "I have dreamt of touching you every day that we've been apart." He continued to kiss her as he stood up and removed the rest of their clothing, throwing it various places across the room. Hugh lifted Zoie and put her on the bed, supporting himself as he lay over her.

Her messy red curls lay all around her, and he took in the sight of her. "You're really here?" He was afraid that she would disappear at any moment. She nodded slowly, and he pressed his lips to hers again.

She moaned into his mouth as they kissed, and he couldn't help but smile. Lips still touching, he asked, "Are you sure you're ready to do this?" When she kissed him and nodded, he pressed himself into her and they both groaned softly.

"I love you," they said to each other simultaneously. Hugh's heart soared, as that was the first time she had ever actually said those words to him. Their kisses became fierce and passionate. They twisted in the sheets, exploring each other, learning whether anything had changed since the last time they were together.

———

As his back hit the bed, Hugh immediately pulled her close to him so she could lay her head on his chest. Their legs twisted together. He took a couple deep breaths, trying to hide the emotions that he was feeling.

She looked up at him. "Are you okay?"

"Zoie… I can't be apart from you." He felt his eyes fill with tears. "I can't ever be apart like that again."

She reached up and wiped a tear from his cheek. "I don't want to ever be apart again either."

He sat up, and she straddled his lap. Hugh wrapped a blanket around her shoulders so that she wouldn't get cold. "You don't want to, but I can't." He kissed her softly. "I… I don't know that I can live without you." He closed his eyes for a moment. "I almost didn't live without you." He admitted, "A part of me, I think, knew that you weren't really gone. That's how I survived. I convinced myself that I didn't believe that you were gone, but…"

She put her hand on his chest. "I know."

"You didn't want me to go that day. You had a bad feeling, and I went anyways." He placed his forehead to hers. "And I wasn't there… I failed you." He took a couple shaky breaths. "And, somehow, you still love me, even though I left you there, alone and vulnerable."

She put her hands in his hair. "Hugh, that wasn't your fault." Pulling him into a hug, she started to cry, too. "You thought I was in safe hands."

Pulling back from the hug, he said, "The only hands you should ever be in are mine." He wiped her tears. "We lost so much time." Putting a hand in her hair, he asked, "Why can't we just pick up from where we were?"

She smiled. "We have to get to know each other again. It's only logical."

"Ah, yes, logic. Because there is so much logic about the dynamics of werewolf–witch relationships. Step-by-step books and everything." He playfully touched her nose with his finger. "You know that I'll take as much time as you need."

While he ran his hand slowly along her thigh, he kissed her neck. She tilted her head back and moaned. "Mmmm… do you not want to sleep tonight?" She smiled.

"No… we… have… to get… to… know… each… other … again." It took time to say with a kiss between each word.

—Zoie—

Squawking seagulls woke Zoie, but she lay there for a few more moments. Her ear was to Hugh's chest, and she could hear his heartbeat. She ran her hand down his chest and stomach just to see if it would speed up.

It did, but it also caused Hugh to stir a little. He moved, swatting her hand away in his sleep, and mumbled her name with a twitch of a small smile.

She giggled to herself and decided to let him sleep. After she got dressed, Zoie pulled the curtains extra tight to make sure Hugh could sleep, then headed downstairs.

Before she'd even rounded the corner on the stairs, she heard Cade laughing and some bubbly giggles—Xariella.

They were sitting across from each other, sharing a dish of fruit. Cade was also eating cereal, and Xariella was eating pancakes.

Zoie asked, "Is Silas still sleeping?"

Xariella fell so silent that she even stopped chewing. Cade bit their own lip and delivered the news. "He's not here."

Zoie's heart broke a little. "Oh." She understood why he had left, but she hadn't wanted him to. She had more to learn from him, but that wasn't why she wanted him near.

"We switched shifts with Xariella, and when I came out to switch again, he was gone." Cade frowned. "I'm sorry, Zoie."

Zoie held her sadness inside, pushing it deep into her heart where no one would ever find it—where even she would forget it, she hoped. She poured some tea and grabbed a pancake. "So, who made all this?"

Xariella smiled proudly. "We did it together."

Zoie smiled. "Well, thank you both. I haven't had a pancake in so long."

Out of nowhere, Cade asked, "So, what's it like to sleep for four months straight? Was it like a coma?"

Zoie choked on her tea. "Um… I don't know. I don't remember being asleep at all. And, to be honest, I didn't feel all that well rested when I woke up."

"That seems like such a waste!" Xariella shook her head in disbelief. "I mean, you should have been ready to take on the world after that kind of rest!"

Zoie laughed. "I couldn't even stand at first!" Cade and Xariella laughed, too. Desperate to change the subject, Zoie asked Xariella, "How are you feeling?"

"I have gotten full mobility back in my arm. Thank you." Xariella looked at Zoie with genuine gratitude. "You didn't have to stop him. I don't even know how you did it. Princess Stevie said that he's one of the most powerful shapeshifters to ever live and that there are legends based on him. How are you not terrified of him?"

Hugh came down the stairs, still putting his shirt on. "She's not terrified of me because she has no need to be." He kissed Zoie's cheek. "The rest of the world should be careful, you two included." Cade scoffed in disbelief.

"So, is it true that if a wolf's mate says their name they will turn back into their human form?" Xariella leaned forward in interest.

Cade interjected. "Why do you ask? Are you going to run back to Stevie and tell her all of our weaknesses?"

She retreated into herself. "No." She frowned. "I was genuinely interested. I don't even think Stevie actually knew my name. She called me Vampira. She promised to help me get my boyfriend freed, but now I don't think she was being honest about it."

Hugh finally answered Xariella's question, perhaps to give Xariella a chance to show her trustworthiness. "Yes, it's true. If Zoie says my name when I'm in wolf form, I will turn back into my human self." He ate some of the breakfast that Cade had prepared and then asked, "Tell me about these legends."

She grinned. "She told us that you used to be a vigilante who killed evil men. She also claimed you were the actual Jack the Ripper. Also that you have ripped people limb from limb. Ummm…"

He stopped her. "I'm definitely not Jack the Ripper. Why would I cut the throat of my victims? That's not my usual M.O. Like you said, I usually rip my victims' limbs off."

"Because you were trying to keep the authorities off your trail." Cayden leaned in, very excited.

"Cayden, you know me." Hugh laughed. He turned back to Xariella. "Yes, I would kill evil men, especially if they were going to harm women or children." Then he leaned closer to her. "And, yes, I have ripped many people limb from limb, as recently as within the last six months. So beware."

Xariella cowered, frightened. Zoie playfully smacked Hugh's arm. "Stop trying to scare her." She looked to Xariella. "He protects those he loves with his life."

"Especially Zoie," Cade warned, obviously still not convinced that Xariella was truly going to be on their side.

"Zoie?" Her voice was quiet and cautious—obviously she was afraid of Hugh, never allowing him to get out of her line of sight.

"Yeah?"

Xariella drew a circle in her left hand with the thumb of her right, looking at the floor. "Do you… do you think that… would you maybe consider… could you maybe help me find a way to free my boyfriend?" She quickly added, "After, of course, we take care of this whole Stevie thing."

Zoie didn't even consult the others. "Of course we can." She waved Xariella over and pulled her into a hug; she trusted Xariella. "The more I learn about this gargoyle punishment, the more I feel it's unjust." She looked at Hugh and Cayden. "Lettie's been captured and imprisoned."

Both of them sighed. Cade said, "We tried to contact her to help her when we saw the alert, but she didn't respond."

"There was an alert?" Zoie asked.

Hugh explained, "I think it was before you were registered, so you wouldn't have gotten the notification." Zoie didn't care about that—she was irritated that Silas had waited so long to tell her that Lettie was in trouble. Hugh must have sensed something was off because he added, "It makes sense that she didn't respond to our messages now that you're back. She was likely afraid that there would be too many connections to you." He placed his hand on her back, comforting her.

"Thank you both for trying to help her." She turned back to Xariella. "I don't know much about gargoyles. What do you know?" She wanted Xariella to feel like she had a say in what would happen in the group. Maybe it would make her want to stay on their side instead of reporting things back to Stevie.

Xariella shook her head. "I just became a vampire like… three months ago. I didn't know much beforehand. I met Tafari, and we fell in love. I didn't ask questions." She hung her head in shame, embarrassed by her rash behavior.

Zoie placed her hand over Xariella's. "Sometimes, when you fall in love, there just aren't any questions that matter." The warmth of Hugh's hand radiated on her back.

She felt Hugh kiss her head and then he stood up. "So… we know that the witches create a spell to entrap the victim."

"Which witch," Cade chuckled at their little accidental joke. "Which witch usually casts the spell?"

"Not sure." Hugh guessed, "Probably Jade."

"Earth magic—that makes sense, with the rock forming," Xariella suggested.

Zoie thought for a moment. "I think it's all three. Ha is a Sun Witch, so she can manipulate time, so she probably locks in the time—the eternity of it all. Chandra probably makes it dark in there—she wouldn't want them to be able to enjoy it. Jade, of course, creates the stone."

Xariella gasped. "So you mean to tell me that Tafari is in that gargoyle, alone, in the dark? And he'll be there for eternity—like there isn't maybe a 100-years and then become fully stone and die thing?"

"What the fuck did you think it was?" Cayden asked. "A damn party? It's solitary confinement. It's torture."

Zoie put her arm around Xariella. "She just told you what she thought it was." She looked at the girl. "It's going to be okay. We're going to figure this out. I know these two very well, and both of them always have a plan." She looked at the pair of them and then back at Xariella. "We're going to have two plans to choose from in just a moment."

Cade and Hugh looked at each other. After sitting in silence for a moment, Cade suggested, "I think we need to start by figuring out where they move the gargoyles to once the big spectacle is over."

Hugh looked up at the ceiling as he thought. "There has to be thousands of them. Where could they hide them?"

Xariella interjected. "All of that is pointless if we don't know how to undo the spell. We have to figure out what to do when we get there first, or the point is moot."

"Hugh—Cade, it seems like the majority of the magic is Earth magic," Zoie pointed out. "Who do you know that could help us?"

Hugh shook his head. "I don't have close relationships with many witches. Lettie was kind of it. Of course, you as well." Cautiously, he asked, "What about the witch that helped when… when you…"

"Claudette?" Zoie shook her head. "Eeehhh, I don't think so. First of all, she's a Sun witch, so it wouldn't help with the Earth stuff…"

"But maybe she knows something," Xariella pleaded. "What could it hurt?"

Hugh quickly replied, "She could tell someone that we contacted her."

Cayden cleared their throat. "Hi, yes. I have another idea to throw out onto the proverbial table."

Hugh, unsure why Cade was being dramatic, actually glared at them. "Out with it."

"Get close to the Shrews." They presented it cautiously but also as if it was the most obvious answer.

"How do you suggest that?" Zoie asked.

Cade suggested, "Inserting one of us into their lives." They glanced at Hugh. "Take the place of someone already in their lives."

Hugh and Zoie both drew in long, deep breaths. On their

exhales, Zoie said, "What are you suggesting?" At the same time, Hugh replied, "Last time didn't work out so well."

Zoie registered what Hugh said, and quickly replied, "No. No way. We can't try that again."

Xariella looked back and forth and even checked behind her to see if there were others who understood what was going on while she didn't. "What is going on? What are you suggesting?"

Cade completely ignored Xariella and looked directly at Hugh. "We don't have to do the same thing. I don't even think that we really have to assassinate the asshole to get him out of the picture."

Xariella's mouth dropped. "Assassinate?!"

"We aren't assassinating anyone," Zoie said. She was saying that to everyone. She didn't want to risk the dangers around that again. This time, one of them really could die.

Hugh looked directly at Xariella but said to everyone else, "I don't know if we should discuss this any further."

Xariella squinted at him. "I'm trustworthy."

"Last night, you tried to kill Zoie."

"Last night, you tried to kill me."

Hugh rolled his eyes. "Wouldn't have had to do that if you weren't trying to kill my mate."

"Look, Zoie saved my life, and I'm indebted to her. Plus, I want to get Tafari back." Her eyes were nearly full of tears. "If you love Zoie as much as you say you do—if your bond is that strong, then you understand that I want my partner back as well." Her chin started to shake. "Stevie had offered to help me once we completed our job, and that is why I joined her." Xariella looked down at her hands in her lap. "I know now she would have never done it."

Zoie thought for a moment and then asked Xariella, "Do you have any special abilities, or did you as a human?"

Xariella shrugged. "I mean, I was always good at math, and when I was little, sometimes I swore that if I made a wish out loud, it would come true. But I had to be singing it. Not any particular song, just sing it. I used to be quite the vocalist. That's how I met Tafari. He heard me singing while I was taking out the trash at the place I worked, and he said it was the most beautiful song he had ever heard."

Zoie asked, "Did Stevie ask you to ever use that ability?"

"Of course she did." She looked down. "She treated me like a court jester in some ways. She would ask me to sing for her; her choice of course…" She paused and looked up. "And every time she did that, that night, another member would join our group."

Zoie looked at Hugh. "Do you think that it's possible that Stevie used her influence to get Tafari captured? Maybe Xariella is some sort of Siren or something? She could draw people in with her singing."

"Are you saying that she used her political influence to orchestrate Tafari's capture so that I would help her?" Xariella slammed her fist on the counter. "She's so fucking evil."

Cayden took a seat next to Xariella. "Xari, I know this seems unbelievable, but Stevie isn't all bad. She's made some bad choices recently, but… I would like to believe that she would have helped you if she really could." They took her hand in theirs, then jumped back suddenly, dropping Xari's hand. Their eyes grew wide, and then Cade finally let out a breath. "I'm sorry. I think I'm going to be…" They ran out of the room, all the way out the back door and towards the water.

Hugh kissed Zoie's cheek. "I'll be right back. I think Cade needs me." He added, whispering in her ear, "Please don't talk about this with her until Cade comes back."

Zoie nodded. "Understood, and I think you're the only person Cade'll want to talk to right now."

—Hugh—

Cayden was pacing back and forth along the shore, picking up seashells and then tossing them into the waves. They did not look happy whatsoever. Hugh could hear their muttering over the gentle waves.

"Hey." Hugh let the word come out as slowly and as cautiously as possible.

Cade didn't even greet him. They just immediately said, "A fucking VAMPIRE?!" All of the seashells in their hands flew free as their arms went up in the air. "What fucking evil prank did the Gods think they were playing on me?!" They started pacing again. "I don't want this. I'm fighting it. Do not tell her. Do not. Do NOT tell her."

Hugh laughed. "You're going to fight it?" He doubled over with laughter. Fighting the mating bond was simply an impossibility. "Good luck with that."

Cade remained standing there, arms folded. Hugh stood up and gathered his composure. "Oh. You're serious?"

"Yes." They threw their arms at their side. "A vampire? They… we're… we are not the same. We do not match."

"Really? That's the route you're going with this? You're not the same?" Hugh asked, "When you went swimming, did you get a giant colorful fin?"

"That's different. Stevie and I… we weren't…"

Hugh forced Cade to look at him. "It will be okay, Cade. It doesn't always mean like me and Zoie. Maybe you'll just be a really good friend…"

"You mean like how Silas and Zoie are friends?" When Cayden was unable to control a situation, they tended to lash out. When it was apparent that Hugh wasn't going to even entertain discussion of that, Cade stated, sadly, "It didn't feel like friend." They groaned. "She's not even alive."

"Looks pretty alive to me, pal."

"They drink blood." Another excuse.

"I know you just saw her eat breakfast. Pretty sure those pancakes weren't made of blood." Hugh then decided to take another route. "Look, I'm not going to tell you what to do. You handle this the way that you see fit to do. It's your life. But no matter how you get separated, it's not easy being away from your mate." He reminded Cayden, "Only a couple months ago, you told me that you wanted a love like I have with Zoie."

"She's too young for me." Yet another excuse.

Hugh chuckled, "I think you can make it work if Zoie and I can make it work." He repeated, "It's your life, and you do whatever you want with it." He turned to walk back inside.

"Does…"

Hugh turned back around. "Hmm?"

"Does Zoie love you because of the bond or because she loves you?"

Hugh smiled. "Simply because she loves me. Zoie and I—" His

heart warmed as he thought about it. "We would love each other even if we weren't bonded. It just wouldn't have moved at such an accelerated rate."

"Do you worry about that Silas guy?"

Since the question was posed differently, Hugh decided to answer. He shook his head. "I know she loves him—I can feel it, and anyone can see that he loves her. But it's not like what I have with her. What we—Zoie and me—have, Cayden, it is untouchable. So, no. Those feelings she shares with him—they are not a threat."

"What if she wants to be with him?"

Hugh shrugged. "We'll figure it out."

"You'll figure it out?"

Hugh just glared at them. The conversation was changing, and it was obviously because Cayden was trying to ignore what was really going on.

"Okay, we're not going to discuss that, I see."

Hugh sighed. "If you were asking for the right reason, I would entertain it." When Cade looked confused, he added, "If we free Tafari and she chooses him, Cade, it will not be easy for you to watch her walk away."

Cayden threw another shell into the water. "Do you think you could have fought the mating bond?"

Hugh shrugged. "I never considered it." He added, "But then again, I didn't want to fight it. The thought never crossed my mind."

"What would you do if you were me?"

Hugh smiled. "I'm not you, Cayden." He looked back at the house and then back at Cade. "My advice is that you should just think about what you want in your future."

"Hugh…"

The wind picked up, and Hugh didn't hear what Cayden said, so he moved closer. "What was that?"

Then Cayden said something that Hugh couldn't recall ever hearing from them before. "I'm scared. I'm scared of this." Cayden was always fearless. They always did everything on their own terms and never even considered what society believed was right—definitely not the human world and not the supernatural one either. They just lived. Without fear.

For a few moments, Hugh just stood in silence, unable to understand what could be scary about this situation. He leaned in closer to his friend. "Being in love, Cade, is incredible. I wouldn't trade a single moment of it."

"What about those months when you thought she was dead?"

Any other person, Hugh would have sent flying into a palm tree. Not Cade. "That's a fair question." He considered what to say, but settled on honesty—Cade would know if he was lying. "Those months sucked. I wanted to die because she, for all intents and purposes of the question, was dead. Yeah, it was awful. However…" Hugh couldn't control the smile that took over. "The time I had before and also have now with her far outweighs that. And, honestly, even if she was truly gone, I would have the same answer." He continued, "Because I let myself love —fearlessly, and no matter what happens, Zoie is and always will be the greatest love of my life."

He saw that Cayden was truly considering what he had said, but wasn't convinced, so he added, "But, Cade, I'm a hopeless romantic. That's not you."

Cade nodded, and as they both started back towards the house, Cade requested, "Please, let me tell her in my own time." Hugh agreed with a simple nod.

They slid the door open, and Hugh followed Cayden in. Cade immediately apologized. "I'm sorry about that. I just…"

Xariella blushed. "I'm sorry. I forgot how the wolves don't like the way vampires smell and I let you get too close… It's just, with you all, I don't feel like… I don't feel like a freak."

Cade shook their head. "Seriously, Xari, this is one of those cases where it literally is not you. It's me. Also, you are a freak!"

Xariella looked sad, and Cade continued, trying to cheer her up, "But but but! We all are freaks."

Hugh leaned over and whispered to Zoie, "Cade will tell her in their own time." She nodded.

Xariella quietly stated, "I wish we could just change the law and get the gargoyles free. Like when they made weed legal and released and expunged the records of anyone with criminal marijuana charges."

"Hugh could do that," Cade said matter-of-factly.

Hugh glared at them. He did not want to risk another assassination attempt on Alvin. "I don't think that's possible at this time. Alvin likely has measures in place to protect himself."

Xariella asked, "Why would simply ousting him change anything?"

"Because Hugh's ass gets to sit in Alvin's chair if he goes buh-byes." Cade poured a cup of coffee and dramatically dropped two cubes of sugar in it.

Xariella' jaw dropped. "Do you realize the kind of change you could make from that seat? Everyone knows—I mean everyone, including me, a total supernatural world novice, knows—that it's the partnership between Alvin and the Abyss that forces all the decisions. They always vote the same. That's on public record."

"But how do we remove him without killing him? It's a lifetime appointment, and, last time I checked, we're all more or less immortal." Hugh sighed deeply. He didn't want to risk something happening to Zoie, again.

Everyone thought in silence for minutes before Xariella asked, "Could we make him look, like, totally unhinged and get him like put in the hospital or something?"

Zoie opened her mouth, but no sound came out. She shook her head and got up to leave. Hugh put his hand around her wrist. "Zoie, what's wrong?"

"I can't do that to someone. I was put in a behavioral health institution because of what happened to my dad, remember? They told me I was crazy and… and I wasn't, and it was horrible." Completely out of character for Zoie, she didn't try to yank her arm free. Hugh pulled her into a hug, and apparently, that was the right thing to do because she slid her arms around him and got as close to him as possible.

Cade wasn't having it. "Zoie, that's ridiculous. This is the man whose son killed you, more or less. He has tried to kill Hugh multiple times in the past, remember? He put a bounty on both of your heads—a ridiculous one, if I may add. This guy has killed dozens upon dozens of shifters so that he can remain in power." They reached over and tapped her shoulder, requesting that she turn around in Hugh's arms. "This guy has locked thousands of innocents up in gargoyle form, including Lettie. He needs to be stopped. He is a fucking sociopath."

She turned around to Hugh and looked up at him. "What do you think?"

Hugh usually sided with Zoie, however, reluctantly, he admitted, "I agree with Cade, but I don't know how we're going to pull it off."

Xariella spoke as if the solution was simple. "We make him see things that aren't there."

Everyone just stared at her. For what felt like forever.

Hugh broke the silence first. "Okay, cool, but how?"

"Well…" Cade looked at Zoie. "You can manipulate time, and I think I remember that you said that you can read memories. You're going to have to get close enough to read some of his memories. Lost loved ones, romantic stuff about him and Edie. I mean, gross, but necessary. Maybe his favorite memories of Miles. Make sure he sees these dead loved ones. Have them talk to him, tell him to do something super unhinged, like jump off a building."

"Whoa! I thought…"

Cade cut Zoie off. "We aren't going to let him do it. We're going to make sure whatever he does is very public. Those assholes at the top can't ignore it—they can't brush it under the rug. Snap, crackle, pop and dear old Alvin is locked up. Magic stripped. Done." They turned to Hugh. "You get your ass in his chair and find out where the fuck those gargoyles are stored."

"What about Jack?" Zoie asked. "Couldn't they try to make a case to put Jack there instead of you, Hugh?"

"Who's Jack?" Xariella asked.

Cayden turned to her and explained, "Jack is Alvin's dad. He's a bit of a drunk, so no one takes him seriously, but if we go by the book on this one, he does kind of outrank Hugh, and this may be the one time that they'd actually put him in the seat, because he could easily be controlled."

"We eliminate him," Hugh said. "We completely get rid of him." He looked at Zoie. "I'm sorry, but Cade's right. They don't want me to have any influence, so they may do put him on the chair." He sighed. "I'm so tired of the powerful few having control over the many."

"How do you kill a werewolf?" Xariella asked. "I mean, I know what Stevie was planning on doing. The plan was to tear Hugh apart, but she knew that she would have to seriously overpower him. That's why she had a lot of variety in the team—so he would never be able to anticipate everything. It was when Zoie was found to be alive that…"

Zoie actually cut her off. "I don't want to know what they were going to do to me. We'll discuss that situation later. We need to figure out this one and then we can make sure that the puzzle pieces are in place for that one."

"Stage an accident," Cayden suggested. "We'll stage an accident for when he's in human form."

"Couldn't he just… turn into a wolf and avoid death?" Xariella asked.

Cade nodded, but added, "Zoie, you can get into people's minds, right? Just, like, block his ability to shift during the accident."

"That's not as easy as it sounds, and I'm not the strongest witch at, well, anything that I actually can do. I don't know that I'll ever be."

"You can do it, Zoie! You just need practice," Xariella reassured her. "You fixed me."

Cade agreed. "Fixing Xari was a big deal. She was pretty messed up." They glanced over at Xariella. "I'm sorry, but you were."

"I would say I'm sorry. A bit of me is," Hugh admitted. "But I want to see if you're really on our side before I determine if I'm actually remorseful."

Zoie rolled her eyes at Hugh. Then she asked, "When do we do all of this?"

"I think we need to gather some intel on Jack and Alvin." Cade looked at Xariella. "Honestly, I think you're the only person who can actually do that."

"Absolutely not!" Hugh protested this wholeheartedly. He

didn't trust Xariella whatsoever. She hadn't proven herself beyond the fact that she hadn't run away the previous night—that wasn't good enough for him.

"Hugh, she's the only one Alvin hasn't seen," Cade said. "Alvin definitely knows the two of us, and he's seen Zoie—our entire world has. Xari is the only one who could get close enough."

Zoie pondered this, obviously unsure. "Xari, I want to know more about your special skill. Your singing. Tell me more about how Stevie used it to get what she wanted."

Xariella explained, "So, if I sing a wish, it will come true, but I have to really, truly want it. So…" She paused. "Stevie would convince me to want something—through a reason, sometimes, but also sometimes she had to promise me things that I wanted." She admitted, "I can't wish for big things like someone's death or love or anything major like that. Also, it has to be a pure wish. Like, nothing bad can happen to a person. In middle school, I wished for Geri Gibson to trip and fall and break her nose, and that didn't happen. But it should have. That bitch stole my boyfriend right in the middle of a school dance!"

Zoie laughed so hard that she started coughing. "That's more my speed for the type of wish I would make, to be honest. There's someone I know who always stole my boyfriends, and I really did wish the worst for her at times. It's probably a good thing I didn't have that power."

The girls shared a little laugh, and once they contained themselves, Zoie requested, "So, give me an example—don't sing it. Just give me an example of something that Stevie wanted but you really didn't, but you were still able to make it happen." For once, Zoie's endless line of questioning was getting them new information, instead of just teaching her something.

"Oh, that's easy," Xariella replied. "When we wanted…" She hesitated and then frowned. "She really did set up Tafari's capture to get what she wanted."

Cade made their way over to her and cautiously touched her hand. They pulled back for a moment as the bond between them was obviously overwhelming for Cade. Immediately, they tried it again, pushing through the sensation. "I'm sorry she did that to you." They reached over and touched her shoulder. "Xari, we need this information to help free Tafari. We aren't like her. We will help you."

She nodded slowly. "When she wanted to add a member to our group—it was actually the one you call Rosalie. Her real name is Stella. Stevie wanted someone who was skilled at masking spells. She told me that if I brought her someone who could do those kinds of spells, she would help me free Tafari."

Xariella looked at her hand in Cayden's, and then she looked up. "For that wish, I sang the words 'I wish to find the witch who produces the strongest masking spells so that I can save Tafari'."

"How quickly does it work?" Hugh asked. "When does it yield results?"

She shrugged. "Usually within a week, unless it's something like 'I wish to get perfect grades in high school'. That would take all four years."

Zoie looked to Hugh. "Is this a unique skill?"

He searched his memories for anything like this. "I've never met anyone with this particular skill. Witches and warlocks can manifest, but this is something different. It doesn't take as long, and, from the sounds of it, she gets what she desires, without the work."

Zoie asked one more question. "Your wish that ended with 'so that I can save Tafari'—what will happen now that you are not working with her?"

Xariella shrugged. "Look, I'm new to this—to knowing that it's actually a power, rather than a coincidence, but I think that it will still come true because I didn't ask for Stevie's help. I just asked for it to happen."

"This is a really interesting power, but I honestly don't know how we can use it right now." He tried to think of a way that it could be pure and beneficial at the same time, but he couldn't.

Cade interjected, "I don't think the girls should do any dangerous parts of this by themselves. I know I said that you, Xari, have to be the one to do some really sneaky stuff, but I think that Hugh or I should be there with you."

Zoie went to speak, but Cade continued. "Xari, you're too new into this world to know some of the ramifications of your actions and also what some of the other beings are capable of, and Zoie, I'm sorry, but you've not really developed your powers enough to protect yourself. I just don't think it's a good idea, and I'm sure Hugh will agree."

Hugh nodded, but Zoie spoke. "Of course Hugh is going to agree. I'm his mate, and he doesn't trust Xari yet. It only makes sense. But I also don't know if it's a good idea for Hugh to be my partner on…" she tried to think of a word. "On missions. He may insert himself into situations too soon because he wants to protect me, but it may be something I could handle or it could compromise the mission."

"No. No way. I'm not letting anything happen to you." Hugh was firmly against letting Zoie out of his sight. He had lost her once, and he wasn't about to do it again.

"Hugh, that's precisely my point." She reached over and took his hand. "You would step in at the first sign of danger, and that could ruin everything. I have to be able to get close enough to

Alvin to insert visions into his head, and I can't do that if you get in the way."

"I don't like that." He was shaking his head repeatedly. "No."

Zoie smiled. "But notice that you aren't trying to state that my point is invalid."

His jaw tightened. She was completely correct. "You'll take Cade with you?"

She drew an X over her heart. "I will take Cade with me on missions. I promise."

Cade added, "Hugh, you'll go with Xari?" It was obvious to everyone but Xari that Cade was unable to fight the mating bond, despite wanting to. Xari was either ignorant of mating bonds or just plain oblivious because she didn't react whatsoever. In fact, she was picking at a dry pancake, barely paying attention.

Unable to hide his joy about his friend finding their mate, Hugh smiled. "Of course." Hugh didn't trust Xari, but he would never risk her life knowing that she was Cade's destiny.

Zoie and Hugh finally sat down and started to eat breakfast. Zoie was a handful of bites in when she said, "Wait. Did we actually create a plan?"

Xariella looked up and blurted out, "Stevie said a couple times that she wanted her revenge completed before some big event that was coming up—some ball. She wanted to use it to quietly celebrate her victory."

Cade frowned. "Around this time each year, the Abyss holds a black-tie Gala each year to raise awareness about climate change and the effect it has on the oceans. I attended it as Stevie's guest for several years, and it was always very awkward for me. There's always a lot of powerful people at this event."

Zoie and Hugh looked at each other, obviously thinking the

exact same thing. Hugh said it out loud for Xari and Cade to hear. "That's the day we need to make the big stuff happen." Hugh looked at Zoie. "I think step one is you getting into my memories and seeing what Edie looks like, and her mannerisms."

Zoie sighed. "I'm not sure how strong my memory invasion skills are, first of all. And, also, everyone's memories are skewed by their own experiences—even unrelated things that happened previously." She looked at Hugh, "You need to be careful as you choose which memories you share with me."

Hugh nodded. "Okay, so I'll spend the next couple days trying to recall some memories. Then we can spend maybe a week while you try to retrieve them and also perhaps share the memories with…" He paused to decide. "With Cade, for practice." Zoie nodded. "In the meantime, Xariella can maybe do some investigation to find out Jack's whereabouts."

Cade interjected, "Should be easy enough. I swear the wooden barstool at the tavern has molded to his ass because he sits there so much."

After a chuckle, Hugh continued with laying out the plan. "Here's the issue: Zoie needs to be messing with Alvin's mind while we stage an accident for Jack. That's a lot for one person to do."

Xariella asked, "Do you two have special skills?"

Cade responded, "Hugh can run really, really fast and he can see very, very far in the dark."

"What about you?"

They shrugged. "I can make a really great breakfast."

Hugh chuckled. "Cayden is being modest. Their abilities include empathy and the ability to solve puzzles in record time. I don't mean jigsaw puzzles—though, yes, them too—but if we get into a bind, they can find the way out faster than anyone else could. Also, that's why they are so good at making plans like this. And Cayden can rebuild an engine unlike any mechanic I've ever seen."

Cade blushed. "Thanks for the compliment, and while I can admit I have an aptitude for puzzles, I don't know that the empathy thing is true."

Hugh looked them straight in the face. "Did you or did you not know exactly what I needed at every turn for the last several months? That's just one example."

"We're best friends and have been together for decades."

Zoie interjected, "No, Cade. You're being modest. At first, I thought it was just compassion, but I think that it's why you are a magnet for other people. You have an ability to just… make people feel comfortable. They know you care. You're unbelievably honest—sometimes to the point it could be hurtful, but in those moments, that's what the person needs. You always know how to help someone. Sometimes just your presence is enough."

Despite having her question answered, Xariella sighed. "Neither of those things help, unless, Cade, you can get Jack to open up to me."

Hugh looked at Zoie again, and they silently communicated with each other. Zoie spoke this time, "That's not a half bad idea. We could at least try it." She suggested, "Just go to the tavern. Set Xariella next to him at the bar, but you, Cade, can sit at a table elsewhere with a direct line of vision. You may be able to send calming vibes so that he opens up to her?"

Cade scoffed. "I doubt it. I've never even attempted something like that."

Hugh ordered, "Then practice. Go people watch and try it out."

Xariella interjected, "They're not Jasper from Twilight. It's not like Cade can just send calming vibes." Hugh saw Zoie's eyes light up—she had a new best friend.

Zoie did her best to not react any further. "I think I should get some herbs and maybe Xariella can put something in Jack's drink and then it may be easier to stage some sort of incident."

Xariella nearly spit out her drink when Cade added, "The dude has an iron liver. I don't know if that will work."

Hugh rolled his eyes. "Let's get Plan A down first and then think of Plans B, C, D, and E. Okay, so, I guess we aren't going with the pairings we discussed earlier, but I see this is the only way this part of things is going to work. So while Xariella and Cade are working their magic with Jack, Zoie will be practicing memory work with me. Then once Jack's out of the picture is probably the best time to start working on Alvin because he'll already be a little bit mentally vulnerable."

Cade suggested, "And then at the Gala, Zoie, do you think that you could get him to do something very public and very incriminating? Perhaps you could give him have a vision and maybe he'll make a scene?"

Zoie took a deep breath. "Look, I'll do my best. But I don't have a lot of practice with this stuff, and, beyond that, I'm still a little uncomfortable with the idea that I'm going to put someone in a mental institution who isn't truly in need of going there."

"If there's another way, we'll take it." Hugh didn't know if there was another way to make this happen, but he understood Zoie's apprehension. He wanted to support her, but he also knew that she didn't want to assassinate Alvin. Further, Hugh was certain that there was no way to get Alvin to resign from his post. Alvin had been hungry for power long before Hugh had entered his life; there was no way that he was going to willingly give up the very thing that got him out of bed in the morning. They were backed into a corner, and, if they wanted this to work, it was the only way.

—Zoie—

Back in Birmingham, and after a few days of combing through her spell books, Zoie had compiled a list of herbs she would need for their plan. In fact, she had at least four contingency plans' worth of supplies, just in case.

The only place to get everything she needed was in NightBrooke, so she took a trip to Storyteller Fountain, alone for the first time. Since it was going to be a quick trip, she didn't ask anyone to accompany her. She was registered and no longer on anyone's radar as a fugitive. A trip to the Witch's Coven Shoppe was a normal, everyday activity for any witch or warlock, so she didn't expect it to draw any attention.

Zoie ran her fingers along the bottles of herbs, as if she could tell which one would work by just touching the bottles. Maybe touching helped her better pay attention to the labels. She had already found chamomile and lavender, but she wanted something a little stronger—and that's when she saw a dusty bottle in the back. Magnolia bark. She grabbed it and put it in her basket.

To not look suspicious, she also grabbed some fresh basil, rosemary, thyme, and one herb that she picked with her eyes closed. She also put some cloth and ribbon, a feather, one raven's foot, and some assorted candles in her basket.

When Zoie handed the items to the shop worker, theysaid, "Oh, Magnolia bark. We haven't had a purchase of that in years." Shit.

Zoie nodded and replied, "I've never seen it before. I'm always looking for something to add to my kit." She handed over the money and started towards the door, but a deck of tarot cards caught her eye. Zoie stopped in her tracks. Her hand grabbed them on its own; something about them called to her. She bought them as well. The shop worker complimented the purchase and offered her an altar cloth, which Zoie declined.

Zoie left the store, pondering how to get these herbs in Jack's drink without anyone noticing. He would be easy enough to find—he was almost always at the tavern—but the tarven always had a lot of people there. Thankfully, she had time to research. They weren't going enact their plan for another week.

To her surprise, Jack came stumbling out of the tavern, right in front of her. He hadn't seen her, though; he was too busy finding a place to puke. She hid out of his line of sight and waited for his retching to stop.

He wiped his mouth with his sleeve and headed further into an alleyway. Zoie quietly and cautiously followed him. Knowing where he was going might provide a place other than the crowded tavern for her part of the plan.

Jack stumbled further and further into a forest. It was getting darker with every step. When he started to take strange turns, Zoie realized that she was lost—and that Jack had caught on that someone was following him.

She panicked and realized she'd lost Jack. She looked around and backed into a tree. When she turned, a huge werewolf was leaned over, his face right in front of hers, snarling.

He growled. "Stop following me."

Zoie panicked and lied, "I'm sorry. I was lost in the woods, and I saw you and started following you in hopes that you would get me out of it."

He stood up taller, towering over her. "You've been following me since at least the edge of the tree line." Jack glared at her, raising one hand to attack her, moving the other to grab her arm.

Zoie dropped her bag and ignited a fire in her hand. "I don't want to hurt you. I just want to get out of here." She backed away, feeling her arm get caught on one of his claws. She hoped her palms of fire would convince him to let her go and that she could wander until she found her way out.

No such luck. Jack lunged at her, so she shot fire at some dried leaves in front of him, igniting a wall of flames, possibly singeing some of his fur. This didn't stop him. He just went around the flames and came for her again.

Zoie ran, but soon tripped and scraped her hands on a rock and grazed her head against a branch. She glanced over her shoulder every once in a while to shoot flame in his direction. It was inevitable that he was going to catch her.

She heard leaves and twigs in front of her rustling, and there stood Jack, having jumped over or flanked her at some point. "You can't escape, girlie." He circled her, taunting her. "I can either kill you and leave you here, or I can leave you within an inch of your life and send you back to your coven, witch."

She didn't answer. His circle became smaller with every time around. When he was just in front of her again, Zoie closed her eyes in preparation for what was surely going to be her real death.

Eyes still closed, she heard a struggle and Jack growling and thrashing. She opened her eyes to see. Branches were growing from the trees and wrapping around his wrists and ankles. A dark, thick fog formed across the forest floor, and black vines started to grow and wrap their shapes around Jack, lifting him until he was suspended between two trees.

Zoie fixated on what was happening. The vines wrapped around him, pulling more and more tightly as they climbed his body. She gasped as the vines tightened around his neck, causing Jack to strain to breathe until his throat was entirely crushed. The black vines crawled into his nose and then out of his mouth. Then, they suddenly stopped growing.

Stunned, Zoie stood still for a moment, not sure how to make her feet function, until she felt a hand on her arm, turning her. "What are you doing out here? Why were you following him alone?"

Zoie turned and for a moment, just stared into his eyes—it was Silas. "I…"

He put his hands on either side of her face. Still panicking, he looked in her eyes. "Are you just entirely reckless? He could have killed you!" Without any further hesitation, Silas leaned in and kissed her.

She didn't fight him. In fact, Zoie leaned into the kiss, pulling him closer by his pockets. She felt his hands on her back, pulling their bodies closer together.

"Zoie." His forehead rested against hers. "Why were you doing something so stupid? Why were you out here?" He kissed her gently again.

She didn't answer him. Silas hadn't been privy to the plan to take Alvin's political influence from him. Instead she asked, "What were you doing out here?"

Despite putting a some space between them, he still had a hand in her hair. "I was tasked to protect you, Zoie." He smiled and looked away. "I will always come to your rescue."

"Then why did you leave me?" She started to cry.

He shook his head. "You know why I left." He wiped a tear from her cheek. "I couldn't watch you with Hugh." He asked her again, "Why were you following him?"

"I… I shouldn't have been." She felt foolish to even think that it was a good idea for her to follow Jack. Especially alone—and, even if the plan was to follow him alone, she should have let someone know where she was going. "Is he…?"

"Zoie, when was the last time that you saw someone survive branches in their throat, their bronchial tubes, and their nose?" He looked Zoie in the eyes and sternly said, "We need to get out of here before someone finds us." Silas slid his hand down her arm and took her hand in his. "Where's Hugh?"

"At home."

He took her other hand in his. "Hold on." Reluctantly, he transported them out of the forest.

Zoie felt her body get sucked into the darkness and reassemble. When she was whole again, she immediately recognized where she was. She looked to the right, just in time to see Xariella drop her fork to her plate with a clang.

"Well, that's a neat trick." Xariella's face was glued to the spot where Zoie and Silas stood. A spot that had been empty only moments before.

Cade called down the hall with urgency. "Hugh!"

Hugh walked to the kitchen at a leisurely pace, thinking that Cade was just being dramatic about seeing an insect. "What do you—" His attention immediately shifted to Zoie. "Why are you covered in dirt and ash? Are you bleeding?" He ran over to Zoie, stepping in between her and Silas.

"I was picking up some herbs—oh I left my bag in the forest!" She started to panic, but Silas disappeared and reappeared within seconds, bag in tow. "Thank you," she said politely as he placed it on the counter. "Did you…"

"Yes." Silas continued, "I used the shadows to suck the oxygen out of the area and kill the fire."

"Silas." Hugh slammed his hand on the counter. "Tell me what happened. Now."

Hugh hadn't addressed her, but Zoie tried to speak. Her recount was coming out jumbled, her mind replaying the image of the vines crushing Jack. It finally hit her what had really happened and how much danger she had been in.

Silas held his hand out towards the couch, using the shadows in the room to pull the throw blanket to his hand. He put it around Zoie's shoulders and then summarized the events. "Zoie followed Jack into the forest in NightBrooke, and he didn't like that, so he attacked her."

"Zoie, why would you follow him when you were alone?" Hugh started washing the dirt, ash, and blood from her face. "Cade, get the first aid kit from the cupboard." Hugh looked at the blood on her arm. "Did he scratch you?"

She nodded slowly, but still lied, "I'm not sure if it was a branch or him." She wasn't sure what Hugh's reaction would be. She worried that he would somehow blame himself.

As Hugh cleaned her arm, he frowned. "That's not a branch. It was him." He turned to Silas. "Where is he now?"

Flatly, Silas responded, "Suspended between two trees by the vines that crushed him to death, as if he was trying to personify the cross that Christ was crucified on."

Xari laughed and then tried to cough to cover it up. Hugh shot her an angry glare and then turned to Cade. "I need you to stay here with Zoie for a moment." They nodded.

—Hugh—

"You." He pointed at Silas. "With me." Hugh walked out of the house, and Silas followed as if his body wouldn't let him make any other choice. He led Silas to the garage.

Silas looked around. "Look, you could probably kill me with your bare hands. You don't need all of this shit." He picked up a wrench and then it slipped out of his hand, landing on the dirty cement floor. Silas picked the wrench up and cautiously placed it back where it had originally been.

Hugh turned to him, unamused. He decided to just cut right to the chase. "I know that Zoie can make plants grow and shrink. Were those vines that killed Jack yours or hers?"

Silas nodded, knowing what Hugh was really asking. "Oh, totally me." Silas looked directly at Hugh. "She's not going to have it in her to kill anyone violently. I don't even know that she could do it for mercy." He shook his head a little. "It's admirable in a way, but she's going to get herself hurt—or worse—if she's not willing to protect herself."

Hugh paced. "And your feelings for her…"

Silas didn't hesitate. "Yeah, I love her."

187

Hugh's jaw clenched and his eyes narrowed. "How far, then, are you willing to go to protect her, Silas?" Hopefully death.

Silas chuckled. "I just killed a prominent political figure's father to keep her safe, Hugh. I mean…"

"Death? Would you risk your own life?" Hugh folded his arms across his chest as he stared him down.

"Hugh, I just did. I've done it lots of times. What are you trying to accomplish with this line of questioning?" Silas scoffed. "You're so fucking possessive of her, y'know? It's concerning." He rolled his eyes.

Hugh closed some of the distance between them, attempting to intimidate Silas. "I'm not going to risk her safety." He added, snarkily, "Besides, my overprotective nature, is it actually worse than, I don't know, toying with her emotions by being hot and cold with her, repeatedly, especially when you are in a position of power over her, and she's essentially held captive by you for months?" Hugh wished that his glare came with a thousand knives that he could direct right at Silas.

Silas was silent. Checkmate. Finally, Hugh was able to knock this insufferable menace down a few pegs.

He looked Silas up and down and tried to evaluate him and his loyalty. "I need to know if your commitment to her wavers. Ever."

Silas sighed. "Hugh, I know that the wolves believe in the mating bond…"

"It's real."

Silas rolled his eyes. "Whatever." After a deep sigh, he continued, "What I was going to say before you so rudely interrupted me…"

"Get on with it, Silas."

"Zoie and I don't have your alleged mating bond, but no matter what happens or doesn't happen between the two of us, I will always treat her with respect. I will always care about her."

Hugh pondered for a moment. "Then I need you to do something." The look on Silas' face told Hugh that there wasn't a chance in hell that he was going to do anything that Hugh asked. So, he added, "For Zoie."

He raised an eyebrow, suspiciously. "Go on."

"I need you to make sure that there isn't a single fucking shred of evidence that Zoie was in that forest today. And then," he drew in a deep breath. "And then, I need you to make sure that Jack is found. Hanging there." He added, "Bonus points if it is Alvin Irving that finds him."

Silas narrowed his eyes, questioning Hugh. "Okay, something big is happening here, and I want to know what I'm getting involved in before I agree."

"Just do this for Zoie so that she doesn't get a target on her back."

Silas shook his head. This dude is relentless, Hugh thought, getting more and more annoyed by the millisecond. Finally Silas explained, "I'm not going to do anything unless I know what I'm getting involved in."

Hugh decided to be fuzzy with the details, but he needed Silas's help to protect Zoie from being connected to Jack's death, so he had to give him something. "I'm working on getting Irving out of the Council."

Silas grinned, and stated with no further hesitation, "I'm in."

Shocked to discover how easily Silas agreed once he knew the high-level overview of their goal, Hugh said, "What's in it for you, if he's no longer in power?"

"Oh, come on, Hugh. Everyone knows that he always votes with the Abyss, which makes everything split at best, giving Reon the ultimate say. The Abyss has too much power." Silas asked,

"Anything else you need from me?"

Hugh shook his head. "Not right now," he replied cautiously. Hugh was once again suspicious of Silas's motives.

"Then I'm going to get started on this clean-up job. I'm not going to let you know when it's done and I'm going to keep my distance. I think it's better that way."

Pleased with the last bit of what Silas suggested, Hugh nodded. "Agreed." And then Hugh was alone in the garage.

He made his way back into the house, where Cade and Zoie were still sitting in the kitchen. Zoie's head was on the counter, one hand on a mug of tea. He ran his hand up and down her back. "Do you want to talk about it?"

She turned slowly. "He was going to kill me."

Hugh nodded. "Yes."

"He was going to kill me, and I couldn't even really attack him. I just lit some leaves on fire." She cried. "I think that even if I had enough power to do some real damage, I wouldn't have fought back. Maybe I wasn't ready to return…"

Hugh took her hand in his. "No. No, Zoie. You were gone far too long. And you had more training than most when they discover their abilities."

Cade motioned to Xariella that they should leave; Hugh nodded goobye, and the two of them snuck out the front door.

Hugh focused entirely on comforting Zoie. "Your innate desire to avoid physical conflict is one of the things that I love the most about you." He ran his hand up and down her arm, accidentally grazing the bow that either Xari or Cade had fixed to the bandage wrapped around her scratch. Zoie winced at the pain. Hugh frowned again. "I'm sorry that you got injured."

"Is it going to be yellow and green like Stevie's?" She seemed to be asking for informational purposes only. Perhaps after getting some sleep and letting this all sink in, she might care about having a permanent scar.

Hugh nodded very slowly. "I'm sorry that I got you involved in this world and now you have a scar that will never fade because of it."

She shook her head. "I love our world." Then Zoie added, "and there's nothing wrong with having a scar."

He smiled at her. "My love, right now isn't about making sure that I feel comfortable. If you're upset about having a nasty werewolf scar on your arm, I promise that I won't be offended." He admitted, "It took me a really, really long time to accept that no matter what I did, even being a werewolf with an accelerated healing rate wasn't going to make the scars on my face and shoulder disappear."

She looked around. "Where did everyone go?"

"Cade and Xariella went out for a bit. Silas is taking care of the Jack situation." Hugh pushed some of Zoie's hair behind her ear. He leaned in to kiss her cheek.

She admitted, "I kissed Silas."

Hugh sat up, removing all points of touch from Zoie and closing his eyes. "Alright." His heart started to pound, and his breathing worked harder to accommodate the change in blood flow. "When?" His body temperature started to rise.

"You're angry with me, aren't you?" She bit her lip nervously.

"No…" He proceeded cautiously. "I'm… hurt." He tried to remain calm. "I'm sure that it was just a one-time thing, and if we talk about it…" Hugh began making plans to rip Silas to shreds after everything was settled with this situation.

She shook her head. "Hugh, yes, it was once in the forest after he killed Jack, but I also tried to kiss him once after Rosalie walked in here…" Zoie tried to hold in tears, but Hugh knew that it was because she felt like she had no right to be upset.

Hugh swallowed hard. "Well, both of those times were highly emotional moments for you, and…"

"No, Hugh. Please, let me try to explain." She tried to touch his hand, but he jerked away. "Hugh, please."

Hugh didn't understand what she would need to explain—or how anything that she had to say could make things better. He had already given her the best out—emotional overload—and she wasn't taking it.

The moment that Zoie could no longer fight her tears, Hugh started to cry as well. "Are you in love with him?"

She shook her head. "I don't know. But this isn't really about him."

Hugh stood up and turned away for a moment before turning back and asking, "If it's not about him, then who is it about?"

"Me."

Hugh scoffed. "'It's not you, it's me.' Okay. Cool, cool, cool."

"No, Hugh, listen, please."

He paced. "No, Zoie, you listen. I've never been unfaithful to you. When I was with Rosalie, I thought you were dead. Dead, Zoie. But in both of these moments you had with Silas, we were together. In a committed relationship. A monogamous, committed relationship."

She raked her hands through her hair, then grabbed a ponytail holder and put her hair up. "That's the thing, Hugh. I have a problem."

"Do you not love me anymore?" His heart broke at the mere thought of it.

She groaned. "Ugh, Hugh, shut up and let me speak." She started to cry. "This is really hard for me."

"Are you breaking up with me?" Hugh had been spending the last several minutes trying to avoid shifting into wolf form, but he suddenly realized that he needed to concentrate on breathing. He was starting to panic. He couldn't lose Zoie again.

She slammed her hand on the counter, winced from the pain, and then ordered, "Let me speak." Hugh sat down but slid his chair back so that she couldn't reach out and touch him. "Hugh, I detest unfaithfulness, so I feel extremely filthy right now. Please know that. What happens to me in relationships is that I meet someone and everything is going great, and I get comfortable. Then, sometimes, I meet someone else, and I want them, too, or we become friends and I start to develop feelings… but I still have feelings for my partner…" She shook her head. "It doesn't make sense, I know. But I get so angry at myself that I punish myself and then it ruins the relationship that I have with my partner…"

"What are you saying, Zoie? I'm so confused." He leaned towards her, finally reaching out to touch her hand. He needed her touch so that he could ground himself—so that he could determine if this was a nightmare or reality.

"Hugh, I should have told you early on, but I thought that I could suppress it once I met you and fell in love." She started to cry, so he moved his chair closer to her. "I'm so in love with you, Hugh. I just…"

"Just tell me, Zoie." Whatever was going on with her was destroying her, and he suddenly realized that this wasn't about him at all. He needed to know what was eating away at her so that he could help her beat it.

Trying to gather herself, she finally said, "I'm polyamorous, and I think that we should discuss having an open relationship."

Hugh stood up so fast that his chair slammed to the ground. "No." He could feel his blood boiling again, and he caught in the reflection of the microwave that his eyes were glowing. "Zoie, that is not the terms of our relationship." He pulled his hair back, ready to do battle for their relationship.

"That's why I'm asking us to have a conversation and perhaps change our relationship so that we can both be…"

"Happy? Faithful?" He shook his head. "No, Zoie. I would be miserable thinking about you with someone else, and I think that you just don't want to have to put in the work to be faithful to me." He bitterly said the most hurtful thing that he could think of. "You are used to the drama in your life. Your mother instilled that in you. So, the moment that things get calm, you get bored, and you look to create more drama." He could feel himself losing control, so he walked out the door, slamming it, leaving Zoie to cry alone in the kitchen.

———

For hours, Hugh walked around Birmingham. Eventually, he stopped at a bench and sat for a while before texting Cade to ask for them to meet somewhere.

Once they agreed to a place, Hugh headed directly there. He arrived first, so he started doing some research on his phone about polyamory and open relationships.

"Hey, you seemed pretty upset. Are you okay?" Cade slid into the seat across from Hugh.

Hugh looked up from his phone. "Zoie wants to discuss having an open relationship."

"And you're not okay with this, I take it?" Cade waved a waiter over. "Guinness for each of us. Appetizer Sampler. And… some buffalo wings and fries. Oh, and water."

Hugh frowned. "Should I be okay with it?"

Cade sighed. "Okay, so why did she want to open up the relationship?"

Hugh rolled his eyes. "She just wants an excuse to be able to be unfaithful and fuck that Silas guy. You were right; he is a threat."

"Wait a minute here. That doesn't sound like the Zoie that I know." Cade asked again. "What was the real reason?"

"Well, I guess, she has trouble having feelings for just one person at a time…" He looked out the window. "I just don't know how anyone could agree to this."

Cade put their hand up, stopping Hugh. "First of all, I don't think Zoie 'has trouble' having feelings for one person at a time. I think it's possible that she has such a capacity to love that sometimes it can't be focused on just one person at a time."

Hugh rolled his eyes. "The mating bond…"

"Is a wolf thing," Cade reminded him. "She's not a wolf, Hugh." As soon as the waiter brought over the order, Cade dug in, immediately getting their face covered in buffalo sauce. "I do know she feels the bond you have with her. I once heard her tell Stevie that you ignite a fire in her." They shrugged. "But she's not a wolf; she doesn't have what we feel for our partners." They rubbed their eye and immediately regretted it. "Ohmygodohmygod. Napkin!" They dipped the napkin in water and tried to wipe the sauce from their eyelashes.

Hugh chuckled, forgetting that he was upset for just a moment. Then he admitted, "I don't know if I can watch her be with someone else."

Upon clearing the sauce from their eyes, they tried to wipe the sauce off their face but kept making it worse. Cade finally gave up and grabbed one of the moist towelettes. "Why would you have to actually watch her?"

He shrugged. "What if he picks her up and I'm there, or …"

"Let me stop you right there." Cade took a drink. "You two

would set boundaries and ground rules. You need to tell her your concerns. Honesty and understanding is really important. Wait—when she told you, what did you do?"

Embarrassed, Hugh sighed and admitted, "Essentially, I called her a whore and then got up and left."

"Hugh, I'm actually shocked that you would leave her in that moment." They shook their head in disbelief. "She just, more or less, came out to you, and you insulted her and walked away?" Cade let out a deep, angry sigh.

"Oh."

"Yeah." Cade shook their head, disappointed. "Hugh, do you remember when I told you that I am gender fluid? You were so supportive. You actually congratulated me for being brave enough to own who I am." Another disappointed sigh. "I can't believe you reacted so poorly to her. I mean, think about this for a moment. Imagine the courage that it took for her to stand in front of the person she loves most in the world—the person she's probably the most scared of losing—and admit not only that she made an error and was unfaithful, but also admit a huge facet of her sexuality to you." Yet another deep sigh. "And then you walk out on her." They shook their head again.

Hugh frowned. "I have to fix this." He stirred a mozzarella stick in the marinara listlessly. "I don't even know where to begin. She probably hates me. I mean, I hate me right now."

Cade pressed their lips together. "Hugh, this isn't about you. It's about her." They frowned. "Look, I can't tell you what to do, but if you truly love someone, don't you think that you should love all parts of them? Even the parts you don't agree with?"

—Zoie—

After a few hours, Zoie assumed that Hugh wasn't coming back any time soon, so she resigned herself to going to bed, even though it was still light out.

After a quick shower, she crawled into bed—and for the first time at Hugh's house, she felt as if she didn't really belong there. She crawled under the sheets and grabbed Judy.

Zoie closed her eyes but couldn't sleep. At first, she just watched the colors dance behind her eyelids. After what felt like an era of watching a purple wolf jump through trees while it chased a star, Zoie decided to check her phone. No messages or missed calls. She turned her phone over and stared at the ceiling.

She heard the front door open and shut and recognized the walking pattern, so she rolled over and pretended to be asleep.

The door to the bedroom opened slowly, and then she felt Hugh get on the bed—but he didn't crawl under the blankets. As he lay down and put his hand on her arm, he whispered, "I'm sorry."

Instead of continuing with the charade, Zoie rolled over. "For what?" It wasn't that sweet, innocent version of the question; it was angry and hurt.

"I reacted very poorly." Damn right he had.

He reached over to push some of her hair behind her ear, and she swatted him away and then sat up. "Do you think an apology is going to fix this? You said some horrible things to me and then you walked out." Her chin started to wobble, so she turned away from him.

Hugh cleared his throat. "No, Zoie, I don't think an apology alone is going to make up for how I behaved." He quietly admitted, "I was afraid you wouldn't be here when I got home, and I wouldn't have blamed you for leaving."

Coldly, she replied, "I didn't have anywhere else to go."

"So… you're still here because you had no alternative? Not because you want to be?" He looked away and softly said, "I see."

She scoffed. "Of course I want to be here. I just didn't think I was welcome here anymore."

"Zoie, you belong where I am, always. This is your home." He moved to take her hand, but then retreated. "I know that the things I said today did not show you the depth of my love for you, and I don't think that there are words that can make up for it."

"There aren't." The conflicting emotions were fighting in her stomach, and Zoie felt as if they were going to escape her body. She was trying to suppress them. If she let them take over, what would happen?

Zoie got out of bed and walked towards the bedroom door, and Hugh stood up. He begged, "Zoie, tell me what I can do."

She turned. "We could have a conversation about polyamory and open relationships; what happened when I told you my truth; and how we both felt about it, instead of you just trying to apologize and skirt around the topic." She opened the door and walked out to the kitchen to make some tea.

Hugh followed her. "Okay, yes, let's have that conversation."

She put the kettle on and turned to him. "I'm happy to have the conversation, provided that you are honest and don't just try to say the right things to make up with me."

"You think I would do that?"

She nodded. "You've done it several times. You coddle me at times, Hugh."

His jaw dropped. "If I do that, I don't mean to."

Pulling the mugs out of the cabinet, she calmly stated, "Well, whether or not you intend to, you do." He went to speak, but she loudly interrupted him with "For example," and continued, "I know that you told me that we'd try to do something else to get Alvin out of the way because I was against putting him in a mental institution. You just wanted my buy-in." She pulled out two tea bags.

"That's caffeinated and it's almost nine…"

She cut him off. "I know what time it is. We're going to be up for a while." The only way that the conversation would be shorter would be if one of them gave up. She refused to give up on them.

Hugh pinched the bridge of his nose. "Zoie…"

"Oh, you don't want to have this conversation? Was that just lip service?"

He sighed. "Zoie, of course, I want to have this conversation, but I was hoping that we could rest beforehand so that we had clear heads."

"Oh, I see. Your," she looked at the clock, "five-hour break from the situation wasn't enough to clear your head?"

He groaned quietly. "Okay, Zoie. Is that how this is going to be? You're going to mask things with sarcasm, and I, apparently, am going to coddle you and then we'll move on?"

She folded her arms across her chest. "Hugh, you hurt me. You hurt me terribly. I've been terrified to talk to you about this entire thing. Your words were like daggers to my heart. But you know what made it so shockingly awful?" She wiped a stray tear from her cheek. "I thought you were going to be furious over the kiss with Silas, but I thought you would be reasonable about my desire to have a discussion about the dynamics of our relationship." She shook her head. "You completely subverted my expectations."

"Zoie, I was livid about the kiss, but I wasn't angry at you. I was angry at him. It wasn't like he didn't know that you are my partner. He did it intentionally." He shook his head. "You sandwiched these two things together—this epic fucking kiss that happened after he saved your fucking life in the middle of an enchanted forest and then you suddenly wanting an open relationship…"

"First of all, Hugh, the kiss was nowhere near epic—whatever that means." She continued, "And I didn't suddenly want…"

He cut her off. "It was sudden to me."

She paused and took that in. After a few breaths, she said, "That's fair. But your reaction was not."

"You're right. I overreacted. I lashed out because I was hurt. Zoie, I don't get it, though, Carol's behavior—it makes you so upset. So how are you okay with asking for an open relationship?"

The kettle started to scream. She poured water into her cup. "Her relationships are different. With the exception of Bradshaw, who's been around for nearly a decade, Carol uses all those men to fill a void. She slept with my boyfriends—including my fiancé, and I wasn't in an open relationship with any of them. She knew that and did it anyways. I don't think that any of them—besides Bradshaw—knew the style of relationship they were entering, because it would always end in dramatic fire. She preyed on young men and destroyed my life. Carol is disgusting, and I hate her. I actually hate my own mother."

Zoie sighed. "That's what makes this difficult for me. It doesn't make sense to me, even. You know? I hate her behavior. I really do. She has a right to her relationship style, but she is always so dishonest about it. I know that, for me, I only want meaningful relationships that everyone consents to. I don't think it makes sense that we only love one person for our entire lives…"

"Zoie, I don't know if I can watch you go out with someone else or even think about you loving someone else." He pulled his hair back. "I mean, just the thought of…"

"We can set boundaries so that we are both comfortable." She reached over for his hand. "Hugh, if we discover that we need to alter some things, or if we discover that this doesn't work for us, we can talk about it and make the changes."

He nodded and gently held her hand. "I will think about it. Is it okay if I say that I'll think about it and we come back to it later?"

A small smile found its way to her face. "Yes. But can we maybe revisit sooner, rather than later? Or you can ask questions as much as you want until we make a decision?"

"Yes—but in the meantime… are you… are we…"

She couldn't help but chuckle softly at him. "Yes, we're still in a committed, monogamous relationship at this time."

Quickly he asked, "Could we still get married?" She turned to him, confused and shocked. "What I mean is, is this the reason you didn't want to get married? And if I agree to this relationship, is marriage still off the table?"

She took a deep breath, feeling as if she couldn't fill her lungs entirely. "Okay, Hugh, I think there's another question in there that you don't want to ask. Or maybe you don't know how to ask." Zoie gnawed on her lower lip for a moment while she thought about how to reply. "I declined your marriage proposal because it was far too soon and for the wrong reason. If you would have asked me yesterday, I still would have declined again, because of this big secret I was harboring. If you're asking me if marriage is still entirely a no for me: it is something that I would consider, after some serious discussion about what marriage means for both of us and what our long-term goals are." Then she added, "But I think you're more likely asking if there's a way to show that our relationship comes before all the others, and, Hugh, that's easy. You will always be my primary partner, even if there's no official legal documentation to go with it."

His lips curled into a small smile for the first time in hours. "That is what I was trying to ask." He motioned for her to come closer to him, and as he wrapped his arms around her, Hugh joked, "It's like you can read my mind."

She rested her head on his chest. "I can."

Hugh jumped back. "Excuse me?"

She laughed. "I'm joking! Just memories, remember? And even that, I'm not that good at."

Returning to their previous conversation, he pulled her back into the hug. "I am truly sorry for the awful things I said to you and that I walked out on you. On us." He moved back a little so he could look her in the eyes. "I will try to be better." He ran his thumb over her cheek. "I cannot promise you that I'll be perfect. But I will try to be better."

At first, Zoie was going to respond to his apology, but then she went back to the mind-reading comment. "Why were you concerned about my reading your mind? Do you have thoughts you don't want to me to know about, Hugh Davies?"

He laughed. "I'm simply afraid you'll find out that I'm not the brilliant professor you fell in love with." Leaning over as if he was going to kiss her cheek, he whispered in her ear, "And I don't want you to know how many times a day I think of different naughty things I want to do to you."

As his lips touched her neck, their disagreement nearly melted away from her thoughts. She caught herself and considered whether she had moved forward too easily. There were probably many people who would tell her that she was foolish, but those people weren't in their relationship, so she decided to push those thoughts out of her mind.

"I don't know that I ever thought that you were a brilliant professor," she teased. He pretended to be offended, and she added, "I definitely thought you were fun and a little bit dangerous."

He touched her arm where Jack's nail had ripped through her skin. She had used her ability to manipulate time to try and heal it, but it had gone as far as she could take it—leaving a green-and-yellow stripe in the valley of the scar.

Hugh frowned. "You were wrong about the level of danger."

"Maybe a little." She hugged him, and as soon as his arms were around her, she said, "I think it's possible that I overestimated the level of danger. I've always felt safe in your arms."

"I will spend the rest of my ridiculously long life making sure you feel safe, whether you are in my arms or not." Hugh looked in her eyes. "Not just the physical idea of safe. I will work extremely hard every day to make sure that you feel like it's safe to tell me anything. I am so sorry about my reaction. I want you to be able to trust me to never walk away again."

Zoie wouldn't have forgiven anyone else, but she knew Hugh's heart. She knew he was sincere. Still, she didn't want to give him an easy out. "I'm going to need you to work hard at that." She looked him directly in the eyes. "Do not ever walk out on me again, Hugh."

"I won't. I promise." He paused for a moment. "How much of that tea did you drink?"

"Shit! None. I let it go cold." She frowned, disappointed. "It's probably bitter from steeping so long, too." As she discarded the tea bag, she apologized. "I'm so sorry I wasted this."

He chuckled. "We literally have hundreds. It's fine. Plus, it works out because I am mentally exhausted." Hugh faked a pout. "Can we go to bed?"

As she put the mugs in the dishwasher, she turned to Hugh. "We have hundreds?"

Holding his hand out to take hers, he replied, "Yes, we." He pointed between the two of them. "They are ours."

"Is this your way of asking me to move in with you?" Zoie found herself strangely excited about this idea, despite the disagreement they had just started to navigate through.

The confused look on his face caused Zoie's heart to drop out of her ribcage. He paused for a moment before saying, "I assumed when you came back to me that you were living here."

She hesitated, "I thought that you were letting me stay here while I found my own place. I…" she quickly came up with a realistic reason so that she seemed aloof. "I didn't know if the university would approve of your living with a student."

"Well, they probably wouldn't approve it if you were one of my students, but you're not my student." When they were halfway down the hall, he stopped and started going through a couple drawers in a piece of furniture. "Besides, Zoie Seavers is deceased, so you're going to have to reapply, and perhaps your forged documentation will not be sufficient for the English Department. We're snobs." He winked at her. Then, with an "A-ha!", Hugh turned to her, holding a key out. "Zoie, will you move in with me? Officially?"

She squeaked with excitement. "Yes!"

He laughed. "I had no idea you would be so excited about that."

Zoie admitted, "I didn't know either." She grinned and then skipped a little towards the bedroom. When she got to the door, she stopped. "I don't have any other keys. Or a keychain to put it on."

Hugh fished through the drawer and tossed her a keychain. "That's the Scottish flag, and the other keys are the car and the bike." He caught up to her and gave her a kiss as he opened the door.

"Ooh, you're letting me have a key to the bike."

He chuckled. "Yeah, but you're not even close to being tall enough to support it, so you'll never be able to use it."

When he tried to lead her into the bedroom, she put all her weight into staying in place. "Well, now that I know you weren't sincere about the bike, I want to make sure this is really the key to the house." She started towards the front door.

He laughed loudly. "Zoie, it works. But if that's what you need to do, please feel free."

She placed the key in the lock and made sure it worked—even though she knew it would—and then ran back to Hugh and jumped into his arms. "Okay, it's official-official!"

Holding Zoie in his arms and kissing her, Hugh kicked the bedroom door shut. When they were next to the bed, he requested, "Please, get Judy out of our bed, and make sure her eyes are shielded. What's about to happen in this room is not for someone as innocent as her to witness."

—Hugh—

"Are you sure you're okay with this?" Zoie was seated at one end of the couch as Hugh took a seat at the other end.

Reaching over and taking Zoie's hand, Hugh replied, "You are the only person that I would ever even consider willingly letting run around in my head." He didn't want Zoie to know that he was worried about what she would find—but in a few minutes, what Hugh wanted might not matter.

While he and Zoie had discussed what it would be like for her to try to read his memories, this was the first time they were attempting it. Zoie had never thought to ask Silas what it felt like to have his mind read. Hugh was going into this blind.

She had explained to him that, while she had practiced unlocking Silas's mind, Silas had never intentionally tried to let her in to find particular memories. In fact, he tried to block her more often than not. The memories that she found were only by her own navigation. She admitted that she still didn't truly know how she managed that.

"Are you sure that you don't know of anything that I can do to make the process easier for you?" Hugh asked.

Zoie's eyes scanned Hugh for a few seconds. "Relax. Maybe…"

she paused. "Well, we're trying to find memories of Edie and Alvin together—when they were happy. So, maybe you could focus on a particular memory?" She added, "Don't fight it."

"How could someone fight it?"

He didn't have a chance to get a response from Zoie. She had started to try to enter his mind when he wasn't paying attention so that he wouldn't block her.

Hugh felt like he was stuck in his own head with no choice as to where his mind wandered. Paralyzed as he travelled through his memories, amidst a storm.

The first stop was actually one of his worst memories—the night that he got in a bar fight and died and became a wolf. They didn't hang out in that memory for very long; Zoie already knew that story, and she was kind enough to not make Hugh relive it.

Hugh felt like he was spinning in his own head for a few seconds, and then he was in another horrible memory—Alvin had just shifted into his wolf form, attempting to attack Hugh. Edie was in this memory, but this wasn't one that Hugh wanted Zoie to see. He attempted to walk out of the memory—to change it—but he didn't have control over it anymore. It was only a few seconds when dream-Hugh turned his focus to Edie, who was using her magic to try to hold him down, or maybe it was to stop him from taking on his wolf form. She hadn't been able to restrain him, so his wolf form lunged at her, and as she tried to run away, he reached out and took hold of her long brown hair, yanking her back towards him. When her legs flailed and kicked him, he slammed her to the ground and stepped on her, still having a hold of her hair and yanking. Just as he threw her head across the room, the shadow of a small boy appeared in a doorway.

"Stop!" He screamed, and he felt himself gain control. Hugh was back in his living room, with Zoie on the couch beside him.

"Why did you stay in that memory?"

She took a deep breath. "Your mind is really hard to navigate, for several reasons. You've locked away so many memories, or maybe it's because you've lived so much life. Perhaps the mind can only hold so many memories—I don't know. I just wasn't sure if we'd get another opportunity for me to see her."

Hugh took a drink of water and closed his eyes. "What if I just really focused on a memory with Edie?"

Zoie shook her head. "I don't know, Hugh. It's extremely intense in your mind. It's like being in one of those… you remember those dome toys that had electricity sparks in them? If you would touch it, it would focus the spark on your hand or finger? It's like that everywhere. It's coming for me as I run through your mind." She hesitated to speak further.

Hugh grumbled a little, knowing the unspoken part of her thought. "That electricity is our bond. That's why you didn't find that when you went into Silas's mind." He looked over at her. "Let's try again."

When Zoie nodded, Hugh closed his eyes and tried to concentrate on the one memory that he knew, for certain, brought joy to Alvin.

Still, when Zoie entered his mind, she didn't go directly for it. She found the memory of Edie and Alvin helping Hugh a few days after he had become a werewolf. She stayed there for a few moments, and then she went a few years in the future to another memory, and then a few years further.

Hugh figured out that she was trying to see Edie at different stages of life so that when she inserted Edie into Alvin's dreams, it would be accurate. Hugh went spinning again, and finally, Zoie stopped on the memory he had hoped for.

Edie was lying in a bed, holding a little bundle, and Alvin had just dragged Hugh into the room. He introduced Hugh to the little bundle—Miles. It was the happiest that Hugh had ever seen Alvin. In fact, when Hugh turned in his memory, Jack was there—sober, for one of the rare moments in his life. Alvin's family had been perfect, and Hugh had been lucky enough to see that.

Suddenly, Hugh was sucked out of the memory and spun into blackness. He was confused, until he saw Zoie, in his mind, reaching out towards some of those electricity sparks that she had been describing. He tried to call out to her, but he was too late.

The moment that her hand collided with the electricity, he was sent spinning through every memory he had of her, starting with when she handed him the apple that he had dropped in the hallway at work.

He almost got whiplash with how quickly it sent him through all of the times that they had been together; it was as if he was remembering everything at once.

When Zoie finally vacated his brain, Hugh was dizzy for a moment, but then he looked over at her as she took in a deep breath. It appeared as if she hadn't taken in air for several minutes.

She turned to him slowly. "Is that how you feel every time that I touch you?" He didn't reply, so she elaborated. "Like you're being struck by lightning the entire time? But in a good way? A way that makes you feel so…"

"Alive?" He smiled as she nodded. "Yes. It radiates throughout my entire body."

"How do you manage like that?"

He got up and moved to her side of the couch, leaning towards her, placing a hand in the hair on the back of her head. "I'm not just managing, Zoie. I love it. I actually live for it." Hugh leaned over and kissed her. The electricity from their bond shot through his entire body and back to his heart.

"So, do you love…"

He cut her off. "I love you. The jolt of adrenaline I get from the bond is a bonus." Hugh had come to grips to the fact that he would have to explain this for the rest of his life to anyone who'd never felt a mating bond with someone.

"It's just so intense." She moved closer to him, crawled onto his lap and began kissing him.

Hugh chuckled softly at her. "Now you understand why I'm all over you all the time? Maybe why I'm a little territorial?"

"Yes to the first question, and it will always be a no to the second because I feel that there is no excuse for anyone to be territorial over their partner."

He pushed her hair behind her ear. "Did you get what you needed while you were in my head?" Hugh quickly added, "Which is trippy, by the way, on this end. It's like one of those—have you ever been on the teacups at Disney World? The spinning from the cups and also the floor below the cups in the opposite directions—that combo—that's what it feels like."

"Yes, I think I've got enough." She continued, "And for me, I get sucked through a tunnel into your brain, and I feel like I'm in the memory with you. Right beside you or behind you, as an observer."

There were two quick knocks on the front door and then it opened. Cade and Xariella came barreling through, giggling—and carrying some sort of baked good and a gift.

Xariella handed Zoie the gift while Cade ran the baked good to the kitchen.

Zoie looked around, and then quietly asked, "What's this for?"

"Cade told me that Hugh told them that you've officially

decided to move in together! So exciting!" Xariella nudged the gift. "Open it!" She clapped a little.

Zoie blushed. "Okay!" The warmth in her cheeks was not only because she hated the attention, but also due to the fact that she was actually excited about moving in with Hugh. "Aww! They are His & Hers tea mugs!" She showed Hugh and then hugged Xariella. "Thanks so much."

"When Cade told me that you were moving in together, I was very surprised. I thought you lived together already." She led Zoie to the kitchen so that everyone could enjoy mini-cupcakes—the baked goods that Cade had smuggled in.

"I thought we lived together, too," Hugh admitted with a chuckle. Placing his hand on Zoie's back, he looked in her eyes. "But I'm really happy that we've decided that we officially do." He put some icing on his finger and touched Zoie's nose. When she went to playfully scold him, Hugh leaned over and kissed the icing away. "This icing is really good."

"You should taste the cupcake," Zoie suggested, lifting one to feed him. Just as he went to open his mouth to take the bite, she moved and shoved it in his face.

Hugh laughed. "Why do you always do that?"

Cade doubled over in laughter. "Dude, you fall for that every time from her."

He wiped his face off, smiling. "That's because I love her and trust her to not try to embarrass me."

"First of all: from her? Who else is feeding you cake? Secondly, I hardly think you could be embarrassed in front of Cade and Xariella." She got on her toes and kissed the corner of his mouth, where there was some lingering icing. "Besides, I wouldn't have done it this time if you wouldn't have put the icing on my nose."

Hugh ignored the first question because Zoie had been obviously sarcastic. "You did it last time in front of the Royal Family, so I don't know what will stop you." Hugh shook his head as he chuckled. "You're so very lucky I love you."

She looked up at him, and his heart overflowed with love when she replied, "I am."

Cade began retching, and Xariella reached over and touched their back, not realizing that they were faking it and being dramatic. "Are you okay?"

"They are just so over the top." Cade pointed at Zoie and Hugh and shook their head. "It's too much."

Xariella smiled and blushed. "I think it's really nice, and I wish I had that."

"You do?" Xariella nodded in reply and went back to happily eating another cupcake.

Hugh and Zoie shared a secret smile, knowing that Cade was likely unintentionally taking notes. Regardless of Cade's belief that they could fight the bond with Xariella, Hugh knew it was impossible.

Cade suddenly snapped their fingers. "Oh, the real reason we came over." Cade pulled out their phone. "Stevie sent me a message, inviting me to—no, reminding me of—the Gala. So now I have the location."

Finding out the location, date, and time of the gala sped up their plans. Zoie wasn't sure that she was ready. Scratch that—Zoie knew that she wasn't ready. She had never even attempted what they wanted her to do.

Could she find a memory? Sure, either completely by accident or if she already knew that she could get in someone's mind. It wasn't a guarantee. Even after all of the practice with Silas, and even if she'd had the opportunity to have weeks of practice with Hugh, it still wasn't a certainty.

So it was even worse that their entire plan hinged on her taking a memory from Hugh and building on that to place a vision in Alvin's mind. She hadn't even worked out what the vision should do. Even once she had that part, they didn't know how she was going to get close enough to Alvin to accomplish it.

The last time she had tried to get close to one of their victims— yes, victims, and Zoie felt horrible about that, too—she'd nearly been killed. The time before that, she had been killed, technically speaking.

This was going to end in a disaster.

The four of them sat in Hugh's living room, Zoie sitting on one end of the couch, cross-legged, facing Hugh. Xariella and Cade squeezed onto the oversized chair together.

"Does it hurt?" Xariella asked, preparing for Zoie to try and insert a vision into her brain.

Hugh replied, "It didn't exactly hurt when she tried to read my memories. It was just… wild. You'll feel the emotions of the memory."

Zoie worried. "Hugh, what if I can't do this? Alvin's, what, 300? 400 years old? I'm sure he's seen power like this before and knows how to block it."

"If Hugh doesn't know how, then it's doubtful Alvin does," Xariella encouraged. "I mean, Hugh's ancient too, right?" Cade tried without success to suppress a laugh.

Hugh simply said, "Cade. You're only 40 or 50 years younger than I am, so I wouldn't be laughing too hard." He looked at Xariella. "I'm somewhere between 190 and 200."

"Who forgets their birthday?!"

Zoie laughed. "I asked that too!"

"Cade, when's your birthday?" Hugh smirked.

"Uhhhh…"

"Exactly." Hugh turned back to Xariella. "Alvin knows a lot of things that I don't know. He's privy to things we can't even imagine. Still, as a shifter, we don't have many extraordinary powers. I mean, running fast, seeing in the dark and for long distances. Strength. For me, super stubbornness."

Zoie interjected, "That has nothing to do with being a wolf. It's because you're Scottish."

He didn't miss a beat. "It got worse after my first death, so I think it's a superpower, okay? I've never known any of us to have the ability to intentionally and completely block someone out. Plus, Zo, he'd have to know it's coming."

Xariella said, "Well, I know it's coming, so I'm going to try and put my brain on lockdown. Try to change what I see."

Zoie closed her eyes for a moment, and when she opened them, she looked directly at Xariella and concentrated on getting into her mind.

She felt herself getting sucked into the tunnel, but she was blocked from getting in. She should have been able to go further. There was a path that continued, but every time she tried to move further, she bounced back, as if she was running into a painting on the side of a brick wall.

"Nothing," she and Xariella said in unison.

She tried Cade's mind next, with the same result. Frowning, Zoie asked, "Why can't I do this? I can get into your head, Hugh, easily."

"Maybe we can't count on what worked with me."

All four of them said at the same time, "The bond."

"Then why did it work with Silas?" she asked.

Hugh frowned. "Maybe it's time to accept that you have a bond with him, too." He stood and walked into the kitchen.

Zoie looked at Xariella and Cade. "Excuse us for a moment."

She followed Hugh. He was standing at the sink, looking out the window, so she walked up behind him and slid her arms around him. "Hugh."

He turned around. "What if I agree to this open relationship thing, and you fall more in love with someone else?"

"That's not going to happen." She looked up at him.

He shook his head. "You don't know that, Zoie."

"Yes, I do." She moved back and took his hands. "Hugh, I am completely in love with you."

"Then why, Zoie, am I not enough?" He quickly turned around again.

She touched his arm. "Hugh, you are enough. You're more than enough. There is nothing deficient about you." She softly added, "I've felt broken my entire life because of this."

Turning him around again, she looked him in the eyes. "I have known that I was in love with you since the moment you walked through the door at the safe house the night that you first took me to Nightbrooke." She placed her hand on his cheek. "I knew in that moment that I couldn't imagine my life without you in it. That hasn't changed, and I will never, ever love someone more." She held her pinky out to him. "I pinky promise."

He linked his pinky with hers and then leaned down and kissed her. "You can't break a pinky promise."

They made their way back out to the living room and sat down on the couch. "I'm sorry I failed and destroyed our entire plan," Zoie said everyone.

Xariella asked, "When you go in someone's mind and see their memories, can you manipulate them at all?"

Thinking about it a moment, Zoie replied, "I mean, I've never really, really tried. I've tried to call out to people, but I've never tried to take control or add or remove anything." Thinking a few moments more, she added, "But, if I can't enter to add anything, maybe…"

Motioning for Zoie to stop, Xariella shook her head. "No, listen. You were trying to add something to my mind. Like, specifically create a memory that wasn't there." When Zoie still looked confused, Xariella took a deep breath and tried another way. "You can find memories. You don't go in there and find knowledge. Like you don't try to find out if Hugh knows what two plus two is, am I right?"

"Right." Zoie wasn't sure where this was headed or how what Xariella was saying was any different than what she was trying to do and failed at.

"Go into my brain, in search of a memory. Then once you find it, that's when you add something in." She squinted a little, trying to determine if Zoie had gotten it—she hadn't. "OK, imagine that you're trying to go through a door that is perfectly shaped for you. Like, you in a t-shirt and jeans. But if you try to walk through it with, I don't know, too many clothes on—a ball gown—it's not going to work. You aren't going to fit. There's too much material— too much bulk. But if you take the dress off, walk through and then bring the gown through separately and get dressed on the other side, it will."

Zoie thought about it for a second. "So, you're saying maybe there's a very narrow crack that I can get through, and I'm already trying too much before I get to the opening."

"Exactly. Do what you know, and then try to build upon that." Xariella sat up. "Try it on me."

Zoie nodded and then focused on Xariella. She got sucked into the tunnel that led her into Xariella's mind and was immediately brought into a memory of a small table with paper on it. Xariella—a very young Xariella, maybe five or six—grabbed some crayons and started to draw.

She asked, "¿Mamá, puedo tomar un poco de leche?"

Her mother simply turned and raised an eyebrow at her and said her name—pronouncing it the traditional way—Har-ē-ā-ya— with a hint of disapproval. Little Xariella added, with a dramatic sigh, "Por favor." Zoie had never seen such skilled eye-rolling from anyone, let alone a small child.

Zoie decided that this was the moment to insert something in the dream, so she changed what Mamá handed Xariella.

She was taken out of the memory when Xariella—real, live, adult Xariella—started to laugh. "Zoie, did you change the milk into a green lava lamp?"

Zoie clapped excitedly. "Yes! Yes, I did!" Then she frowned. "Are we saying your name wrong?"

Xariella shook her head. "My mother is the only person who ever pronounced it that way. I mean, I guess she named me, so technically it is the right way to say it." She shrugged. "The kids at school always picked on me for it. Called me Hairy-ella. I would go home crying." She sighed a little. "So, when I was about 12 and we moved, I ended up starting at a new school. I told them that my name was pronounced Zar-ē-el-ah because, well, it was easier, and I liked it better."

Xariella still looked sad, so Hugh motioned for Cade to comfort her. They hesitated, and when they decided to try, it was too late and the moment had passed. It would have just been awkward.

"Do you want to try again?" Xariella asked Zoie.

Zoie shook her head. "I'm afraid that if I practice it too much on just the three of you, it will have negative effects on your mental health." She frowned. "Sometimes I would find memories that Silas didn't want to remember, and it would really mess him up for a couple days, having to relive some of those moments from his life." She added, trying to put a positive spin on things, "Besides, now I know I can do it, and doing it on one of you isn't going to prepare me for trying to do it to Alvin. I will just use the same technique." She smiled at Xariella. "You're really clever, y'know?"

Blushing, Xariella replied. "Oh, I don't know. I just started asking a lot of questions. Does that really mean I'm clever?"

Hugh looked up. "Do you think that Zoie's clever?" When she nodded and smiled enthusiastically, Hugh replied, with a chuckle, "Well, Zoie asks 800 questions a minute, too, so yeah, you're both clever."

Zoie hit him with a throw pillow. "I feel like that was a backhanded compliment."

Snatching the pillow from her hands and hitting her back with it, he replied, "Then that's a you problem. You are clever because you ask questions."

Seemingly out of nowhere, Xariella asked, "Not to, like, shoot myself in the foot here, but, um, when did you all start trusting me?"

"What do you mean?" Zoie asked, sad that Xariella still felt like an outsider.

"You're letting me in on your plan. Like really in on it." She motioned to Hugh. "I mean, it's a long way from wanting to kill me."

Hugh smiled, "You're not going to betray us." He looked over at Cade and then back at her. "Besides, what makes you think that we don't actually just have Cade assigned to you? Maybe that's why they are following you like a shadow?"

When she didn't answer but looked at Cade in hopes that they would deny being her handler, Hugh leaned forward and firmly asked, "Should I not trust you?"

Not letting Xariella respond, Cade interjected, "Cut it the fuck out, Hugh. She is trustworthy."

"It's okay," Xariella smiled, "I used to think that he was big and scary, but last night, when you showed me that text message and how many exclamation points he used, I realized that he is just a big teddy bear."

Zoie excitedly reached her hand out to Cade, doing a gimme-gimme motion. "Show me! I have to see!"

"Please don't," Hugh requested. More like begged.

Zoie turned to him. "Are you going to show me?" When he didn't respond, Zoie started with the gimme-gimmes again. Cade handed it over, laughing the entire time. Zoie chuckled. "Professor

Davies, I don't think this is proper grammar."

He snatched the phone out of her hand. "Language evolves." As he handed the phone back to Cade, he continued, "Plus, it wasn't a formal conversation."

"Hugh, don't be embarrassed. I love how excited you were for us to take a big step in our relationship." She put her finger in one of his belt loops. "If I had any friends, I would have done the same. Plus emojis."

Xariella giggled. "I've never really seen two people so… over the moon for each other." She admitted, "I truly wish that I find that some day."

Hugh looked over at her, doing his very best to not also glance at Cade. "You will." He turned back to Zoie and looked at her, still answering Xariella. "I waited almost 200 years to find Zoie."

"Did you date before you knew you were a shifter?"

Hugh chuckled. "Yes. I mean, in the 19th century, we didn't exactly date like we do now. I actually had just walked a girl home the night I died." He looked up at the ceiling like he was searching a memory. "I think her name was Blanche."

"You must have really liked her," Zoie laughed. "You almost never remember someone's name from that time in your life."

Cade laughed. "Hugh, don't respond! That's a trap!"

Everyone else started to laugh, forgetting for a moment how serious things would be in just a few days.

—Hugh—

Cade sent their RSVP with a plus three to the gala organizers. Xariella—who was quickly becoming invaluable to their group—had pointed out that it would be nearly impossible for them to get close to Alvin prior to the event. Ever since Cade had received the invitation, everyone would know that that they were coming, and Alvin's security team would be on high alert. They had to scrap their plan and decided to just try everything right at the gala.

They had considered sending the RSVP with just Cade + Xariella, but then Hugh and Zoie wouldn't have been able to get in, and it wasn't like they could try to sneak in through the kitchen. They had also discussed Hugh and Zoie doing everything prior to the Gala, but decided that anything that Alvin did privately wouldn't matter anyway. Besides, if the first time he experienced everything was at the gala, the results might actually be better.

As they were getting ready for the gala, Hugh was miserable. He hated getting dressed up for things and had zero interest in attending. Honestly, he had hoped that when things ended between Stevie and Cade, he would no longer have to face going to these endless ridiculous political parties. Of course, they had stopped for a while, but here they were, back where he didn't want to be. Even if it would serve a purpose, Hugh was dreading this. He was dreading the possibility of this becoming a regular thing.

If they succeeded and he took Alvin's place, it would. And it was possible that they would for another reason: Stevie.

Stevie must have been missing Cade because she had started to send them text messages and invitations to events like this. Of course, Cade responded to every message. Hugh worried, for his friend's sake, that these were just ploys to get the lot of them in a place where she could enact her revenge. He had no concern for his own well-being, but he didn't want to see his best friend—a chosen sibling—get their heart broken in front of the most powerful people in their world.

He knew that Cade was mated to Xariella, but even if Cade would never admit it, Hugh believed that a big piece of the reason they wanted to fight the bond was because they had lingering feelings for Stevie. He could see it when Stevie would message them. Cade's face would light up.

The relationship had been fun for Cade. It had been comfortable. Hugh understood why they might want to go back to it.

However, Hugh would never, ever forgive Stevie for what she did to him and Zoie. Even with Zoie back in his life—very not dead—Hugh would never trust Stevie again. But, if she was who Cayden chose, Hugh would do his very best to be civil.

So Hugh took this night—this ridiculous gala that was merely an excuse to party and get buy-in from the richest people in both their world and the mortal world—as an opportunity for Cade to see Stevie again and make a decision. To Hugh, this was even more important than their plan—a plan that he wasn't sure would work. A plan that he didn't even know would work for a single step.

As they got out of the car, Xariella asked, "Do they know?" She was referring to the attendees who didn't have supernatural abilities or genetics.

"Yes," Cade replied. "These are the most elite people in the world. Royalty, billionaires. All powerful people that have been vetted for their discretion."

"That's interesting." Zoie took Hugh's hand. "Aren't most of the powerful people in our world against the mingling…"

"Only when it's convenient." Cade's face wore a disgusted frown. "They play it fast and loose with the rules, remember? Especially when it comes to themselves."

Hugh put his hand on Cade's shoulder. "We don't have to do this, Cade, if you don't want to be here. We can find another way."

Cade shook their head. "I just worry that someone is going to try to pull some bullshit." Cade chuckled when they heard themselves. "I mean, someone besides us."

Xariella let out a small chuckle, but when she noticed how serious Hugh and Zoie were, she stopped.

They continued, and Hugh took Zoie's hand. "Did you even think about our mission here when you were picking out that dress?"

She looked up at him, confused. "I know it's odd to wear something with sleeves to an event at a mansion on the beach, but I had to cover the scar on my arm. If someone saw that cut, they might realize there was something more to Jack's death than just being taken by the enchantment of the forest."

Shaking his head, Hugh clarified, "No. That's not what I meant. Everyone's going to be looking at you because you're so beautiful. If they're all watching you, you can't do your part."

She smacked him playfully with her clutch. "You're silly." Zoie quickly added, "and you're going to have to do better than that if you think that line will get you anywhere."

Pretending to be offended, Hugh replied, "Whatever are you talking about?"

Either nervous or annoyed, perhaps both, Cade turned around to them and said, "Now is the time to start acting ridiculously formal and stuck up." The entrance wasn't more than a few dozen steps away, and they had to put on a facade so it appeared that they belonged there.

Cade's hand instinctively moved to Xariella's back to guide her through the door. As Cade glanced her way, a small smile appeared on her face and her body moved just a hair closer to theirs.

Hugh couldn't help but feel joy in his heart for his friend. He hoped, again, that Cade would get out of their own head and just make the right decision. Hugh squeezed Zoie's hand a little and then motioned very slightly, directing Zoie to what he had seen. She giggled softly and moved even closer to him, as if she wanted to talk about what that could mean for their friends.

The sound of stiletto heels clicking on the floor overtook the sound of the string quartet playing nearby. When Hugh turned to see who was approaching, all of the sunlight coming in the windows reflected off of the silver dress, giving him—and probably anyone else looking in that direction—welder's flash.

The sun went behind a cloud, and then Hugh rolled his eyes and groaned as the vessel for the disco ball of a dress, Stevie, approached Cayden and Xariella. He wanted to step in but Zoie put her hand on his forearm. "No. Let Cade handle this."

While Hugh knew she was right, he couldn't help but focus on the three of them. He needed to be ready to jump in and help, if needed. They had promised each other that they would all stay close, just in case this whole thing was one of Stevie's games.

"Cayden." Stevie smiled the best that she could with the scarred side of her face; the muscles would never fully heal from being torn apart by Hugh's claw. The uneven smile was short-lived, falling into a lopsided deep frown. "Ariana." The disgust was thick in her voice.

"It's…" Xariella began.

"Her name is Xariella," Cade corrected. They stared straight at Stevie, nearly growling as they spoke. "You'd think you would have known her name since you took her in and trained her to fight. But of course, you thought that she would be a casualty in your little game, didn't you?" Cade turned to Xariella. "This part of the room is getting a little crowded. Would you like to maybe step outside?"

Before they could move, Stevie put her hand on Cade's arm. "You can't possibly be happy alone. No one to entertain you at night." She ran a finger down their forearm.

Yanking their arm away, Cade leaned close to her. "I loved you, Stevie, but you betrayed me. What you did was worse—far worse—than anything I had thought you capable of." They glared at her. "You know nothing of my happiness because it never truly mattered to you. What we had wasn't even real. You were so easily swayed to give it up."

"You're making a scene." Stevie plastered a fake smile on her face as she spoke through her teeth.

Xariella's fingers linked with Cade's. "Let's go check out that view, my love."

A smiled curled onto their face involuntarily and they turned. "Of course, my sweetheart."

Stevie snaked her hand onto Xari's wrist, yanking her hand free from Cade's. "You smug little bitch!" Her angry whisper was gaining volume and attracting some attention, so she composed herself. "You will never be able to give Cade what I did."

Hugh watched as any uncertainty faded from Cade's eyes. They knew where their heart truly belonged. Cade wrapped their hand around Stevie's forearm and dug their nails into her skin, knowing that if they pressed any more firmly, Stevie's skin would be broken and more scars would adorn her. The resolve in their eyes let Stevie know that even a simple breath out of line would remove any hesitation. "Touch my mate again, and I will rip your arm from your body and use it as a baseball bat to hit a home run with your fucking head."

Stevie's angry eyes welled up with tears as her hand slowly released Xariella's arm. Trying to act tough, she asked Xariella, "Did you sing a wish to make this happen? Is this one of your enchantments?"

Cade growled low in their chest. "Back off." They squeezed just a tiny bit tighter, and a small, pained whimper escaped Stevie's throat.

Stevie's lip pouted and wobbled and she let out a long, shaky breath, trying to regain some sort of composure. She looked back and forth between Xariella and Cade. "She's really your…?"

Cade smirked. "You heard me." They released Stevie with such force that it appeared as if they were throwing her arm at the floor.

Never knowing when to just give up or walk away, Stevie couldn't just let Cade go on with their life. "I don't care if she is your mate." She made hard eye contact with Xariella. "I'm not a wolf, so I don't give a shit about honor…"

"Obviously." Xari looked her up and down. The teenager who had been loyal to Stevie out of fear and necessity was gone. She stood confident and challenged Stevie without saying a word.

Narrowing her eyes and crossing her arms, Stevie acted as if she didn't have any fear of the young vampire that stood before her. "Cade's heart belongs to me and I will have it, even if it means ending you."

Before Cade could speak, Xariella took two steps towards Stevie. "Outstanding plan, Princess. I'm sure Cade will run right back into your bed after you've taken the very thing that makes their heart beat. And, after that little display, I'm fairly certain that you could physically cut their heart out of their chest, display it in a glass jar on your mantle, and it still wouldn't be yours." She turned around, slipped her hand back into Cade's and then stood on her toes and placed a gentle kiss on Cade's cheek. "I believe we were going to look at the view?"

Cade's free hand moved to Xariella's cheek. "The only view I want to look at is right here." And that was it—Cade could no longer fight what they were feeling.

The sound of Stevie's heels clicking as she marched away echoed, covering the shakiness of her breath as she wiped tears from her cheeks.

In case she decided to come back, Hugh and Zoie closed the space between themselves and their friends. Hugh worried that Stevie would have reinforcements if she was determined to get what she wanted.

As soon as they stepped outside, Xariella asked, "Is that true—what you said?"

Cade avoided the question. "You do look beautiful…"

She shook her head. "No. I don't know why you play so friggin' aloof. You know what I am asking."

Cade pressed their lips together and nodded slowly.

"Why didn't you tell me?"

Cade shrugged and shook their head slowly. "I… I… the timing…" They stumbled over the words, but eventually settled on the truth. "I wanted to see if I could fight it."

Xariella's hand released Cade's, and she stepped back. "You…
you don't want me?"

"The opposite." They placed their hands on the banister and
looked out at the water. "It just doesn't seem fair to have lived so
much life—nearly 150 years—and then tell you that your heart
should belong to me when you're only 19." They added, "Plus, I
know you want to free your boyfriend…"

She put her hand on Cade's. "I do. But…" Inching closer, she
admitted, "I am glad I can stop feeling embarrassed about the little
crush I have on you."

Cade looked down and twirled the toe of their shoe on the
floor. "You have a crush on me?" Their face was getting more red
with each passing moment.

Just as Xariella inched closer to Cade, Hugh's concentration was
broken by the sound of slurred words and a small shove at his
shoulder from behind.

"The hell are you doing here?!" It was Alvin, drunk and angry.

Hugh stole a glance at Zoie—they were supposed to wait a while
to start their plan. She shook her head—she wasn't manipulating
Alvin's thoughts or behavior at this point. He turned to face Alvin
and was cautious to turn at a pace that neither alarmed nor hinted
at a threat to Alvin—neither too fast nor too slow.

Standing calmly, Hugh simply replied, "I'm here to support the
cause. I don't want any trouble."

"You did it!" Alvin growled. He spat as he yelled. "I don't know
how you managed it, but you did it! You killed him! It's always you!"

A woman came forward and tried to put her hand on Alvin's
arm, tried to pull him away. He wasn't having it and shoved her
away, knocking her into some people who had gathered to watch

the spectacle that was about to explode. "Get off me!"

"Alvie, this isn't the time or the place." She smoothed out her dress after regaining her balance.

Hugh quickly looked around the room. The crowd had grown to include members of the Council, who were hiding in the back, trying to stay out of the drama but still take everything in.

"I am going to make sure everyone knows!" Almost as if it were on cue, Alvin's hands dramatically flew up in the air with the word everyone, showering himself and anyone near him in scotch.

"Knows what?" Hugh asked, faking concern as he hoped that whatever came out of Alvin's mouth was completely outlandish.

Alvin turned and stumbled. Yelling out into the open air of the room, he called out, "Tell me, father, did he find some way to manipulate the vines and the trees? Or did he kill you before impaling you in the forest?" Turning towards a waitress, he slammed his empty glass onto her tray. The silver tray flipped through the air in slow motion as everyone watched, and the sound of the crash echoed in the room, which had already been stunned to silence. Glass shattered and sprayed across the floor. Screaming in the waitress' face, Alvin demanded, "Get me another one! And clean this up, you worthless piece of…"

"That is quite enough," Hugh interrupted. Zoie moved to help the waitress, who was visibly shaken, but Hugh squeezed her hand to signal for Zoie to stop. He needed her to be ready to invade Alvin's thoughts and, even beyond that, Zhenga hadn't moved— none of the Council or their mates had. Knowing the results he hoped for from this little incident, both Zoie and he would need to adjust some of their behaviors and habits in public. He turned to another member of the waitstaff. "Water for him, please." Returning his attention to Alvin, he suggested, "Let's get some fresh air." He reached down to help him up.

"So you can finish me off as well? Do you get a prize if you take out all of us?" He yanked his arm away from Hugh's grip.

Hugh frowned. "I understand that this is an emotional time for you. You're grieving, and it can't be easy…"

"Shut up! Just shut up! Stop the fucking act, you miserable fucking bag of evil." He growled. Some of Council Guards surrounded Alvin. They tried to coax him into walking away on his own, but he refused. He purposely spat at Hugh's feet, leaving the guards with no choice. It took six to get him out of there. One on each arm, two behind him and two more to clear the way. The yelling didn't stop, but the orders of "Unhand me at once!" and "You'll pay for this!" and "I'll get my revenge, Davies!" faded as they exited the building.

"Wow." Hugh exaggerated each letter as if it were a syllable all its own.

The woman Alvin had shoved into the crowd approached Hugh and Zoie to apologize. "He's just very emotional right now, and this was just so out of character for him."

Hugh glanced at Zoie, a small smile trying to force itself onto his face. Out of character, my ass. "I'm sorry that things escalated like this. Perhaps, I shouldn't have come, knowing…"

She shook her head and so sweetly—and obviously unaware of the long history between Alvin and Hugh—replied, "No, no. It's wonderful seeing all of the support that the cause has. It's always been Alvie's mission to reverse climate change. So many came out tonight just because they know the kind of man he is; it's not even the cause. And, if you're here, despite the differences you may have had, that's incredible. I mean, you still respect him. It's really just a true testament to the kind of person he is." Someone handed the woman a purse. Upon thanking them, she turned back to Hugh and Zoie. "Again, I apologize for everything that transpired. I really must be getting to my fiancé." Another member of the Council Guard escorted her to a vehicle—without any dramatic yelling or fighting to echo off of the cool marble.

Cade and Xariella hurried to Hugh and Zoie's side. Cade whispered to Zoie, "Was that you?"

She shook her head. "No way. That was all Alvin."

"Do you think it was enough?" Xariella asked quietly.

Hugh shrugged. "Not sure." He cleared his throat to signal the rest of them that they were no longer safe to speak freely. Upon seeing King Reon—Hugh hated that man—and Queen Zhenga approaching, Cade bowed as slightly as protocol permitted, and Xariella followed suit with a curtsey. Zoie went to follow, but Hugh touched her elbow. He wasn't about to let her bow to them; not only had they taken part in organizing what had eventually led to her apparent death, but if Alvin was removed from power, they would no longer be superior to the two of them, no matter what the royal pains in the ass thought.

Zhenga didn't even wait for the formalities to take place. "Zoie, sweetheart!" She held out her hands to take Zoie's. "So good to see you well."

Hugh's jaw tightened. It was difficult for him to let Zhenga take a hold of Zoie; he feared for her safety because he trusted the queen even less than he had before. "Reon. Zhenga. Always a delight to see the both of you."

Reon glared at him. "Have you seen Stephanie? I'm sure she would be ecstatic to see you. She is around here somewhere…"

"We ran into her earlier." Cade scowled.

Reon rolled his eyes—not doubt he was thrilled that Cade was no longer officially in a romantic relationship with his daughter, meaning that he didn't have to even pretend to try to like them. Looking back to Hugh, he stated, "You kept your cool remarkably well there." Glancing at Zoie, he added, "It seems that your gentling influence on him has paid off."

Zhenga waved her hand dismissively at her husband. "Please get all the little jabs out now. You'll be working together soon enough."

"That's yet to be seen." The king smirked at Hugh. "Nothing will be decided tonight." Zhenga waved her hand again, dismissively. Reon had to play neutral, but the strangely redeeming quality of Zhenga had been that she was always a little bit of a wildcard. She had no fear of telling her husband exactly what she thought, no matter what company they were in.

Zhenga then asked Zoie, very genuinely, "Do you think that you can use your magic to help Stephanie? Her face? She's horribly devastated by it. I hear that you are able to wield the power of the sun. Manipulate time?"

Zoie's jaw dropped a little. "Ahh… I don't know, Zhenga. I believe that the type of scarring that she has… I'm not sure that even reversing time could help. I'm just not sure."

"But you'll try?" Her eyes appeared to be full of sincere concern for her daughter.

Hugh could feel the empathy in Zoie's heart rise. "Of course, I will." The words were genuine. He gave her hand a reassuring squeeze. If Zoie truly wanted to help Stevie, he wouldn't stop her. He didn't trust the mermaid princess, but he wouldn't stand in Zoie's way—though he would be right by her side, protecting her the entire time.

"Zhenga, you can't just ask that of her. Besides, how much training has she had? She could make things worse." Reon looked

Zoie up and down. "Perhaps on purpose."

Hugh interjected, "What reason would Zoie have to do that? Stevie and Zoie were always friendly, were they not? I mean, I would dare say that the ladies felt as if they were found family. Surely Stevie hasn't done anything to deserve any sort of retaliatory treatment from Zoie, has she?"

Reon stepped closer to him. "You've already enacted your revenge. Revenge on her. Revenge on Alvin's son." He poked Hugh in the chest with two fingers. "And if it hadn't been proven that something else killed Jack, I would think that Alvin had some truth to his words tonight."

Zhenga let out a scoff. "Gentlemen. Enough of this brute-like behavior. It's embarrassing. It's attracting a crowd. Not to mention, it's completely unbecoming of your status." She turned to Zoie. "Honestly, if we weren't here to knock them down a peg or two…"

Reon grabbed his wife's hand but kept his eyes fixed on Hugh. "You'll be hearing from the Council within a week. Be vigilant for communication. We'll likely want to release some sort of statement about the events of this evening and any planned resolution rather quickly."

"Of course. Wouldn't want our world to think that the Council is weak or has swept anything under the rug." Hugh smirked and then turned to Zoie. "I think that our presence has acquired much more attention than we had desired. Would you like to get out of here?"

She nodded. "But first, please, let me find that waitress who got caught in the crossfire. I want to check and see if she's managing okay."

Hugh brought the back of her hand to his lips for a gentle kiss. "Absolutely."

"Always such a kind heart." Zhenga smiled at Zoie and took her free hand. "Please, tell me that your little disagreement with

Stephanie isn't going to keep you from visiting?"

Little disagreement. Hugh was disgusted by their downplay of the events.

Cautiously and politely, Zoie replied to Zhenga. "Of course."

Hugh wasn't about to let Zoie make any more promises that she couldn't—or shouldn't—keep. "Zoie, let's check on that waitress and then take our leave." Hugh turned to his friends. "Cade—Xariella? Will you be long? Should we all find our own way back?"

Xariella answered immediately on their behalf. "No. We'll leave with you." She took Cade's hand in hers and then clung to their arm as if she were holding onto something valuable in a crowd full of pickpockets.

After checking on the waitress—who was still a little shaken but would be fine—the four of them made their way to the car. Before turning the key in the ignition, Hugh turned around to Cade and Xariella, looking back and forth between the two of them.

"What?" Cade glared at him.

"Are we going to talk about you two?" He grinned widely, excited for his friend.

"Just fucking drive." Cade rolled their eyes.

Hugh grinned. "C'mon. Give me something. You've been all over each other all evening. In fact, really since you met."

"If you don't mind," Xariella replied, "I would really like to talk to Zoie about some things, gal to gal, before anything is decided or said."

Cade smiled gently at Xariella, but Hugh could nearly feel the disappointment in their heart.

He turned around and started the car. He was several miles down the road before the awkward silence started to get to him. He flipped his hand that was on the gearshift and opened and closed it like a claw game; Zoie placed her hand in his and smiled. He glanced at her quickly and smiled. "I adore you."

She turned towards him. "You are like a dream that's come to life."

Cade gagged dramatically. "You two make me fucking sick."

Hugh chuckled. "Make sure you wash that envy off of you the moment we get home. Green is not your color, Cayden." Hugh looked at them through the rear-view mirror.

In true Cade fashion, they replied honestly. "It's no secret that I've been jealous of your relationship since the first moment I saw the two of you together." They shrugged. "It doesn't change the fact that you two are so sickly sweet that I feel myself getting cavities as we speak."

"I think they're adorable," Xariella said, nearly singing it. Before she inadvertently sang a wish, she quietly spoke. "Zoie…?"

Zoie turned a little further. "Yeah?"

"Ummm… you can tell me if you want to answer this privately, but… do you ever… did you…" Hugh wanted to yell for her to spit it out, but he knew that she was trying to protect Cade's feelings. Xariella finally said, "Do you feel like you have a choice to be in your relationship?"

"Of course, I do. Hugh wouldn't have it any other way." She continued, "I did try to not be with him once. Very early on. When he told me that he was a shifter, and I thought he was lying. Any normal woman would have run away, but something pulled my heart to his."

Cade chuckled, "You also declined his marriage proposal."

"Cayden!" Hugh grumbled.

They laughed. "It was fucking hilarious, and you know it." Cade looked at Xariella and took her hand, gently. "You don't have to be with me if you don't want to. I understand if it's too much. I understand if…" They motioned up and down their entire body. "I understand if you aren't into… if you don't want to be with someone like me." They looked down at their shoes.

"A shifter? A wolf?" She shook her head. "Why would that matter?"

"That's not what I'm talking about." They frowned. "Maybe we shouldn't do this right now."

Xariella turned towards them and placed both of her hands around one of Cayden's. "The pronouns you use do not matter to me." She quietly admitted, "I'm afraid that I will never compare to Stevie. That you'll always love her. She's really beautiful and powerful. She's confident and…"

"…and she betrayed my best friend—my brother." Cade shook their head. "Yes, I loved her…if I'm honest, until tonight, I thought that a part of me still did." They looked up and touched Xariella's chin to make her look at them. "But, Xari, comparing yourself to her is pointless."

"I know…" She tried to look away, but they wouldn't let her.

"No, you don't." Their voice softened in a way Hugh had never heard before. "She is merely the piece of dust that catches someone's eye for a moment as it falls through a sunbeam. You are the entire sunbeam. The light. The warmth." Cade took her hand and placed it over their heart. "You are the flame that lights my blood on fire."

"Then why do you want to fight it?" She started to cry.

"Because I'm terrified."

Xariella waited for a few moments. "Of…?"

"You." Slowly continuing, they admitted, "You have the power to destroy me. Your absence…" They swallowed hard. "I saw what being without Zoie did to Hugh… It nearly killed him. I watched my friend go from being the most animated, grumpy person in the room to becoming basically a still life painting." Cade reached up and touched Hugh's shoulder. "I'm sorry to bring this up…"

Hugh shook his head. "You're welcome to continue, as long as it serves a purpose in the point you're trying to make."

"Look, it's no secret that everyone in our world knew that Hugh was a bit of a curmudgeon, but when he did laugh, everyone felt it, and it was infectious. Everyone wanted to try to work their way into our little circle of friends—not because Stevie was a social butterfly or because I am, obviously, impossibly cool. But because despite being the grumpiest mother fucker in the world, something about Hugh drew them in." Cade admitted, "Even Stevie and I initially met because she was hitting on Hugh."

Zoie gasped quietly and tried to cover it up with a fake cough. Hugh squeezed her hand. "I didn't even give her a moment's glance."

"That's true, Zoie. He actually immediately introduced her to me." They looked back to Xariella. "But when Zoie died—kind of died? I don't know. Whatever that was. When Zoie died, Hugh didn't leave his house for weeks. He didn't eat. I don't know if he slept. He definitely didn't take the trash out or shower. He didn't read. Write. Watch TV. Nothing. I watched my friend die, too." Cade shook their head. "I don't want that for me in the case that you don't want me." They sighed. "Sure, when they are together, it's cinematic. But I remember the day that Zoie drowned. Everything that made Hugh whole was left on the pool deck with Zoie's body."

"But you're not even giving me the option to choose. We wouldn't be having this conversation if she wouldn't have grabbed my arm." She yanked her hands away and turned her body to face forward.

"You're 19. You have so much life to live. You have a boyfriend that we are going to try to save. When he is released from that gargoyle state…" Cade turned and looked out the window. "You're going to run back to him, and I'm going to be alone again."

She turned towards him. "You're going to be alone because you won't let me in. You've made the choice to be alone." She mumbled, "So stupid." When the car stopped at the rental home, she got out and immediately started marching to the door of the place.

Cade chased after her. "You joined our cause because you want our help to save him."

"Yeah. Yeah I did," she admitted, trying to get the key into the lock. When she failed for a fifth time, she turned around and handed it to Cade while saying, "But I stay because even if we don't free him, you are all wonderful people. Especially you."

Cade didn't respond, but instead focused on getting the door opened. And continued to fail.

Hugh looked at Zoie as they walked towards the porch. "Do you think we should tell them that they're trying the key to the deadbolt in the doorknob and vice versa?" He chuckled.

Zoie shook her head. "Let them figure it out together." She looked around to the side of the house. "Is there another entrance?"

"Yeah, but I don't think I have a key."

She smiled and lit a ball of fire in her hand to see better in the dark. "I'll just use magic to unlock the door." She was able to easily manipulate the tumblers and they were in before Cade and Xariella had even begun to figure out how to properly work a doorknob. Instead, the two of them were still arguing on the front porch.

"Get your glass of water and come to bed." Hugh removed his tie, giving her a wink. He headed towards their room, and she followed.

In the room, Hugh immediately kissed her and started to unzip the back of her dress. Zoie pushed away a little.

"Did I do something wrong?" He stepped back.

She shook her head. "Was it really that terrible for you? Did you want to…"

Hugh bit the inside of his lip. "Yes."

"Why didn't you tell me?"

He shrugged. "What would it change? You're here now. We'll never be apart again."

"Are you okay? Do we need to… I don't know… slow down? Do we need to talk about it?" Her eyes searched his.

"Zoie, I felt so broken because…" He paused. "Because I really felt like you were still out there, and I just couldn't figure it out. I spent the first few weeks trying to navigate that, and then I was exhausted. When you didn't come back, I figured that I was wrong; you were really gone." He sat on the bed.

Approaching him cautiously, she asked, "Did you try to…"

He reached his hand out to hers and pulled her until she was standing between his knees. "Unless you count fighting Miles and knowing that if he threw me off the City Federal building I was dead, no. No, I didn't try to hurt myself." He looked in her eyes. "I promise you, Zoie, that I am fine. I am whole. I am happy." He stated just to make sure she knew, "I am madly in love with you." He begged, "I've had to be on my best behavior for hours. Please reward me."

She leaned in slowly to kiss him, and just as their lips were about to touch, they heard the front door open and slam shut, shaking the walls, and then something crash to the floor and shatter. That was followed by a muffled, "leave it," a low, playful growl from Cade, and a giggle-shriek from Xariella.

$$—Hugh—$$

For as much as the leaders of the supernatural world loathed the rest of the population, it always astounded Hugh that they chose locations right out in public, where anyone could see, for important things.

He knew that the magic that surrounded the locations would deter those who didn't belong there, but Hugh still felt that it was bold—risky even.

Zoie hesitated before walking down the dark stairs into the abandoned part of the subway system. "Hugh, are you sure? This looks sketchy."

He took her hand. "It's intended to make you feel that way. It even makes me feel that way." He started down the stairs, slowly so as not to make Zoie rush. Once they got to a chained gate, Hugh looked around until he saw some glowing symbols. "Zoie—over here." As she approached him, he reached out for her hand. "They only invited me, so I think you should hang onto me to make sure it lets you in."

"Hugh Davies," she teased, placing her hand in his, "is this just a ploy to get to touch me?"

He lifted her hand to his mouth and gently kissed it. "That part doesn't hurt, but no, my love, I'm being serious. You never know with the Council." He placed his hand over the glowing paw symbol, and the wall split down the center and slid open, revealing a quirky little reception area.

The two of them walked directly to the front desk. The receptionist, a faerie, looked up at them and smiled with obvious insincerity. "Ah, Mr. Davies. You are a little early. Would you like something to drink while you wait?" Hugh declined, and she immediately picked up the phone. "Yes, Mr. Davies and his guest have arrived… mmhmmm, I see."

The small faerie hung up the phone and then looked between Hugh and Zoie several times. "She'll have to wait here." Even the sparkle in her cheeks and the light sound of bells that gently accompanied her movement couldn't hide the fact that she was miserable at her job.

Hugh shook his head. "Where I go, she goes and vice versa." He gently squeezed Zoie's hand. The once overwhelming electricity between them had become a feeling he welcomed. A small smile snuck past his rough exterior, and his eyes turned slightly to look at her.

The faerie sat up straighter in her chair and squared her shoulders. "But they are only expecting you…"

"I'm aware of what they expect." Hugh wasn't afraid of her—even though he knew that he should be. Faeries very often used their powers to get back at those who wronged them. Hugh was never certain if this was because they didn't have anyone to represent them on the Council, so they were trying to rebel, or if it was just their nature. He hadn't known many in his extraordinarily long life.

Nervously, the faerie put her pen down, locked her computer

and then walked confidently through a pair of wooden doors.

Hugh and Zoie didn't even have time to speak a word to each other before the receptionist returned, accompanied by a familiar face.

King Reon politely greeted Zoie and then, trying to keep up the facade, shook Hugh's hand, unable to hide the distaste for Hugh in his glare. "You will not come without her?"

Hugh smiled. "C'mon. We all know you prefer her company to mine, so this would make things a little more bearable for the both of us, don't you think?"

Reon made one last attempt to get his way. "It's not how we typically operate here."

"Things are changing, aren't they?" Hugh squeezed Zoie's hand a little and glanced at her. "Ready, my dear?"

King Reon groaned a little and motioned for them to follow. Once they were beyond the doors, they walked down a long hallway whose ceilings reached to the sky.

Zoie shivered a little, so Hugh shrugged off his jacket and placed it over her shoulders. He noticed that she wasn't looking in front of them, but at the tops of the walls, where different gargoyles perched. Pictures or windows should be in their places. Instead, there were indents and shelves displaying the gargoyles—dozens of them—as if they were trophies. At a quick glance, Hugh knew that this wasn't the full collection. There weren't even enough in that hallway to cover the ones that had been created in his lifetime.

They continued in silence. When they reached the next set of doors, Reon left the couple at the near end of the table and walked around to the opposite side, taking his seat. He was at the far end, as if he was the supreme leader in charge of the entire operation.

And he was—for the moment. Hugh was, finally, ready to change that.

"I'm sure you know why we've called you here." King Reon looked about as pleased as Hugh was at the moment.

His entire life, Hugh had tried—and mostly managed—to stay out of the political world. Of course, there were times where he couldn't just stand by and watch, but, for the most part, he had wanted to stay quietly on the sidelines, where he liked to be. However, somewhere in the back of his mind, he had known that this day would come. Still, he played as if he was clueless. "I received an invitation—I just did as told."

An ancient vampire—probably more than 1000 years old—turned to them. His eyes were bloodshot, and the irises were as black as the night sky. His skin, despite being caramel-colored, was almost transparent. His veins were visible as if they were a roadmap printed right on his body. His distaste in Hugh's presence—and, worse, complete disregard for the rules—was apparent in his voice. "If you do as told, why is your pet here?"

"My mate," he corrected. "And her name is Zoie."

"Are you not going to answer the question?" The relationship with this vampire was going to be rocky at best.

Hugh didn't care. He wasn't there to make friends. He wanted to shake things up, so he decided that he would refuse to issue a response. "Quit pissing around. Why was I called here?"

The Shrews sat in silence, their eyes fixed on Hugh and Zoie. Hugh felt Zoie's free hand move to his forearm, signaling that she was uncomfortable.

King Reon broke the silence. "There is a vacant seat on the Council, and you are the heir to it. But," he smiled, "you can always abdicate and we can move onto the next party."

"Not a chance."

"Not a chance that you'll take the seat?" Reon's eyes lit up.

Hugh shook his head and chuckled. "Not a chance that I would abdicate. The seat is mine. I want it."

King Reon's eyes narrowed and he leaned forward. "I've known you for years, and…"

Hugh put his hand in the air. "You've known only what you wanted to know. That's been the problem with this council for more than a century. You've only paid attention to your personal interests, disregarding what the people want."

"You can't just sit in the chair," one of the witches stated.

Another finished her thought. "There is work involved."

He nodded. "I'm fully aware." He continued, "I don't intend to just fill the chair. I intend to make our world a better place."

The third witch—the Sun witch—stood up and walked towards them. Zoie's grip tightened on Hugh and her heart started to beat harder. The witch got within a few feet of them and held her bony hands out, requesting something from them. "Your arms."

"For what purpose?" Hugh wasn't about to let this old crone touch Zoie without knowing what he was setting her up for.

The vampire answered on behalf of the Council. Exposing the glowing mark on his arm, a dagger—the symbol for vampire—and a black circle. "If you're going to be one of us, you need to add the mark to your arm." He smirked. "It comes with some benefits."

"And Zoie?"

The vampire answered, "She's not your spouse."

Hugh glared at him. "She's my bonded mate, and she will be treated with the respect that comes with it."

Reon ended the bickering. "Hers will be silver, like my wife's." Hugh was shocked that he had stuck up for his bond with Zoie. It could have been that Zhenga truly enjoyed Zoie's company, that Reon preferred Zoie over Hugh, that the vampire was being overly strict, or simply that he wanted this ritual over with and knew that Hugh wouldn't back down.

"And these benefits?"

Reon frowned. "As you can see from the removal of Alvin, you aren't immune to any or every form of discipline, so to speak, but your past indiscretions will be expunged, and, for the most part, you'll be free to act as you see fit—for the benefit of our world."

Releasing Zoie's hand from his, Hugh rolled up his sleeve, presenting it to the witch, who waved her hands over his arm three times, closed her eyes, and then used one hand to grab his wrist while placing her other palm on his forearm. When she removed it a few seconds later, there was a fresh black circle on Hugh's arm.

She turned to Zoie, motioning for her to present her arm. "Ahhh, Miss Zoie Seavers or, according to the registry, LaForge… for now." She smirked and then glanced at Hugh. When she returned her attention to Zoie, the witch slowly added, "Your father was an extremely powerful warlock, but he fell into debt."

Zoie unconsciously took a small step backwards. The witch must have read the specific question in her thoughts. "No, not financial debt. He owed favors that he couldn't fulfill." She must have decided that was enough to tease Zoie with, so, with a smirk, she held out her hand, and Zoie presented her arm. The witch repeated the ritual for Zoie, just as she did with Hugh's, except her hands were reversed.

As soon as the silver circle was completed, the witch leaned forward, still holding Zoie's arm in her hand, and told her, "He'd give his life for you, but you aren't sure if you are ready to accept everything that comes with letting someone love you so completely." She paused. "In fact, you aren't sure that he loves you for all that you are." She touched Hugh's arm. "He does."

She glanced over at Hugh. "You have a decision to make, and that choice will determine if you get the future you want. If you cage that which you love, it will never be free to return your sentiment." She turned and walked back to her chair, as if that wasn't the strangest thing she had done that day.

Feeling that Zoie was embarrassed and completely uncomfortable, Hugh interrupted. "Are we done here, or…?"

Reon stood, and the others followed his lead. "We'll reconvene at a later date. For now, celebrate your glorious ascension." He snapped and the doors opened.

A young woman—a vampire—greeted them. "I'll lead you out of here. It can be quite easy to get lost."

Hugh acknowledged her with a nod, but otherwise the three of them walked with only the sound of their footsteps preventing complete silence until they reached the front desk again.

The faerie working the desk walked them to the door, and, as they crossed the threshold back out into the abandoned subway, she whispered, "I'm looking forward to the changes you may make." Hugh only gave her a small nod. So it was that they didn't have representation.

—Zoie—

Zoie and Hugh walked in silence as they climbed the stairs and made their way back onto the busy streets of Toronto. She felt much more comfortable on a public street rather than in the dirty, abandoned, underbelly of the city.

They had parked the car in a public garage a few blocks away, so it didn't take long for them to get back to it, which thrilled Zoie. She didn't want to be out in the open for any longer than she had to be. She didn't trust the Council to not have minions around to take care of them. She was on high alert until they were in the car, with the doors locked, and on the road.

At first, the two of them sat in silence. Zoie wasn't sure if it was because Hugh was worried that they had someone following them or if he just needed to decompress. As soon as they were out of the city and onto the highway to Niagara Falls, Zoie asked, "How are you feeling?"

Hugh shrugged. "That part was easy. It's not something I ever really wanted to do, but I know it was the right decision." He glanced over at her. "Are you okay? Ha was really… weird today. Even for her."

"Yeah, about the relationship and love stuff... I..." With the uncertainty about the future of their relationship, Zoie really didn't want Hugh to feel pressured to do anything. She truly hoped that they could work through things, but that also didn't mean that she wanted to get married.

Hugh waved that off. "That's not what I was talking about." He took her hand in his. "I know you aren't sure that marriage is in the cards for us, and that's fine. I'm happy just to have you in my life." He glanced over at her. "I meant the stuff about your dad."

Zoie gnawed on her lip. "What if..." She hesitated. "No, that's ridiculous." Zoie stared out the windows at the passing trees. She wasn't sure whether she wanted to dig into old memories to see if she could see something different now.

He let her think for a few moments, but bluntly said, "Zo, since you won't say it, I think I will. I think that there's more to your father's accident than you know or remember."

"I mean, I know that he was being... I don't know that hunted is the right word, but it's the best I've got." She frowned. "Silas and Lettie told me that some powerful people were after my father and that's why Silas was hired to protect me once Lettie could no longer do it."

Hugh hesitated, and then proceeded cautiously. His message to her was serious but he presented it as gently and honestly as he could. "Zoie, I don't know that your father is actually dead. I think he's imprisoned." Before she could argue, he said, "I don't have any proof or anything. It's just a feeling."

She turned her head slowly towards him. "Imprisoned? Where?" She knew where, but she just didn't want to say it out loud.

Hugh took a deep breath. "Where are all supernatural beings imprisoned, Zoie?"

Her entire body turned towards him quickly, causing her seatbelt to lock and nearly choke her. She adjusted it as she said what she really didn't want to admit. "You think he's a gargoyle?"

Hugh nodded. "I think you couldn't save your father because, beyond having zero training, Ha put a block on your ability in the moment, and you were also trying to bring him back to life—but he wasn't really dead."

Zoie put her head in her hands and let out a deep breath she hadn't known she was holding. What Hugh said made sense, and it was something that she had been thinking. "How can we get them to admit this?"

"We can't." Hugh said, very directly. "We just have to free him. We have to free them all."

She adjusted herself in her seat, sitting the proper way and staring out the front window. "I know that Xariella and Cade seem optimistic that we can do this easily, but I don't think it's going to be as simple as we think."

Hugh stared at the road ahead of them for a few seconds. "I think I'm going to have to play the game for a while before they give up the location of where they are all kept. They aren't going to trust me with that level of information instantly."

"And we don't even know how to free them once we know where they are." Zoie shook her head. "I don't know that I want to talk about this right now. We have enough heavy stuff going on just today alone." Looking at the silver circle on her forearm, she asked, "Like, what do you think the price is that we have to pay for these? Certainly sitting in that chair isn't all you have to do."

Hugh shook his head. "I'm sure I'm going to have to prove myself and my loyalty to them. Who knows what kind of shit they are going to make me do."

Thinking about where they were headed, Zoie asked, "Do you think Alvin will give you any insight?"

"I'm not going to ask him." He shrugged. "I don't trust him to be honest with a syllable that comes out of his mouth, and I don't want his advice. I just want to make sure that his threat is neutralized."

They fell silent again. As they made their way around Lake Ontario, Zoie spent most of the time looking out the window.

She tuned out even the sound of the radio. She was too worried to hear it. Zoie was trying to determine how much of herself she was willing to give up to be in this relationship. Hugh more than made up for any loss, but she truly worried that if their relationship didn't include the consent for it to be open, she would destroy it anyway.

When she wasn't thinking about that, she was thinking about Silas. Where was he? Had Hugh asked him to leave—no he wouldn't do that, would he? Would Silas ever reach out to her again to let her know that he was safe? Happy?

Maybe it was for the best that he didn't. Maybe his absence would help her forget about him. Most people would think that this would be the solution to her relationship issues, but she knew differently. Someone else would come along.

For years, Zoie had wrestled with how this was different than her mother's behavior—was she just projecting when she voiced her disgust? She thought about that as she stared out the window. But Carol didn't have the capacity to love any of those one-night stands—not even the boyfriends she stole from her daughter. They were just a blanket to hide the pain of losing her spouse. Sure, Bradshaw had stood by Carol's side for many years, but he knew—and Carol knew—that there was no love involved. They were companions—nothing more. They would never even live together, and there were no next logical steps in their relationship. Further, Bradshaw had to be okay with her mother sleeping with whomever so she could fill a void.

Zoie wasn't filling a void. There was no void to fill. She had a lot of love to share, and she wanted to do that. Her love, maybe, would fill a small void in the world.

Zoie gasped, feeling a warm hand on her shoulder. She turned to see Hugh and realized she must have fallen asleep in the car.

"Zo, it's just me." He smiled gently at her. "We're here. We're going to have to walk behind the falls, and the entrance is there."

"I don't have a raincoat." Zoie didn't want to look like a drowned rat when they got to their destination.

Hugh chuckled. "Can you not reverse time and make the water go back to where it was, thus drying your clothes and hair?"

Zoie nodded, surprised. "I suppose I can!" She laughed a little and got out of the car.

They took the path behind the falls—the water was so loud, Zoie couldn't hear Hugh when he tried to direct her off of the approved path. Hidden further back in one of the openings was another entrance, marked by the usual glowing symbols.

Before Hugh could place his hand on his symbol, Zoie turned her hand clockwise and some rocks rolled to the right.

Hugh took her hand and they walked into the cave. The rocks behind them closed, and they were in complete darkness—even the sound of the waterfall was almost completely muffled. Zoie knew that Hugh could see in the dark, but even with his guidance, she knew with certainty that she would at least roll an ankle, so she lit her palms with some flames.

"Why do they always have to make it so creepy?" she asked.

The sound of water dripping was almost putting Zoie in a trance, as it was creating its own rhythm and melody.

Hugh laughed. "So that if a human does find this place, they will turn the fuck around. We're almost at the end. I can see the door."

"Must be nice," Zoie mumbled.

As they approached the door, Zoie saw the glowing symbols again, and she felt relieved. The door slid open in the manner that the previous one had, and they were finally in a green clearing, with a gravel pathway wide enough for a car.

Hugh shook the water from his body, and Zoie was glad that she waited to dry herself off, because she was victim to some of the wild water droplets flying every which way.

She decided to manipulate the wind, rather than time. Placing one hand over the other, palms facing each other, she turned her hands in opposite directions and a gust of wind circled around her like a tiny tornado, drying her off.

She was impressed with herself.

—Hugh—

"Are you sure that you want to do this?" Zoie squeezed his hand and placed her other on his forearm. "You don't have to."

Hugh felt the gentle current of electricity spread throughout his body. Just knowing she was by his side gave him the strength to do anything. He turned towards her. "I need to do this, Zoie. I have to know that he's never going to hurt us again." His comfortable vulnerability with her gave him permission to admit, "I have to see him—with my own eyes—to know that it's true."

She nodded, squeezing his hand again. "Whatever you need from me, I'm here for you."

He took a deep breath, and they continued down the gravel walkway from the cave door to the long-term care facility. It looked like a manufactured community from a suburban horror film—all of the little buildings looked identical—all appeared to be extra-long ranch-style homes made of red brick. Sidewalks without even the slightest hint of weeds growing between the cement blocks. Benches every 50 feet or so. Trees with little fences around them. Signs telling everyone to stay off of the perfectly manicured grass.

Patients were being pushed around in wheelchairs or were

slowly walking, each with someone wearing scrubs. Those who worked at the facility seemed happy, but it was a mixed bag for those living there. Some seemed deliriously happy. Others looked obviously miserable. Some looked like they didn't even know their own name.

One patient joyously pointed out a butterfly to their attendant, and Hugh noticed braided floral bands around her wrists.

Hugh's attention was pulled away from this by the sound of Zoie's voice. "Hugh, this is Regina, the managing nurse here. She said she's going to take us to visit Alvin."

"Alvin hasn't had any visitors yet, not even his fiancée, which is shocking, given his position—err, former position—in the Realm. I'm hopeful that your visit will lift his spirits." She smiled. "He's mostly healthy. We don't have him hooked up to monitors, but given his recent history, we do have him restrained. I tell you this because I don't want you to be alarmed when you see him."

Hugh didn't care that Alvin would be restrained. In fact, he preferred it. Regina pointed out the door. "I'm going to let him know that he has guests, but take your time and enter when you're ready."

Zoie's hand ran up and down Hugh's forearm. "I'm here for you."

He smiled. "I love you." He entered the room before Zoie, still holding her hand.

Alvin turned his head and locked eyes with Hugh. Hugh momentarily felt sorry for him. He looked pathetic, lying there, restrained at the wrists and ankles by enchanted braids of different magical items, blocking his ability to use magic. Blocking his ability to shift.

His skin was pale—it looked thin, nearly translucent; the area below his eyes looked bruised from lack of sleep. The markings on his arms—the black circle and the wolf paw—had faded significantly. They seemed likely to disappear at any moment.

Alvin groaned. "What are you doing here? Come to rub your new job in my face? That you've finally won?"

Hugh sat in a chair next to the bed, his eyes following Zoie as she took the other one near the window. She looked out at the garden, pretending as if she was giving as much privacy to the two of them as possible while still remaining in the room.

He looked back at Alvin. "No. But I did have to see for myself that you were no longer a threat."

Alvin let out a small laugh. "You always were completely honest. So serious. Even in the first moments that I met you." Hugh didn't have anything to say to that. Alvin continued, "I have to ask, Hugh, why?"

Hugh replied, "Why what?"

"Why did you take everything from me? My wife, my son? I believe you caused the death of my father. And now. Now, Hugh, you've taken my power from me." He looked him straight in the eyes. "Why?"

Hugh leaned forward. "Edie was an accident." Alvin rolled his eyes and scoffed, but Hugh continued. "I know you don't believe me, but she was. You were trying to kill me to gain power. I had no choice but to fight back to protect myself, and she got caught in the crossfire."

"You tore her…"

"I know." He moved the chair closer, scraping it on the floor. "I know what I did, and I live with that every day. It wasn't intentional. I don't expect you to believe me, and I don't care if you do." Hugh looked up at the ceiling for a moment. "Who was next on your list? Oh, Miles, your son."

"My son," Alvin said, weakly, at the same time.

Hugh shook his head. "Everyone—including Miles himself—thought that he killed Zoie. She is my mate, and you know the rules for wolves include never, ever, ever harming another wolf's mate."

"He wasn't…"

Hugh growled back. "I don't care."

"So, an eye for an eye."

Hugh's eyes narrowed. "Again, Edie was an accident. And even though Zoie was your revenge, Miles carried it out." He continued, barely above a whisper. "Miles did it—not you, you fucking coward."

Zoie moved, obviously trying to get comfortable in the rocking chair. Alvin turned his head towards her.

"Don't you even think about looking at her," Hugh ordered. "You keep your focus on me." Alvin's head slowly turned back to Hugh. "I didn't kill Jack." Technically, that was true. Silas had done that.

Standing up, Hugh answered the final question. "And I took your power because you were abusing it." He locked eyes with Zoie, and she stood to approach him.

As her hand met Hugh's, Alvin spoke again. "Before you go, I have one request."

Hugh rolled his eyes. "Of course you do. What now?"

"I don't want to live like this—unable to use my magic, no freedom. Hugh, I can't even take a shit without someone chaperoning me."

"You want me to request a change in your sentence? Not a fucking chance." He turned to leave again.

"No…" He tried to reach out, but the restraints pulled his hand back to the bed. "Help me end my life on my own terms. Let it be my choice."

Hugh chuckled. "Like I said, you're a coward."

When Hugh turned to walk out the door again, Zoie put her

hand on his arm, gently. She pulled him into the corner of the room and whispered, "Hugh, you should consider this."

"Let him suffer," Hugh replied.

Zoie's eyes pleaded with Hugh's. "First of all, Hugh, while you have taken his place, he still has friends in high places. Who is to say he doesn't get freed from this place? Hmm?" When that didn't convince him, she pulled him closer. "You owe the majority of your life to this man. He helped you figure out who—and what—you were when you were completely lost."

He leaned in closer. "What, do you want me to snap his neck? Smother him with a pillow? I think that would cause some commotion."

She shook her head. "Let him die with some hint of dignity. The flowers on the windowsill—I recognize some of them. They are wilting, and some of them could be mixed into some tea, and he could go quietly into the night, when he wants to, on his own terms."

His eyes searched hers. "You think he would decide to do it? Or is it another game for him?" He saw her conviction. "Fine." Zoie exited the room, and he heard her ask the assistant at the desk for some hot water and a few tea bags—or even loose leaf.

A few minutes later, she returned and began crushing up some dried petals and stems. She opened a teabag, added the dead flowers to the mix, and then used a little magic to reverse the damage done to the bag.

After placing the bag into a mug and showering it with the hot water, she placed it on the table next to his bed. "Whenever you're ready, drink this." She smiled gently at him. "You won't feel a thing."

He placed his hand over hers, gently. "Thank you. You are doing me a kindness that I know I don't deserve."

She replied, quietly. "You're right, you don't deserve this

peaceful end." She curtly added, "and I am not doing this kindness on your behalf."

Hugh felt Zoie's hand slide into his, and they stepped out of the room. Glancing back, he saw Alvin reach for the mug.

He felt Zoie gently move her hand—a small twitch, and Hugh knew that she was changing Alvin's vision. They watched him attempt to replace the mug on the table, but instead, it fell to the floor, shattering.

The two of them made their way back through the cave, behind the falls, and to the car. Once again, they began the drive in silence. About ten minutes down the road, Hugh pulled over at a lookout, shutting off the car. Leaning forward, he placed his forehead on the steering wheel.

Zoie's hand ran up and down his back. "Let it out."

He sat up and looked up, trying to hide his tears. "It's finally over. His power over me—and you—it's finally completely gone."

She unlatched her seatbelt and turned towards him, placing a hand on his cheek to catch those traitorous tears. "It's okay to feel a lot of emotions here, Hugh."

He raked his hands down his face, one catching on hers and holding it. "He was like a father figure to me before everything changed. Before he betrayed me." After kissing her palm, he took her hand away from his face. "So much time has passed since then—so much has happened—I don't know why I feel this way. I should be relieved that he's gone." Before Zoie could say anything, he said, "I am relieved, but…"

"But what?"

Not wanting to admit that he felt sadness, loss, and grief, Hugh changed the subject. "What did you make him see?"

"Edie."

"Why?" He asked.

She pressed her lips together, considering her answer. "Because in Romania, I might have been glaring at Miles, but in my mind and heart, all I thought about was whether or not you knew that I loved you. I just wanted to be near you. You brought me comfort."

Hugh looked in her eyes. "Why'd you do it?"

"Provide him comfort?" She shrugged. "It just seemed like the right thing to do. If you mean the tea, That seemed like the best way to not get caught."

"No." He shook his head. "He asked me to do it. Why did you do it?"

She smiled at him. "That's a silly question." He felt the gentle squeeze of her hand again. "Because I love you, and because you needed me to do it." Zoie must have sensed that the answer wasn't good enough for Hugh. "You couldn't make the decision. I could see that in your soul. And I wasn't about to let you struggle with that internal conflict for eternity."

He brought her hand to his lips and kissed it. "I would have been doing it to protect you, so the conflict would resolve itself pretty quickly."

Her free hand went to his chest. "Well, I did it to protect this gentle heart."

He laughed. "That's the heart of a warrior, woman!" He leaned over and playfully kissed her lips.

With their lips still touching and her eyes closed, she replied, "Those two things aren't mutually exclusive, y'know."

Hugh paused, thinking about how Zoie had disregarded her own soul to protect Hugh's. How she would bend her own beliefs—that magic should never be used for dark reasons—to make sure that he felt safe and happy. She would risk an internal battle within herself so that he didn't have one.

He opened his eyes and sat back a little. "I'll do it."

Visibly confused, Zoie asked, "Do what?"

"The open relationship. I'll try." He put his hand on her cheek. "I want you to be happy, and I see now that you'd give anything for my happiness. It's only right that I at least attempt to give you that happiness."

Zoie frowned. "Not at the expense of your own happiness."

"Your happiness brings me happiness." He took her hand in his. "A lot has happened today, though, so I would really like to have a bigger conversation about this—just not right now. But I do mean to really try."

She nodded. "I know." She squeezed his hand.

He smiled and kissed her briefly. "Okay. Onward." As soon as her seatbelt clicked, he turned the car back on and sped off towards New York State and the cafe where they would be meeting Cayden and Xariella.

When Hugh pulled into the parking lot, he saw Cade stand up at one of the outdoor tables and wave them over. Hand in hand, the pair made their way over to their friends.

"How did it go?" Cade's voice was full of concern, but they tried to hide it.

Hugh glanced at Zoie and then replied, "He's gone."

"Like escaped?!" Xariella asked, a little bit more loudly than she should have.

Zoie shook her head quickly, and Hugh leaned forward. "No, he's gone," he whispered.

"Oh." She nodded dramatically. "I see."

Cade raised an eyebrow, and Hugh motioned very slightly— almost invisibly—towards Zoie. Then they couldn't help but laugh.

"Seriously?! That's really unexpected."

"Hush!" Zoie ordered in a loud whisper.

They leaned in. "I want details when we get home."

"I promise," she laughed. "But there's really nothing to tell."

Hugh's heart lifted at the sound of Zoie's laughter. He placed his arm around her, watching her as she chatted excitedly about something on the menu with Xariella, whose other hand was on the table, fingers threaded with Cade's.

He was hopelessly in love with Zoie—something he had never expected for himself before he met her, and he'd certainly never expected that he would be willing to challenge his version of what a successful romantic relationship looked like for anyone. But, for her, he would try. He started to prepare himself, mentally and emotionally, for the challenge that was before him.

His train of thought was broken by the sound of Xariella calling his name. A balled-up piece of straw paper hit him in the face— courtesy of Cade. He threw it back and then turned his attention to Xariella. "Hmm?"

"Now that you've taken over the world, what's next?" She repeated, almost as a plea.

He chuckled. "Well, I think I have some work to do before I actually take over the world. But..." Hugh looked to Cade and Zoie, motioning for them to all lean in more closely. "I think we have to play the long game for this one..." He looked around to make sure that no one was listening too closely. "But Lettie, Tafari, and every other wrongly imprisoned immortal needs our help."

Cade clapped and rubbed their hands together. "Let's do this."